JAMES KOCHALKA

THE GLORKIAN WARRIOR

DELIVERS A PIZZA

PIZZA

:01

First Second
New York

For Eli and Oliver

Special thanks to Mark DeNardo, Miles Tilmann, and
Rich Grillotti of PixelJam for all their hard work on
The Glorkian Warrior and Glorkbot video games.

First Second
Copyright © 2014 by James Kochalka

Published by First Second
First Second is an imprint of Roaring Brook Press,
a division of Holtzbrinck Publishing Holdings Limited Partnership
175 Fifth Avenue, New York, New York 10010
All rights reserved

Cataloging-in-Publication Data is on file at the Library of Congress.

Paperback ISBN 978-1-59643-917-7
Hardcover ISBN 978-1-62672-103-6

First Second books are available for special promotions and premiums.
For details, contact: Director of Special Markets, Holtzbrinck Publishers.

First edition 2014
Book design by Colleen AF Venable

Printed in China by Macmillan
Production (Asia) Ltd., Kowloon,
Hong Kong (supplier code 10)

Paperback: 10 9 8 7 6 5 4 3 2 1
Hardcover: 10 9 8 7 6 5 4 3

BY ART
WE LIVE

CHAPTER ONE

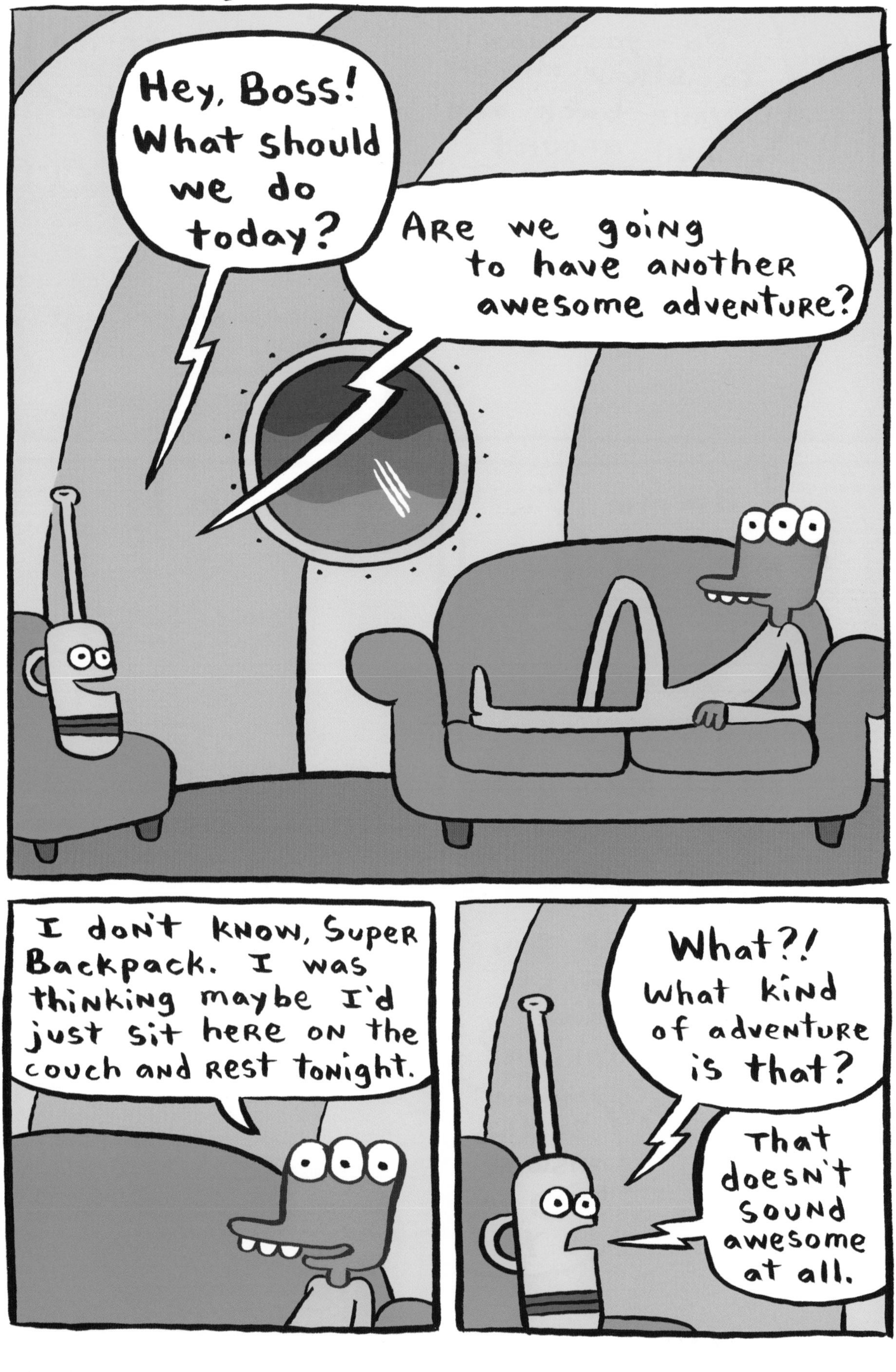
Hey, Boss! What should we do today?
Are we going to have another awesome adventure?
I don't know, Super Backpack. I was thinking maybe I'd just sit here on the couch and rest tonight.
What?! What kind of adventure is that?
That doesn't sound awesome at all.

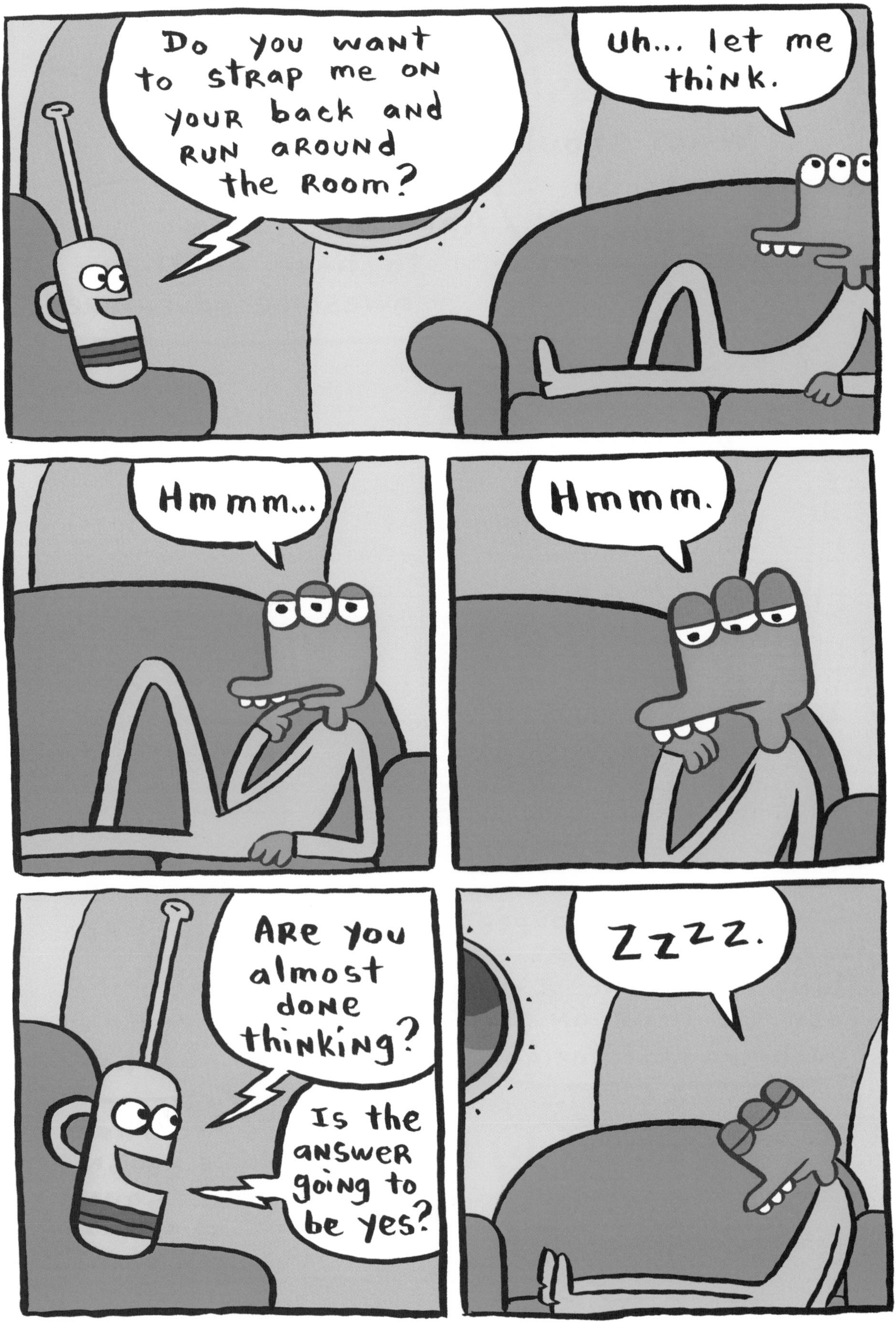
Do you want to strap me on your back and run around the room?
Uh... let me think.
Hmmm...
Hmmm.
Are you almost done thinking?
Is the answer going to be yes?
Zzzz.

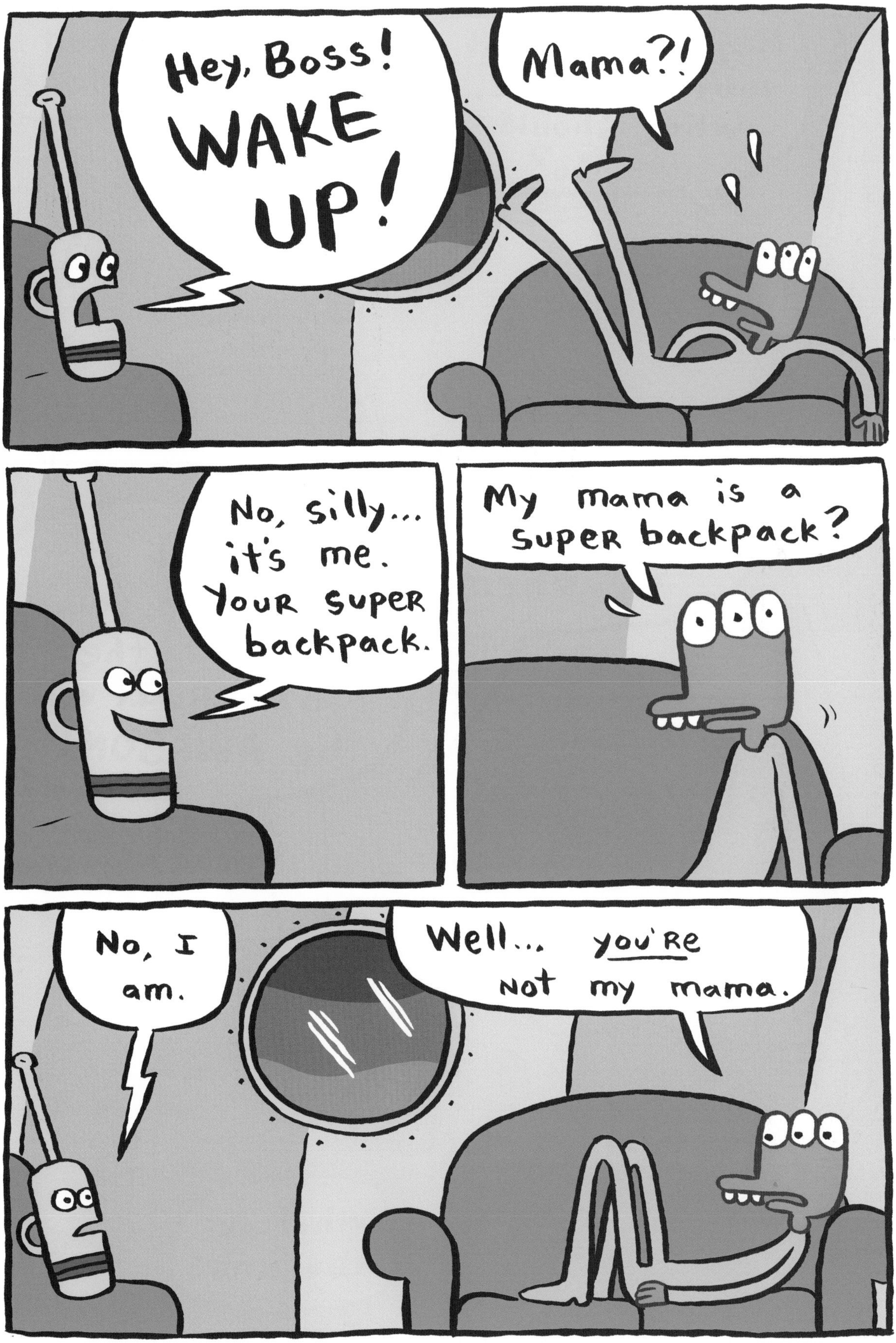
Hey, Boss! WAKE UP!
Mama?!
No, silly... it's me. Your super backpack.
My mama is a super backpack?
No, I am.
Well... you're not my mama.

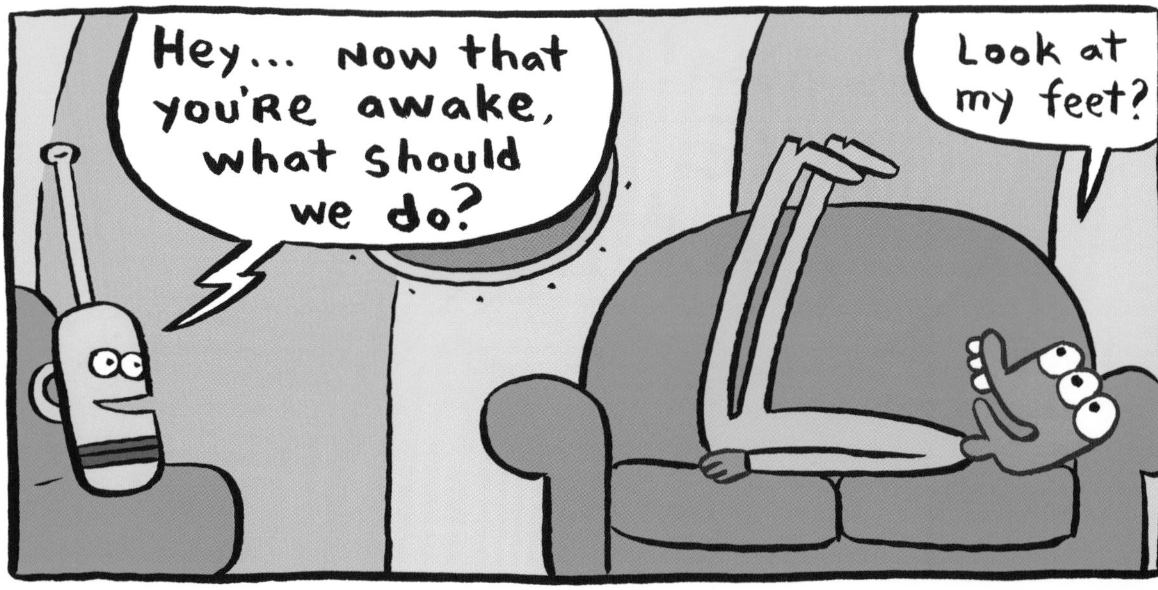
Hey... Now that you're awake, what should we do?
Look at my feet?

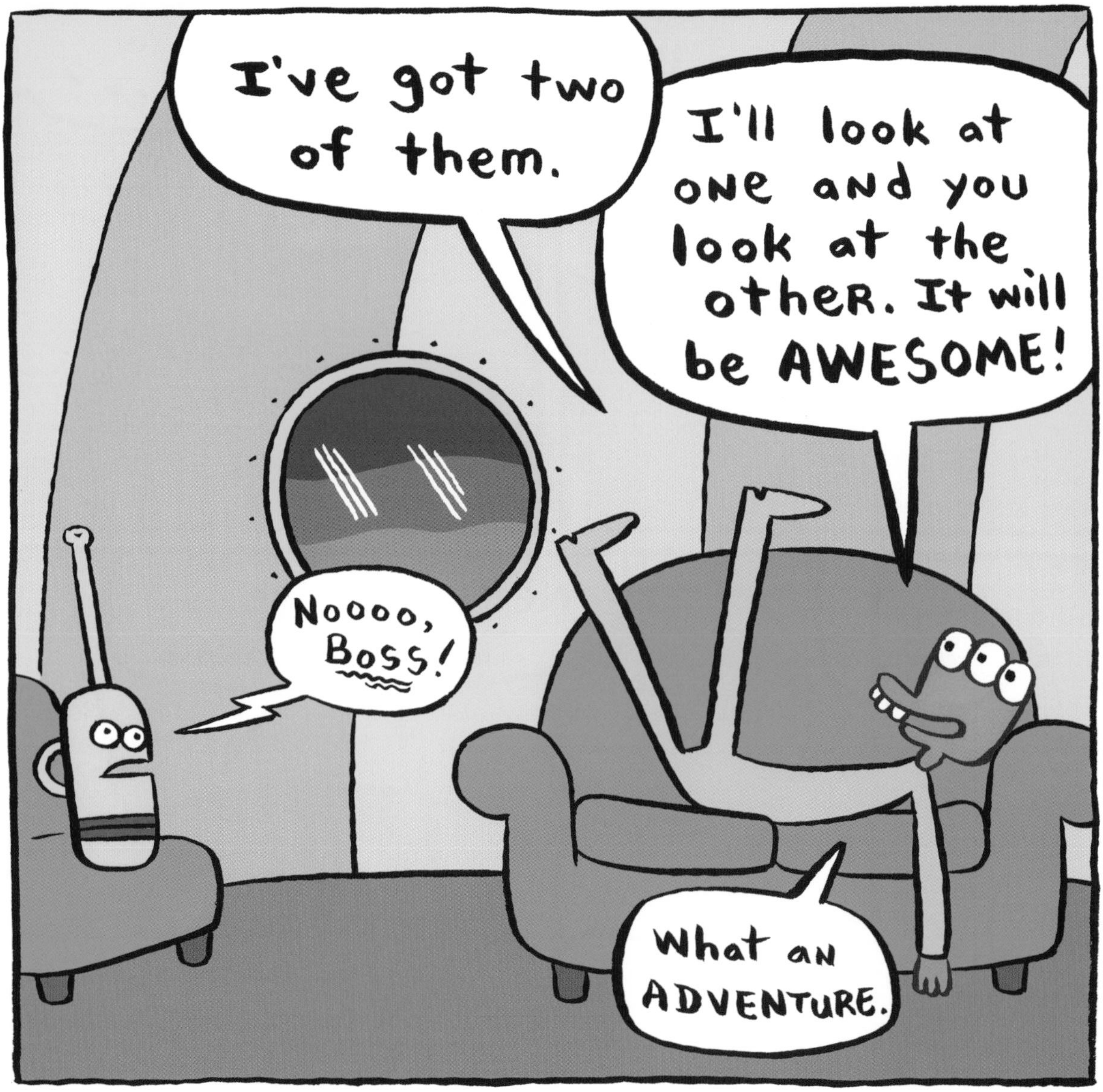
I've got two of them.
I'll look at one and you look at the other. It will be AWESOME!
Noooo, Boss!
What an ADVENTURE.

RRRING
RRRING
Hey, what's that sound?
Are my feet ringing?

No, Boss. That's not your feet!
That's the EMERGENCY SPACE PHONE.

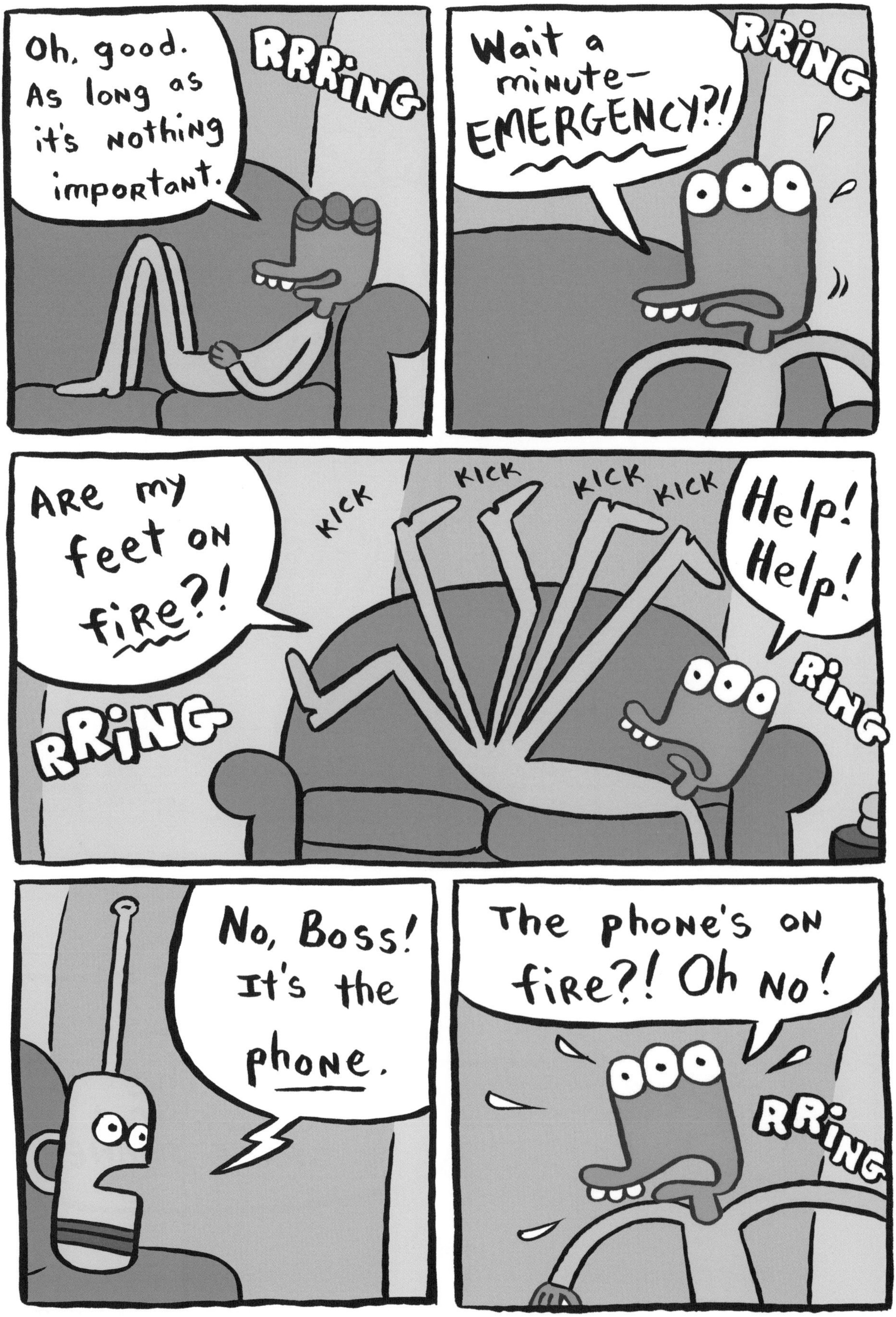

Oh, good. As long as it's nothing important.
RRRiNG
Wait a minute— EMERGENCY?!
RRiNG
!
Are my feet on fire?!
KICK
KICK
KICK
KICK
Help! Help!
RRiNG
RRiNG
No, Boss! It's the phone.
The phone's on fire?! Oh no!
RRiNG

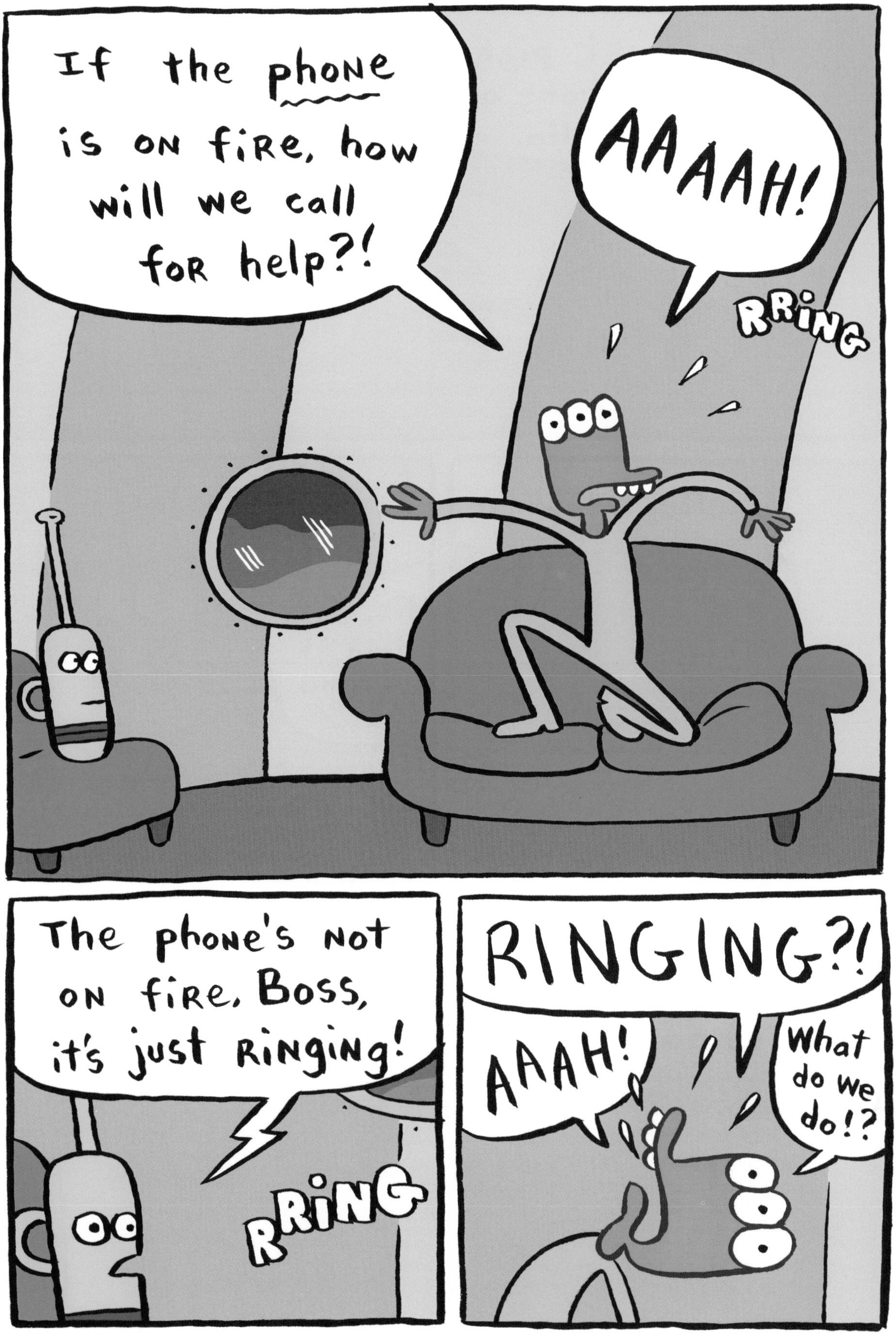
If the phone is on fire, how will we call for help?!
AAAAH!
RRING
The phone's not on fire, Boss, it's just ringing!
RRING
RINGING?!
AAAH!
What do we do!?

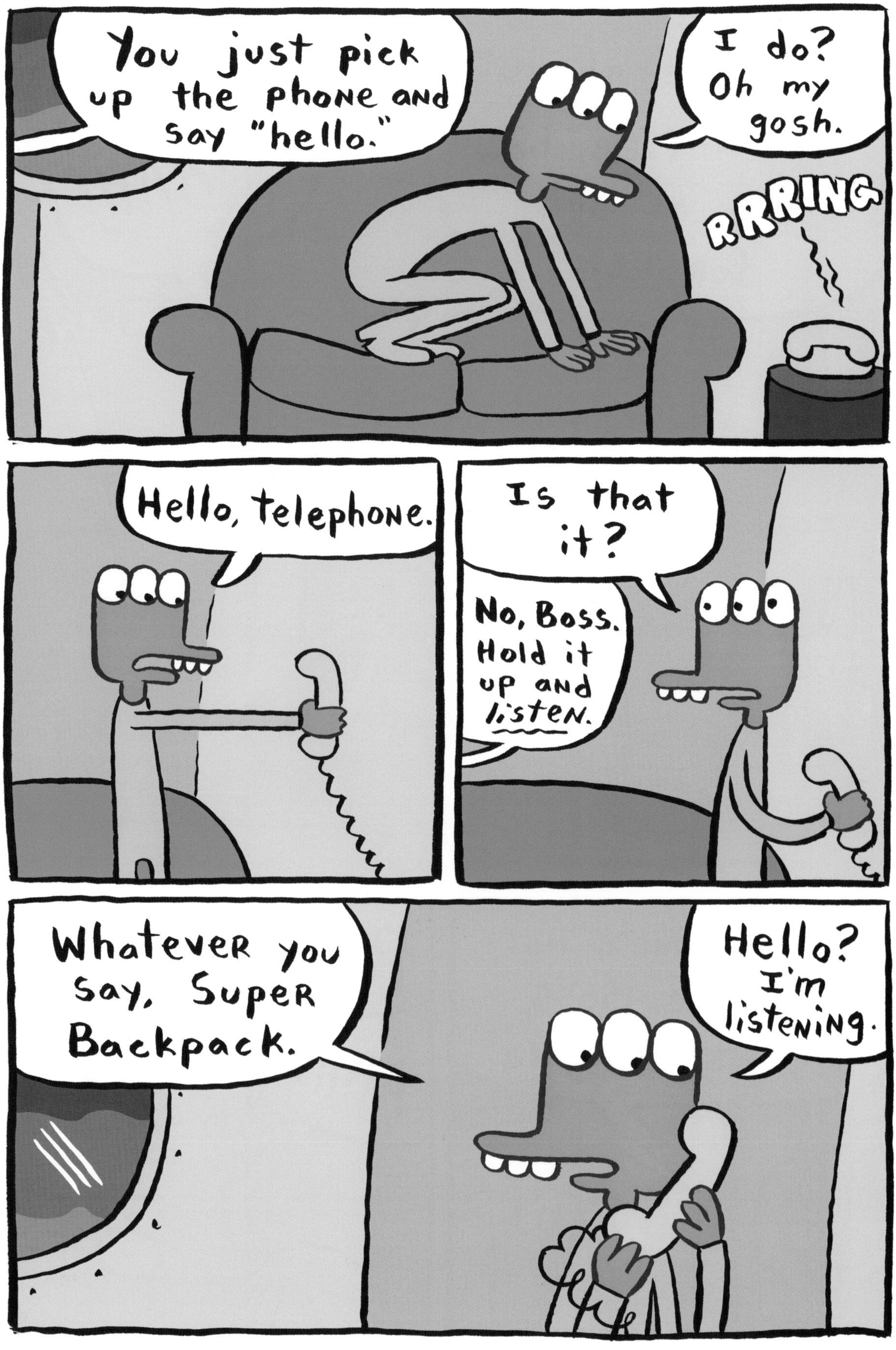

You just pick up the phone and say "hello."
I do? Oh my gosh.
RRRING
Hello, telephone.
Is that it?
No, Boss. Hold it up and listen.
Whatever you say, Super Backpack.
Hello? I'm listening.

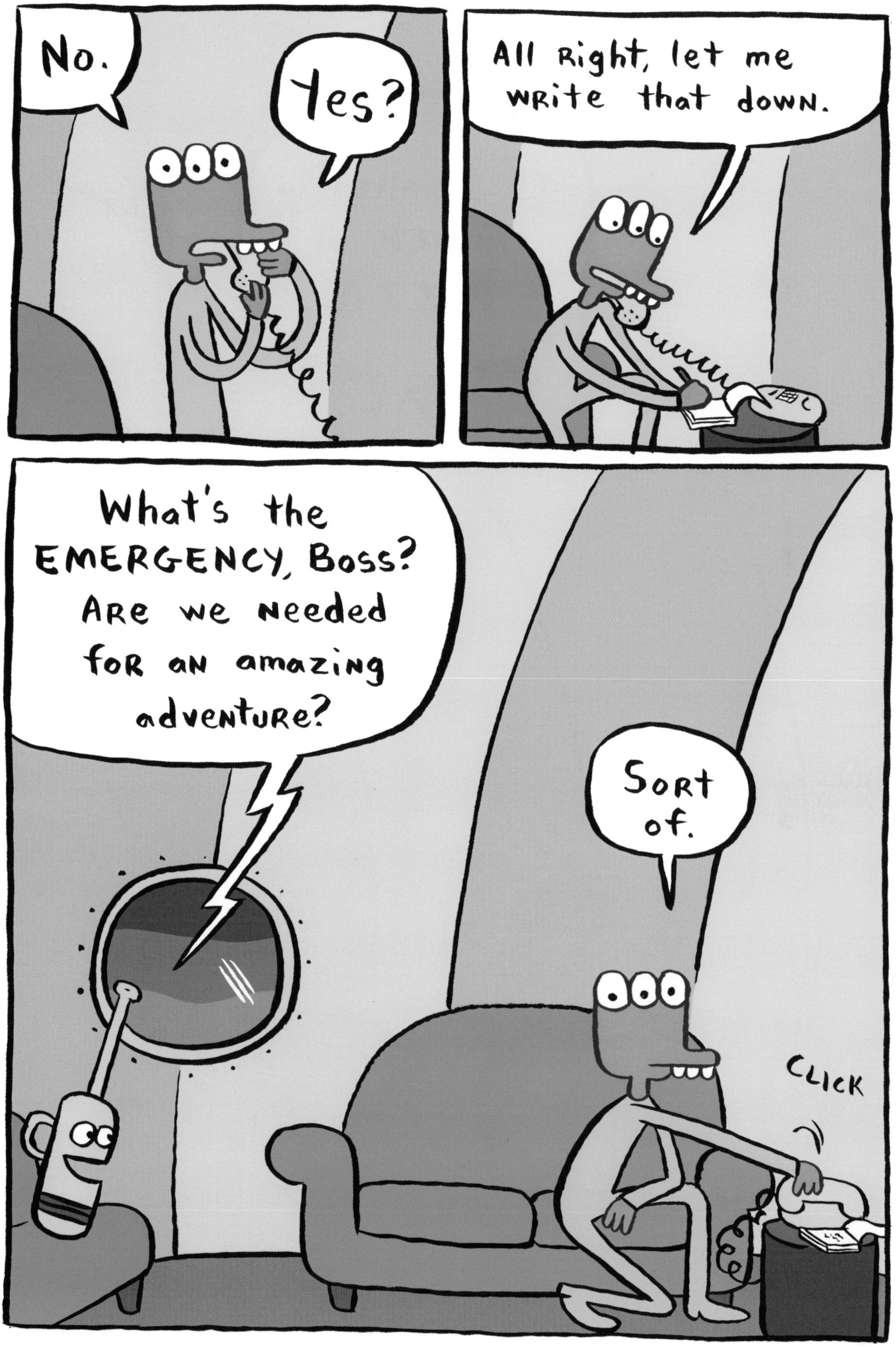
No.
Yes?
All Right, let me write that down.
What's the EMERGENCY, Boss? Are we needed for an amazing adventure?
Sort of.
CLICK

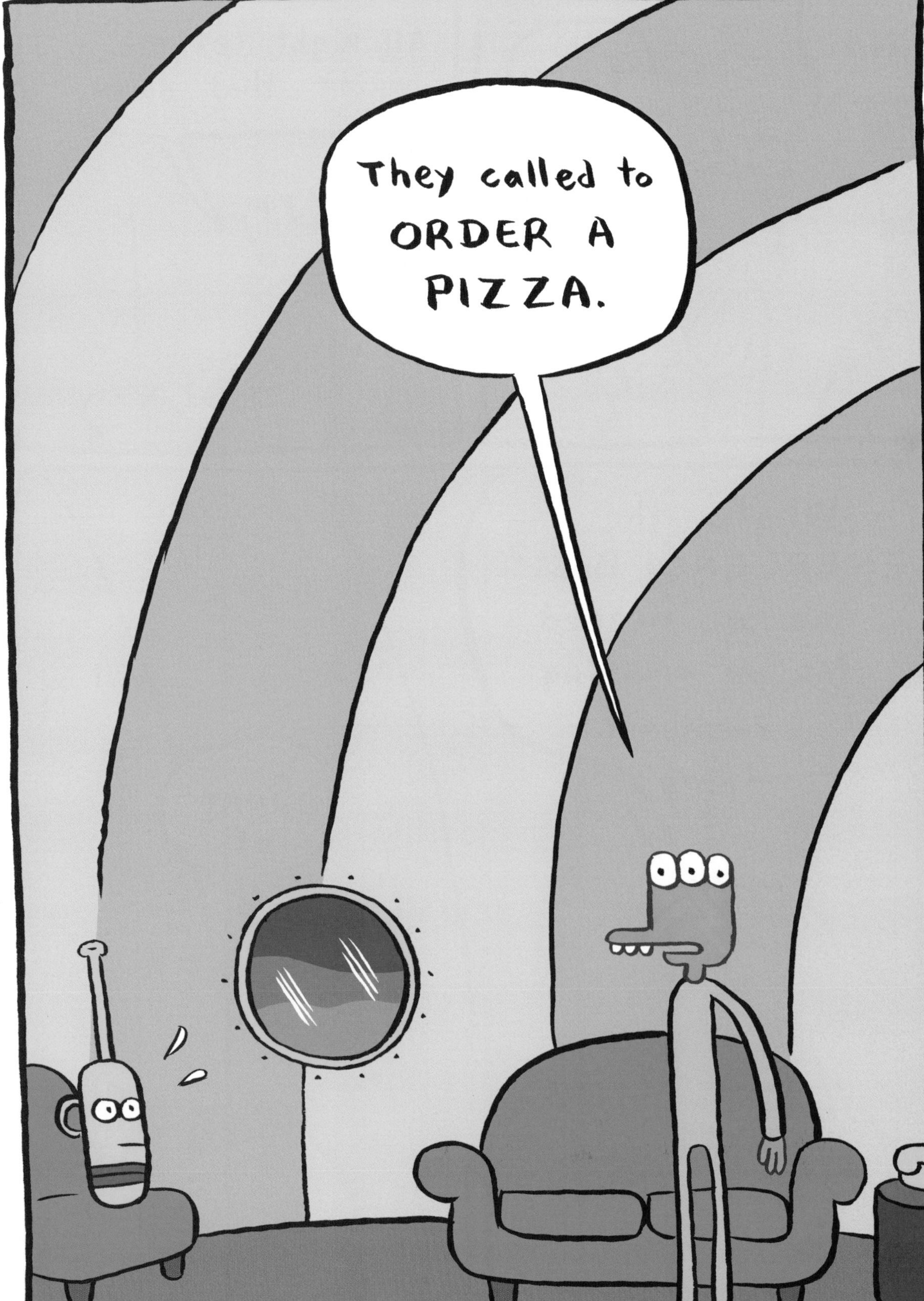
They called to ORDER A PIZZA.

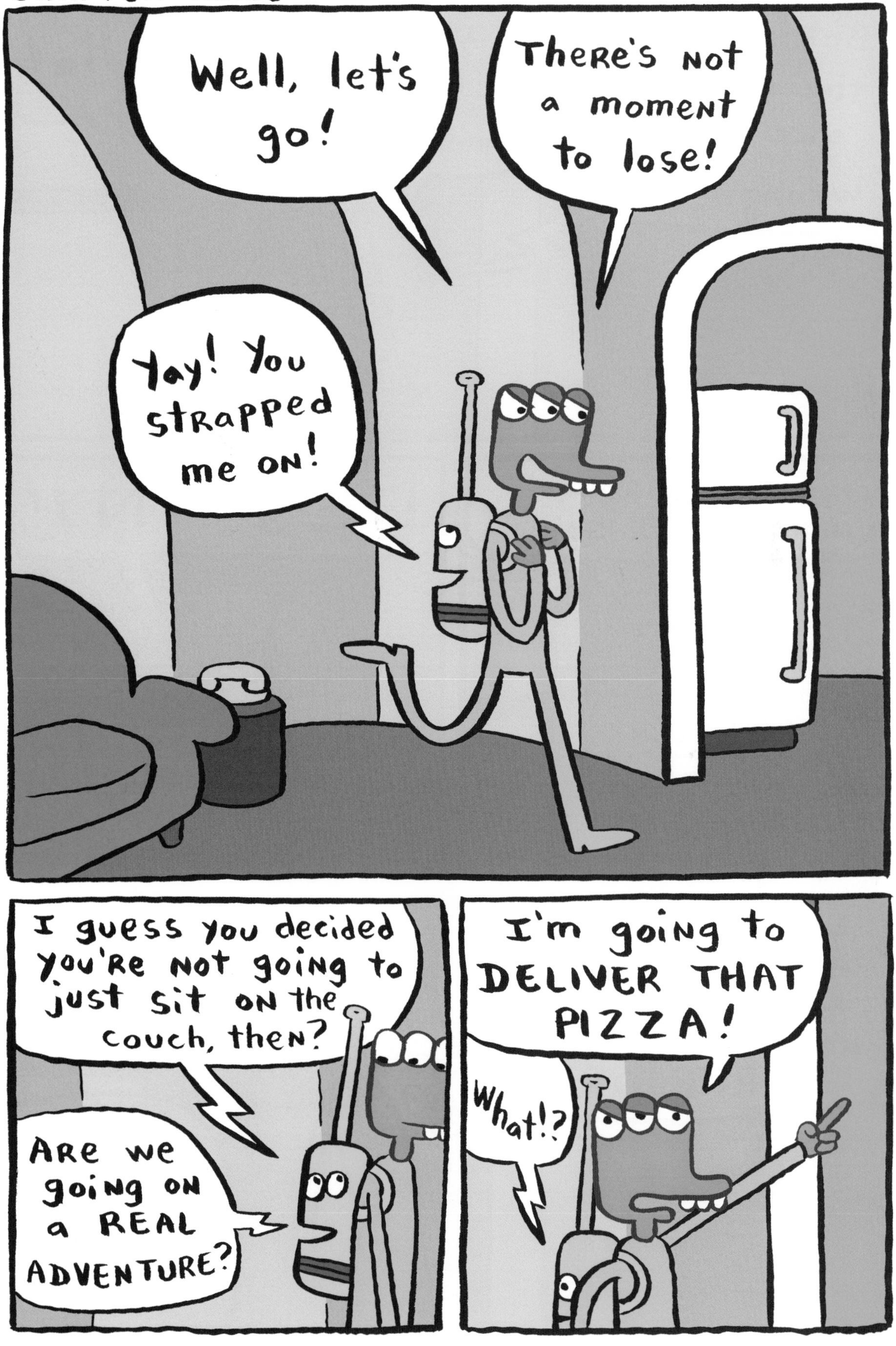
Well, let's go!
There's not a moment to lose!
Yay! You strapped me on!
I guess you decided you're not going to just sit on the couch, then?
Are we going on a REAL ADVENTURE?
I'm going to DELIVER THAT PIZZA!
What!?

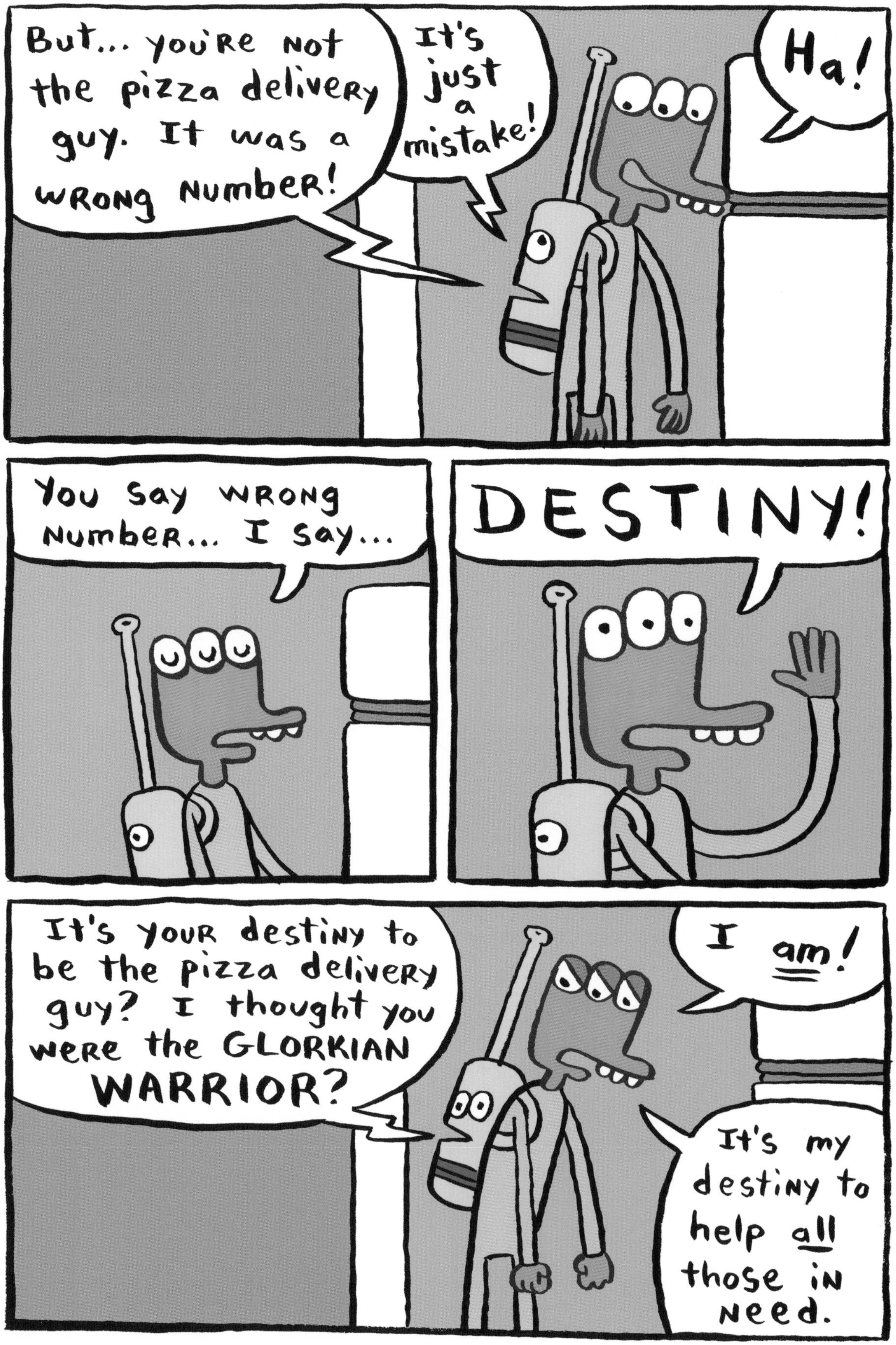

But... you're not the pizza delivery guy. It was a wrong number!
It's just a mistake!
Ha!
You say wrong number... I say...
DESTINY!
It's your destiny to be the pizza delivery guy? I thought you were the GLORKIAN WARRIOR?
I am!
It's my destiny to help all those in need.

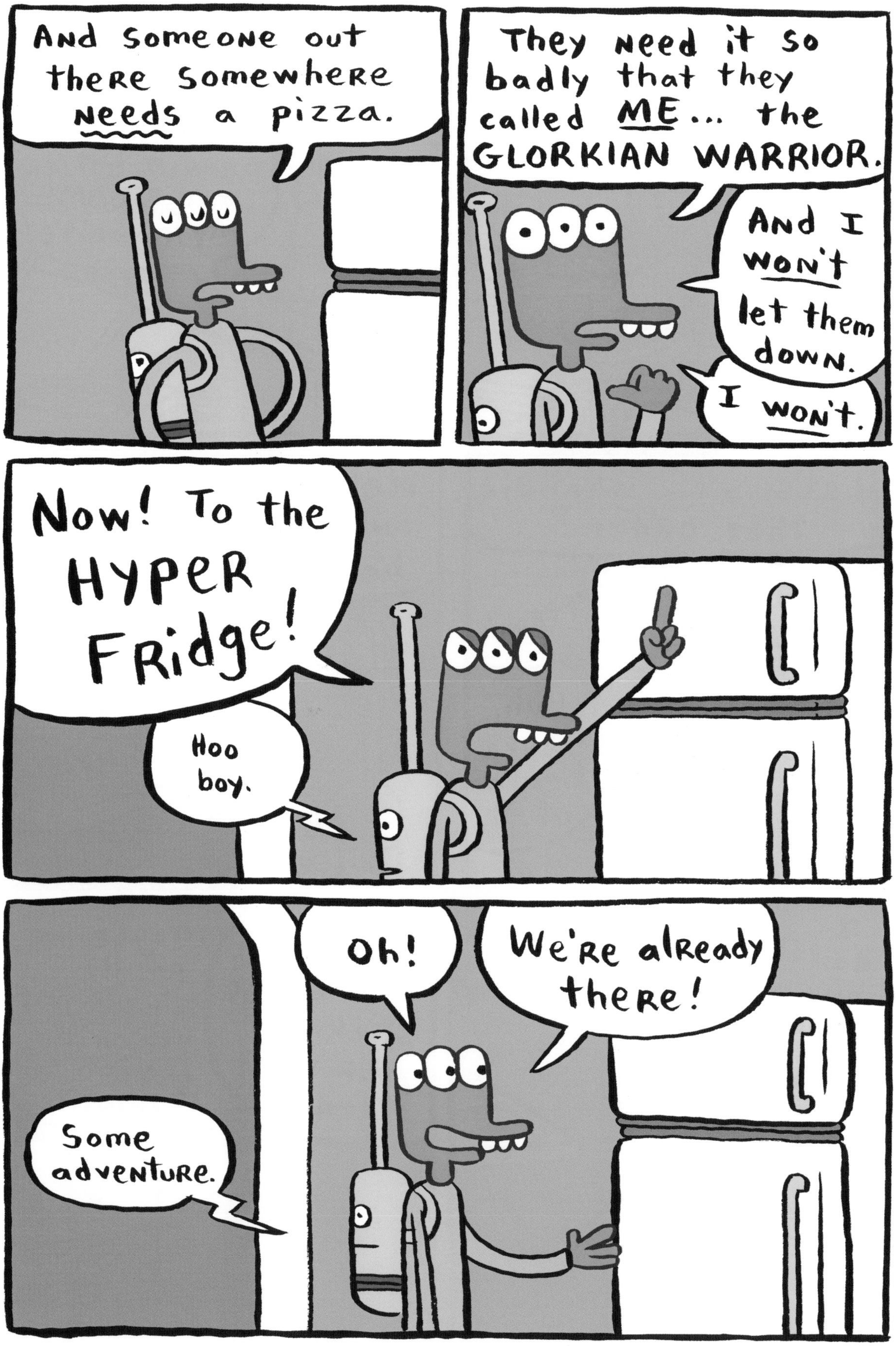
And someone out there somewhere needs a pizza.
They need it so badly that they called ME... the GLORKIAN WARRIOR.
And I won't let them down.
I won't.
Now! To the HYPER Fridge!
Hoo boy.
Oh!
We're already there!
Some adventure.

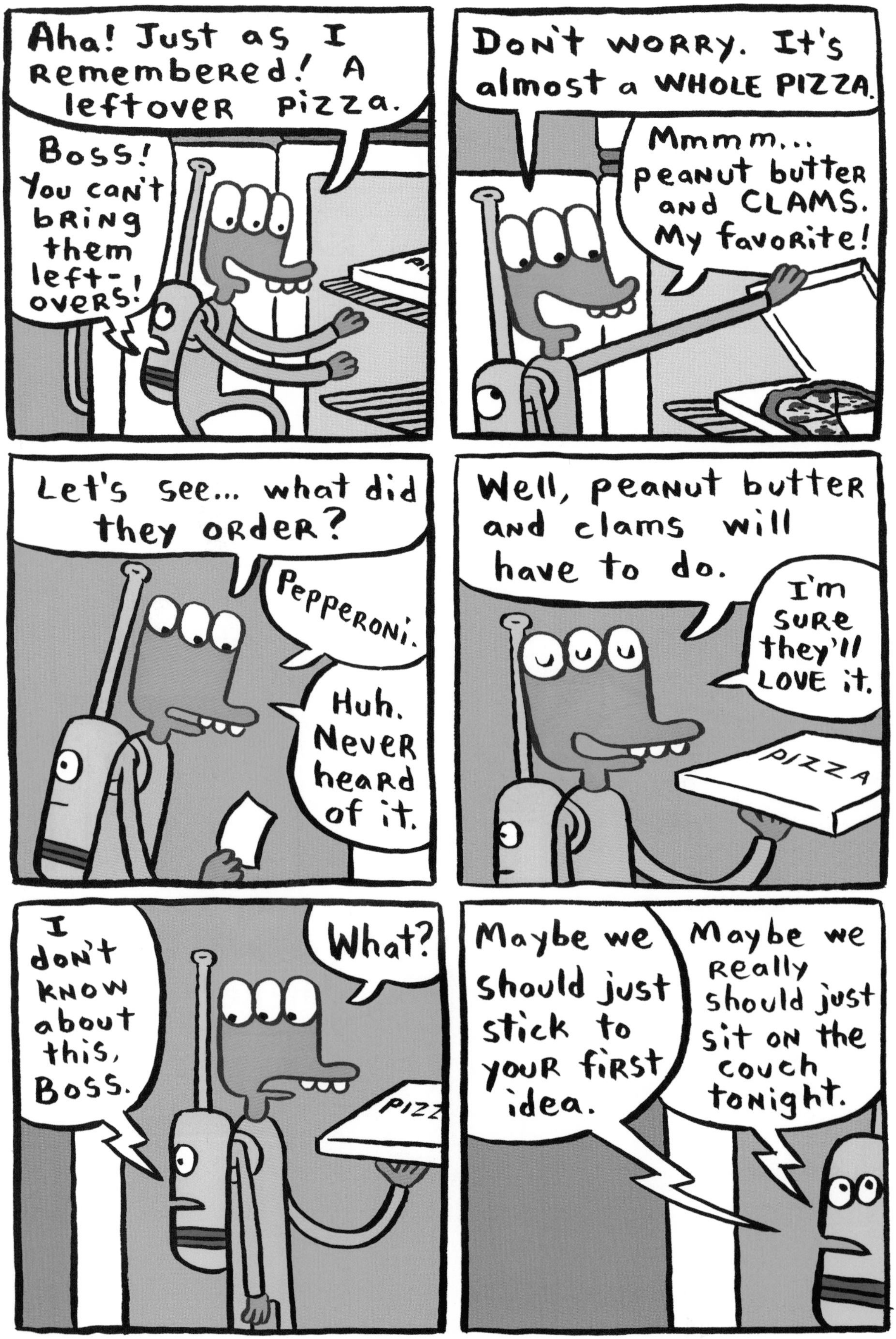
Aha! Just as I remembered! A leftover pizza.
Boss! You can't bring them left-overs!
Don't worry. It's almost a WHOLE PIZZA.
Mmmm... peanut butter and CLAMS. My favorite!
PIZZA
Let's see... what did they order?
Pepperoni.
Huh. Never heard of it.
Well, peanut butter and clams will have to do.
I'm sure they'll LOVE it.
PIZZA
I don't know about this, Boss.
What?
PIZZ
Maybe we should just stick to your first idea.
Maybe we really should just sit on the couch tonight.

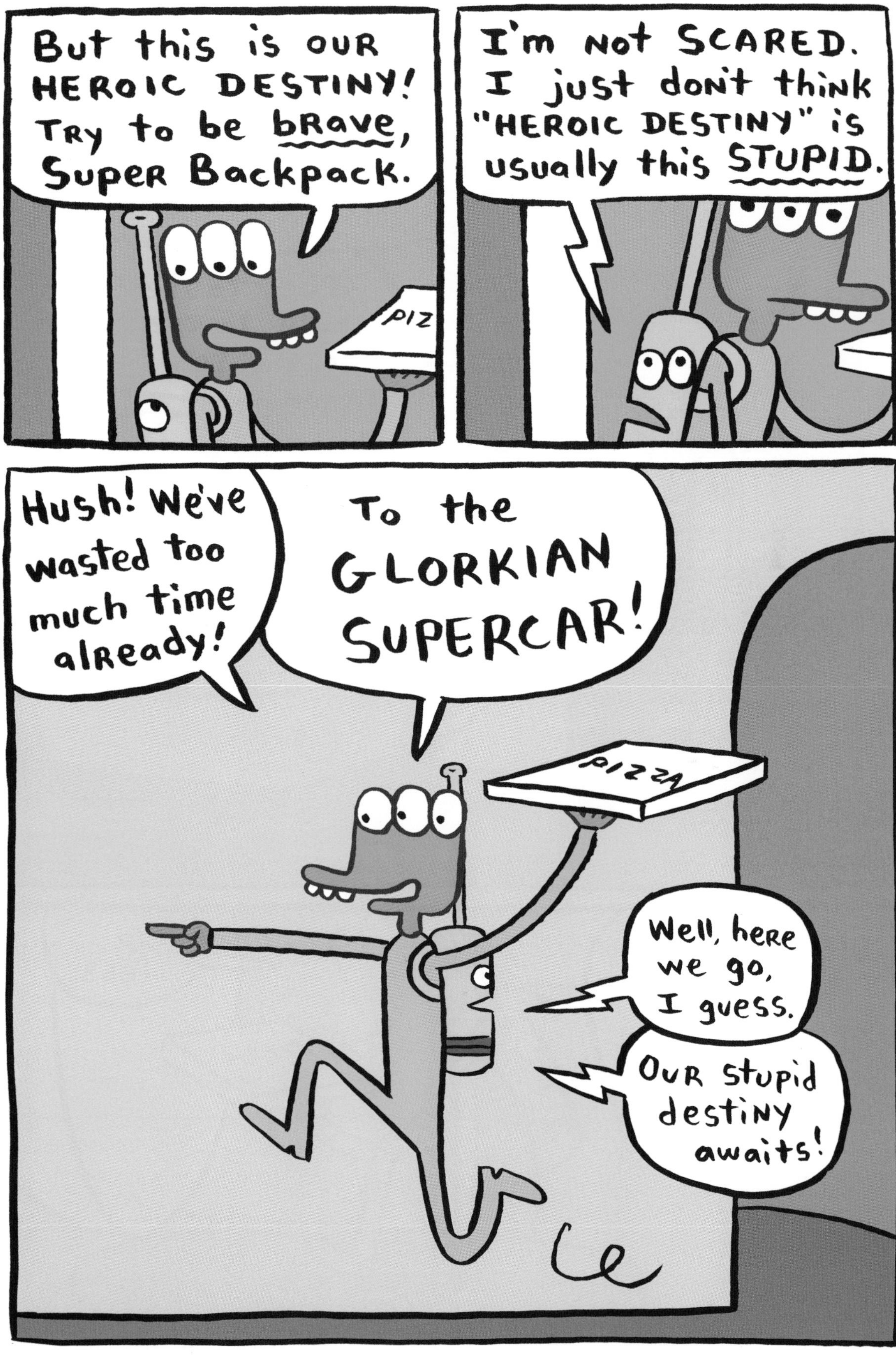

But this is OUR HEROIC DESTINY! Try to be brave, Super Backpack.
PIZ
I'm not SCARED. I just don't think "HEROIC DESTINY" is usually this STUPID.
Hush! We've wasted too much time already!
To the GLORKIAN SUPERCAR!
PIZZA
Well, here we go, I guess.
Our stupid destiny awaits!

CHAPTER FOUR

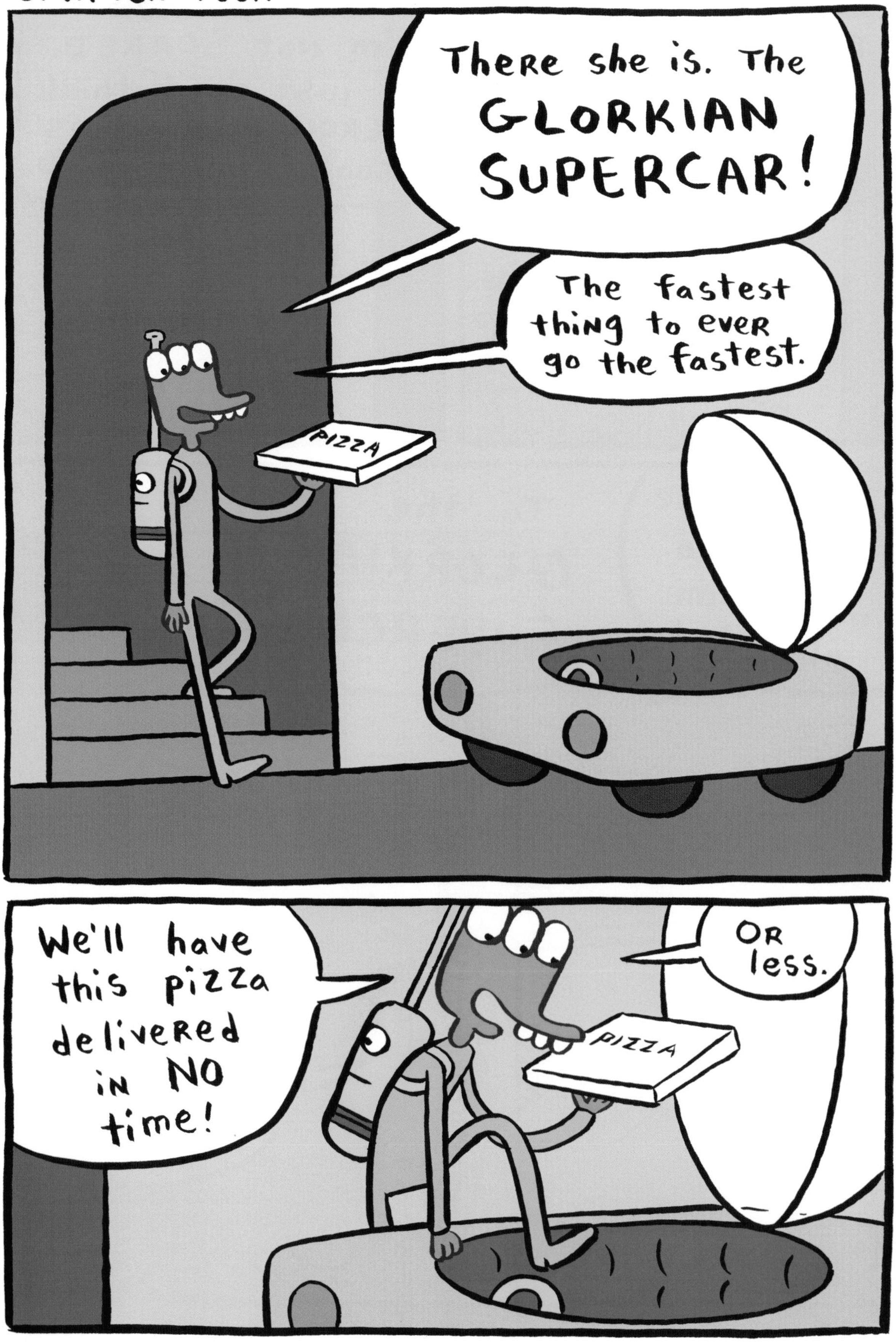
There she is. The GLORKIAN SUPERCAR!
The fastest thing to ever go the fastest.
PIZZA
We'll have this pizza delivered in NO time!
OR less.
PIZZA

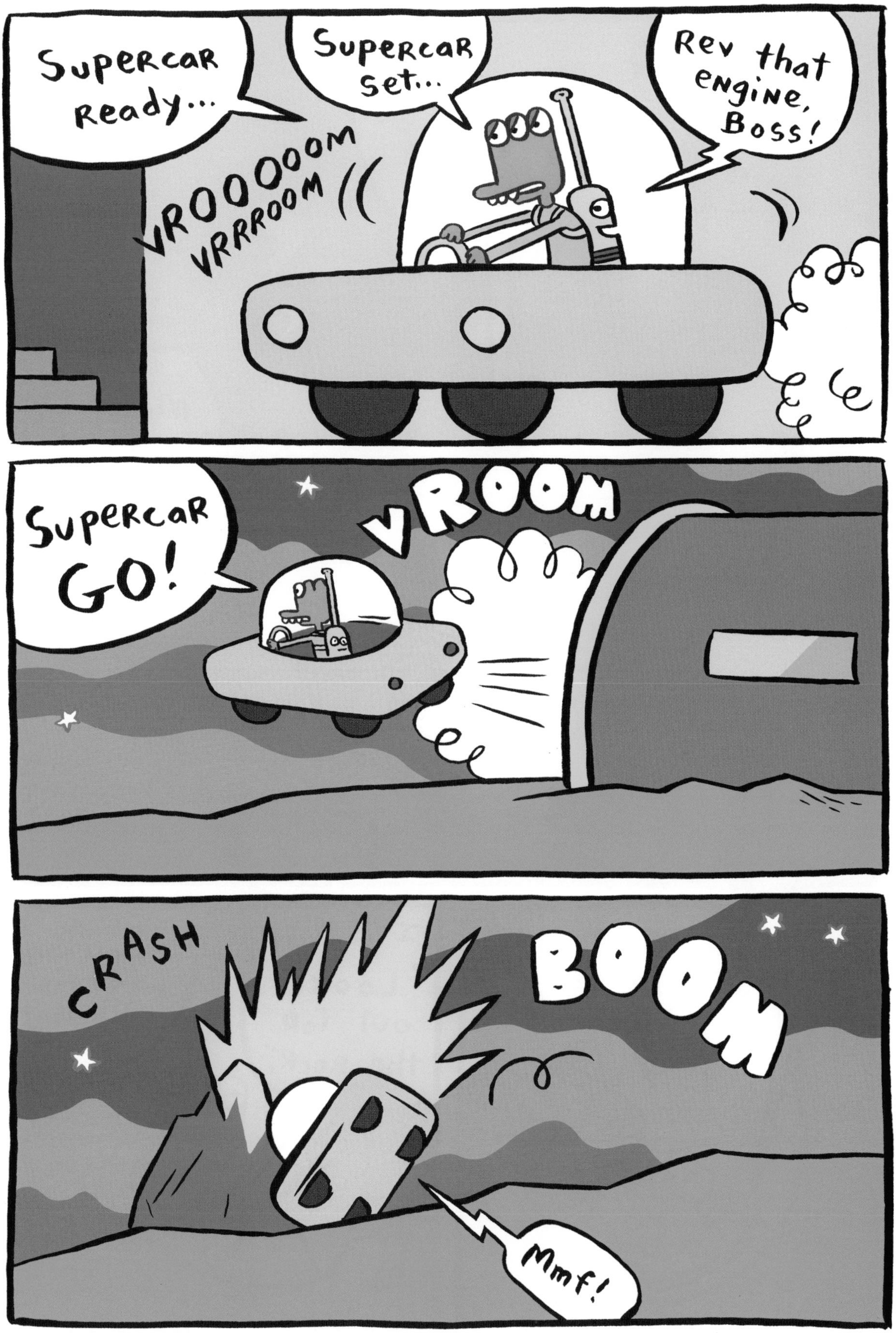
Supercar Ready...
Supercar set...
Rev that engine, Boss!
VROOOOOOM VRRROOM
Supercar GO!
VROOM
CRASH
BOOM
Mmf!

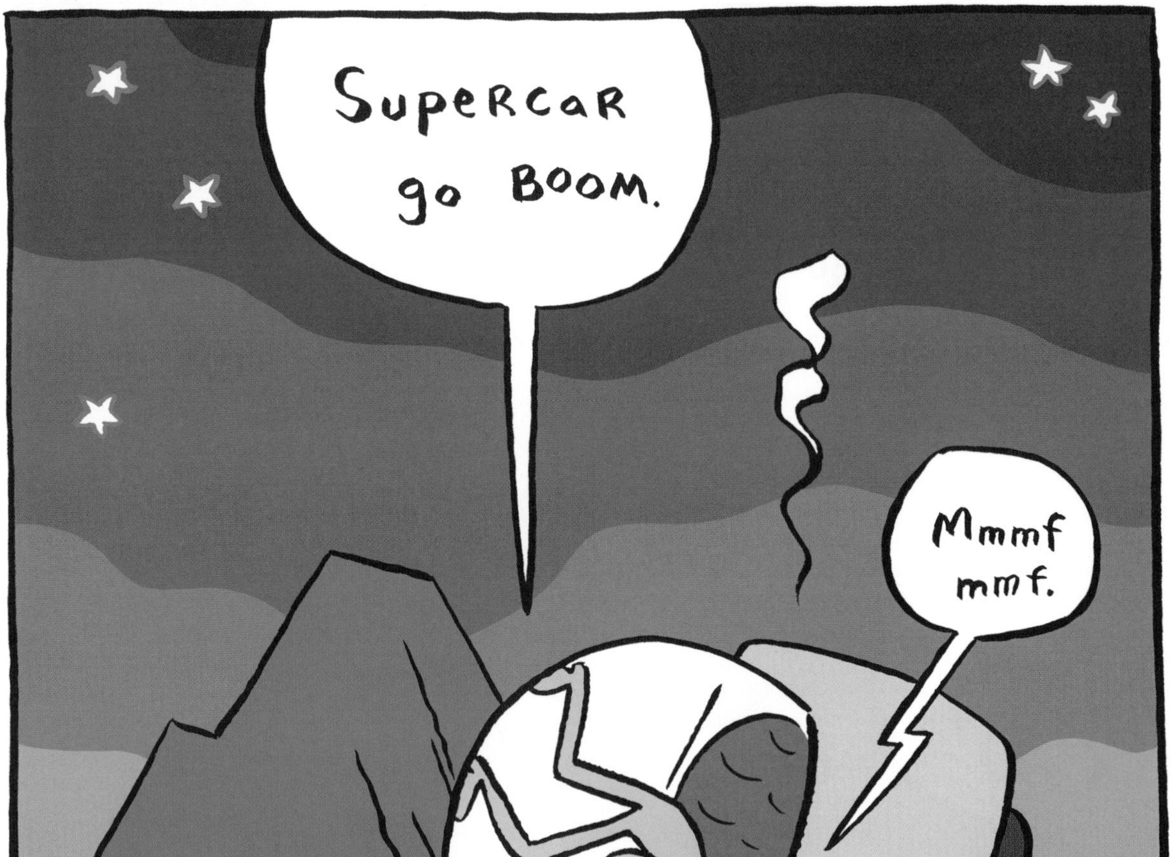
Supercar go BOOM.
Mmmf mmf.
Mmf!
What did you say?
I said, "Look out for the rock."
I think it's a little late for that, don't you?
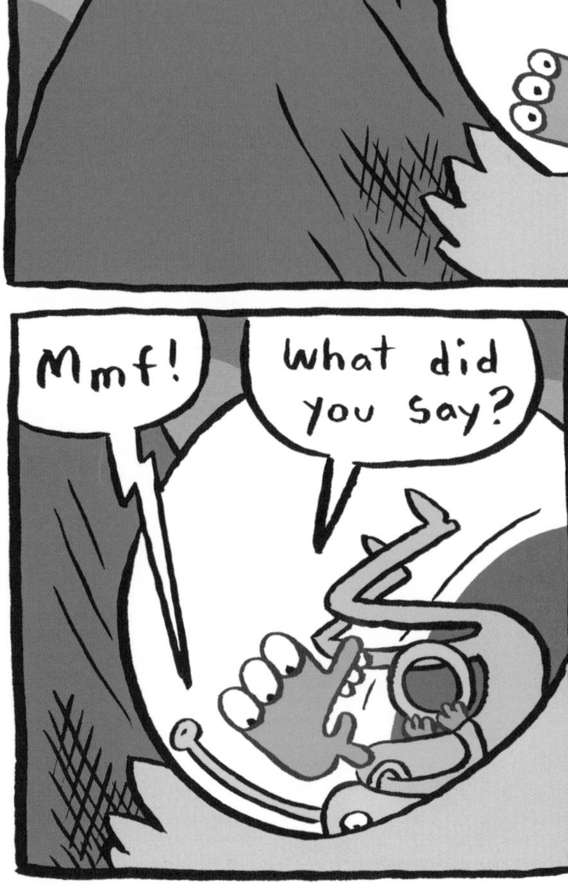

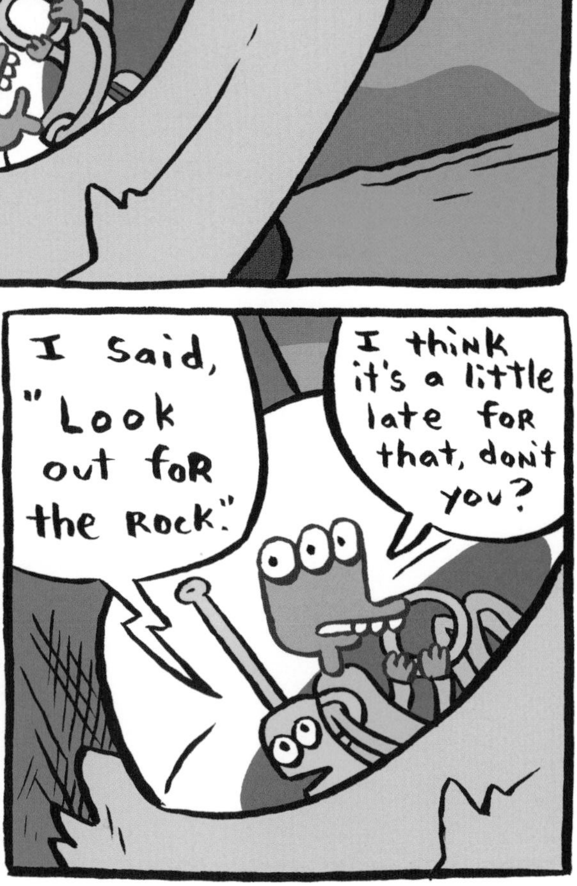

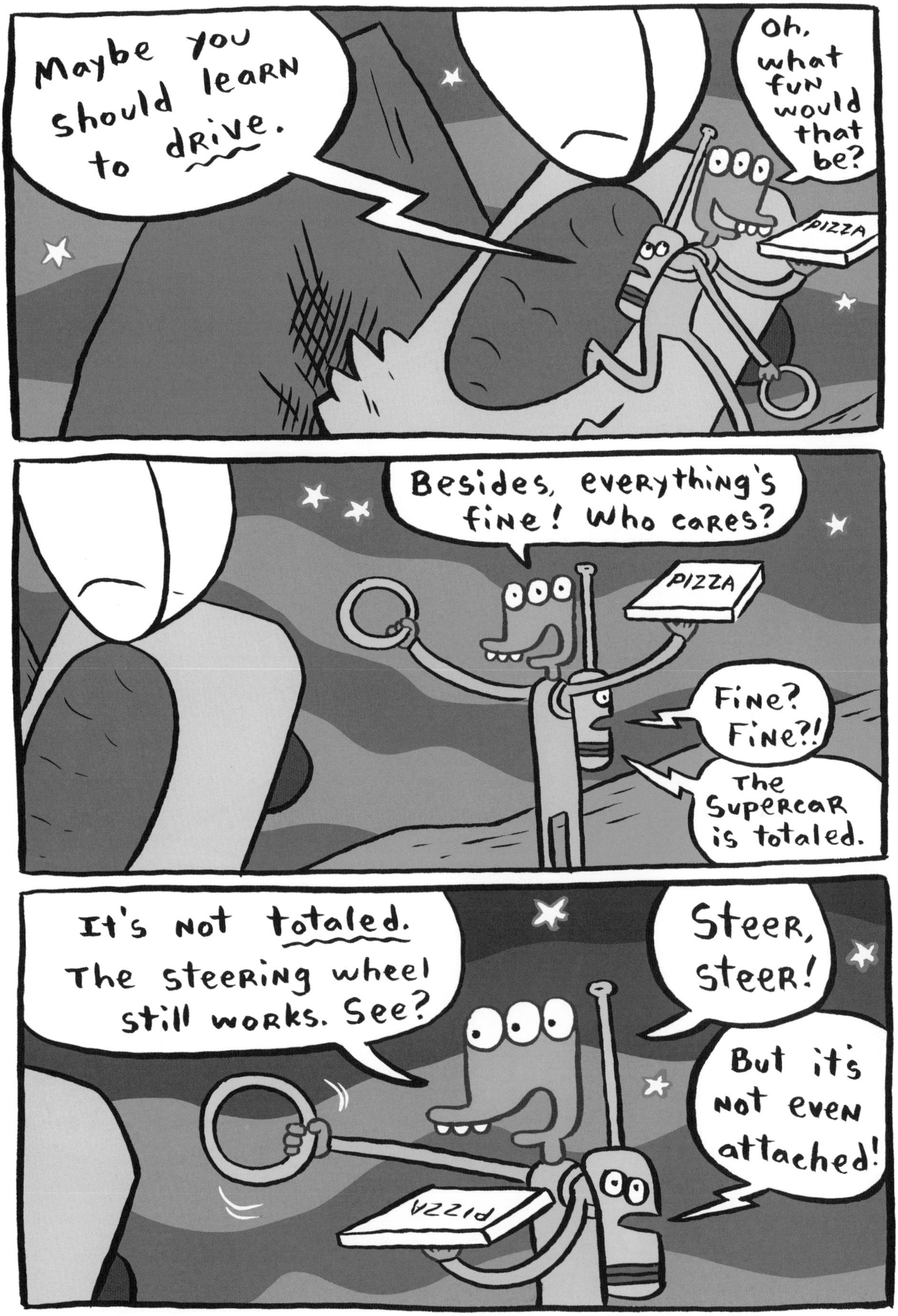
Maybe you should learn to drive.
Oh, what fun would that be?
Besides, everything's fine! Who cares?
Fine? Fine?!
The Supercar is totaled.
It's not totaled. The steering wheel still works. See?
Steer, steer!
But it's not even attached!

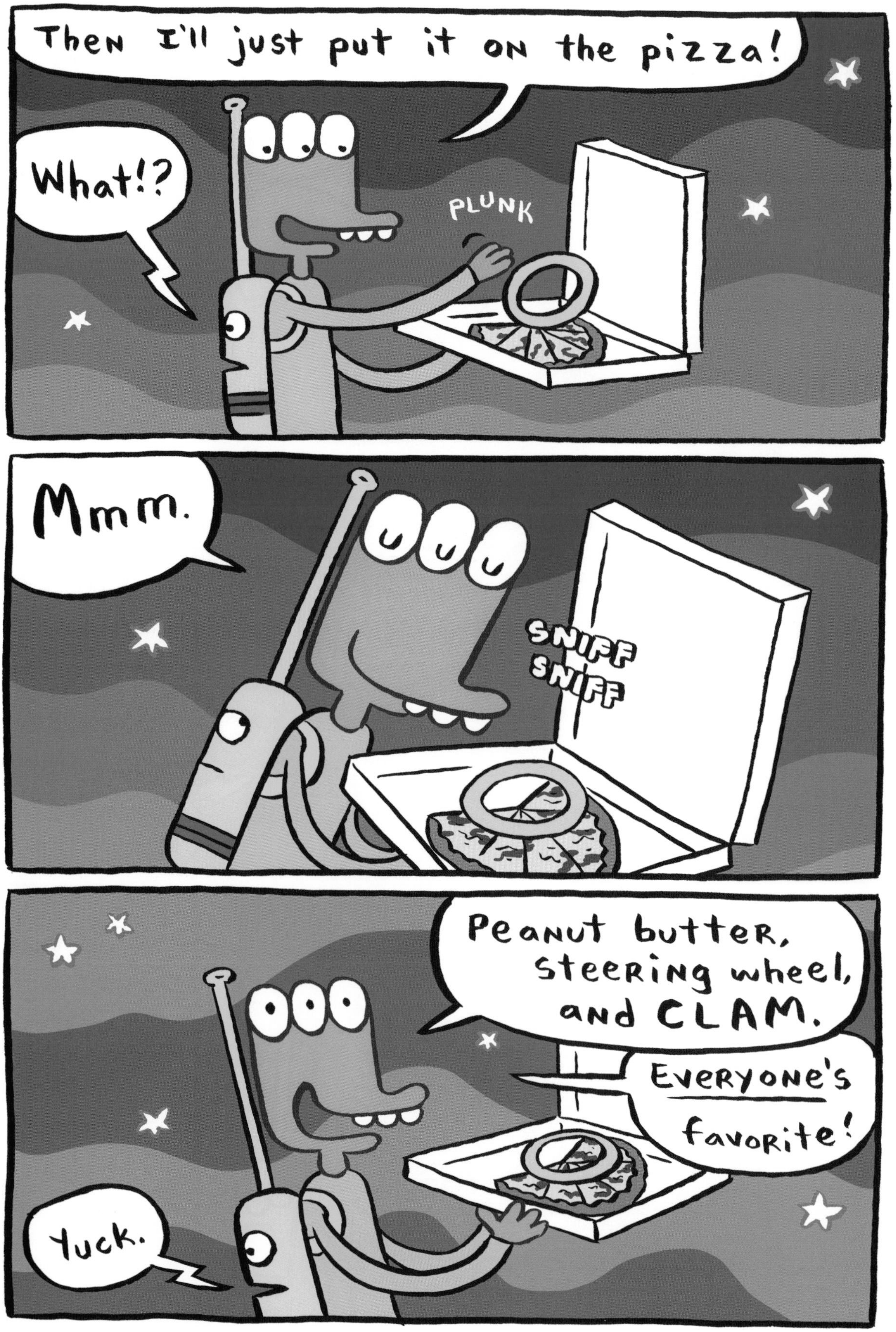
Then I'll just put it on the pizza!
What!?
PLUNK
Mmm.
SNIFF SNIFF
Peanut butter, steering wheel, and CLAM.
Everyone's favorite!
Yuck.

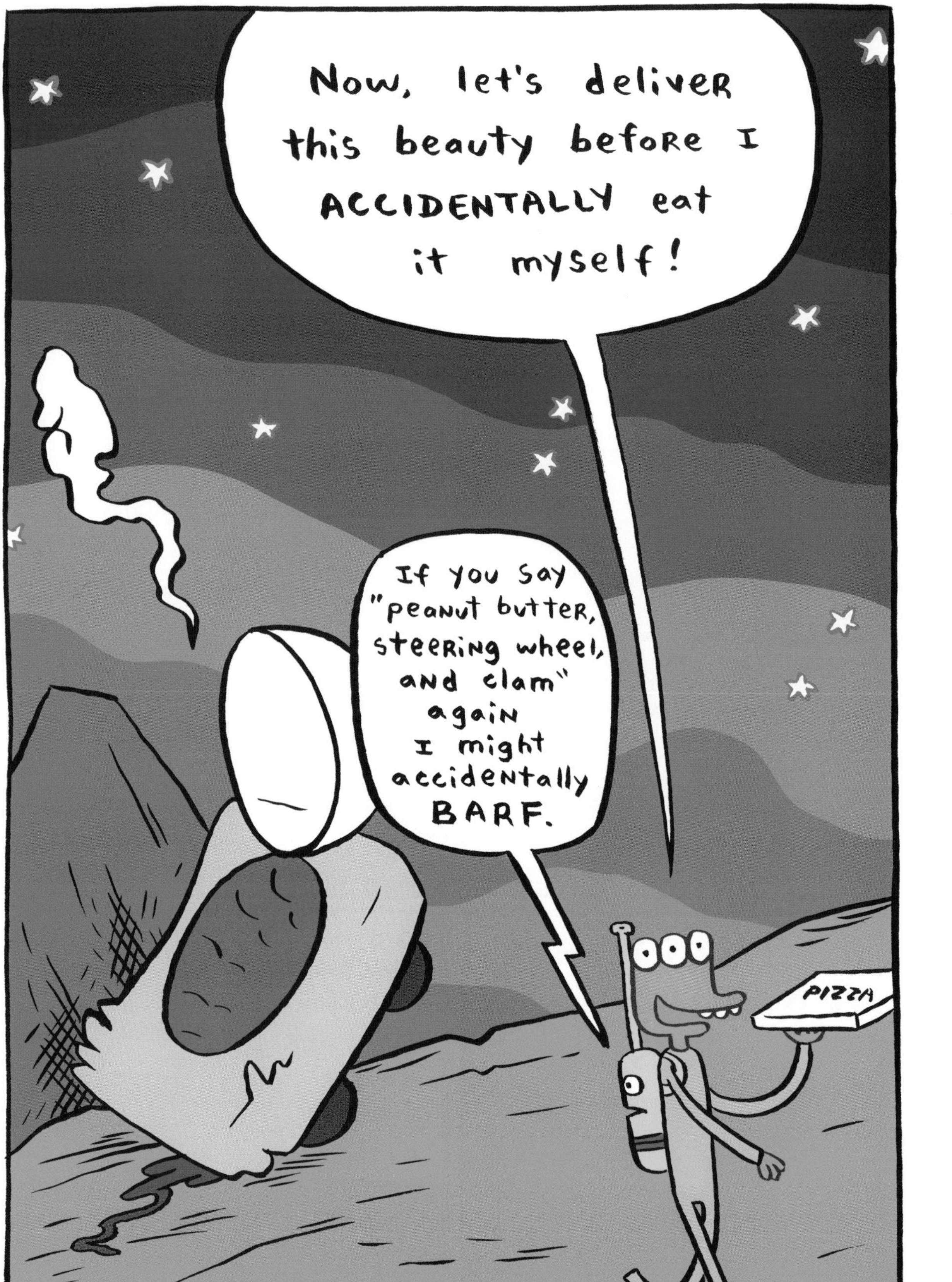
Now, let's deliver this beauty before I ACCIDENTALLY eat it myself!
If you say "peanut butter, steering wheel, and clam" again I might accidentally BARF.
PIZZA

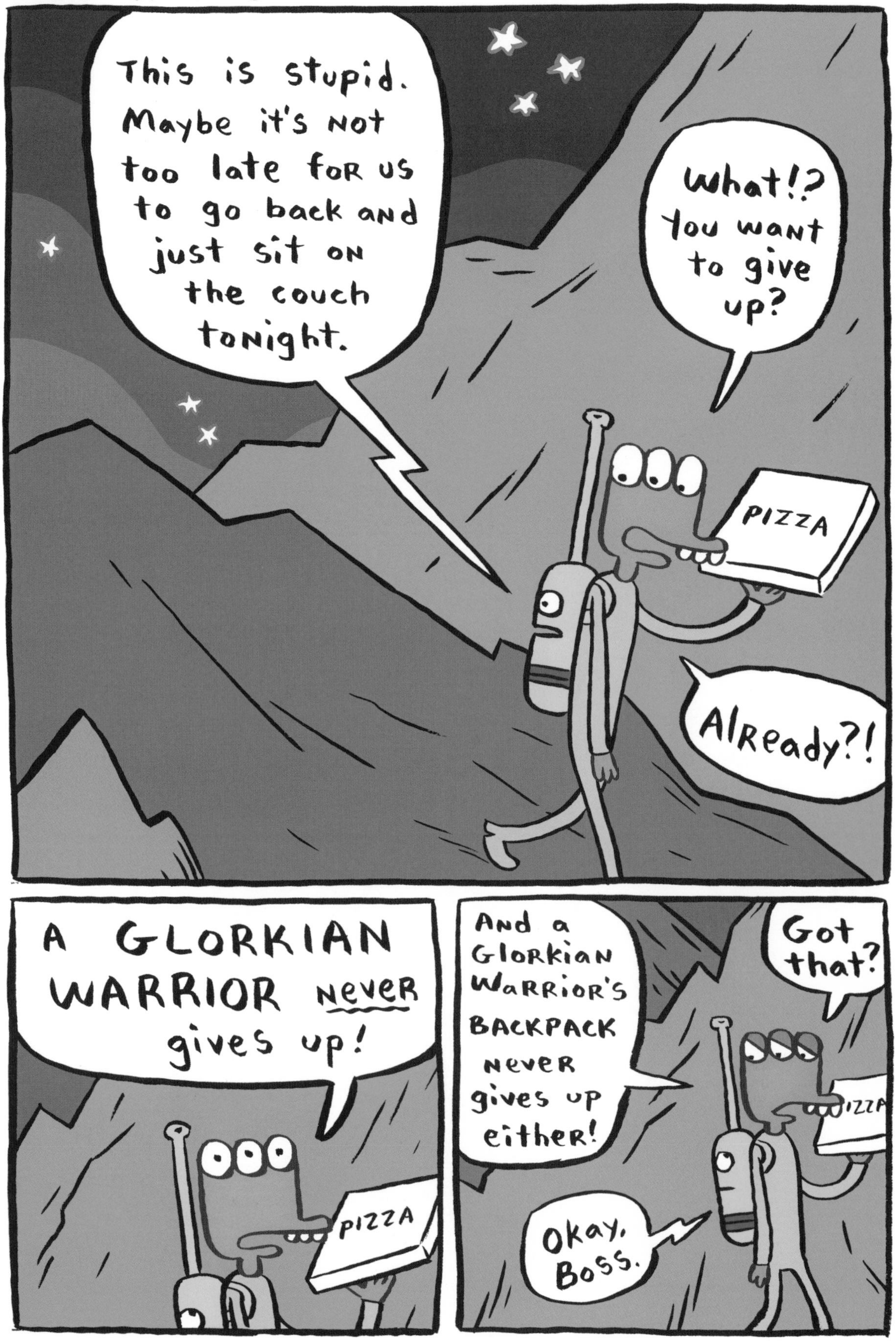
This is stupid. Maybe it's not too late for us to go back and just sit on the couch tonight.
What!? You want to give up?
PIZZA
Already?!
A GLORKIAN WARRIOR never gives up!
PIZZA
And a Glorkian Warrior's BACKPACK never gives up either!
Got that?
Okay, Boss.

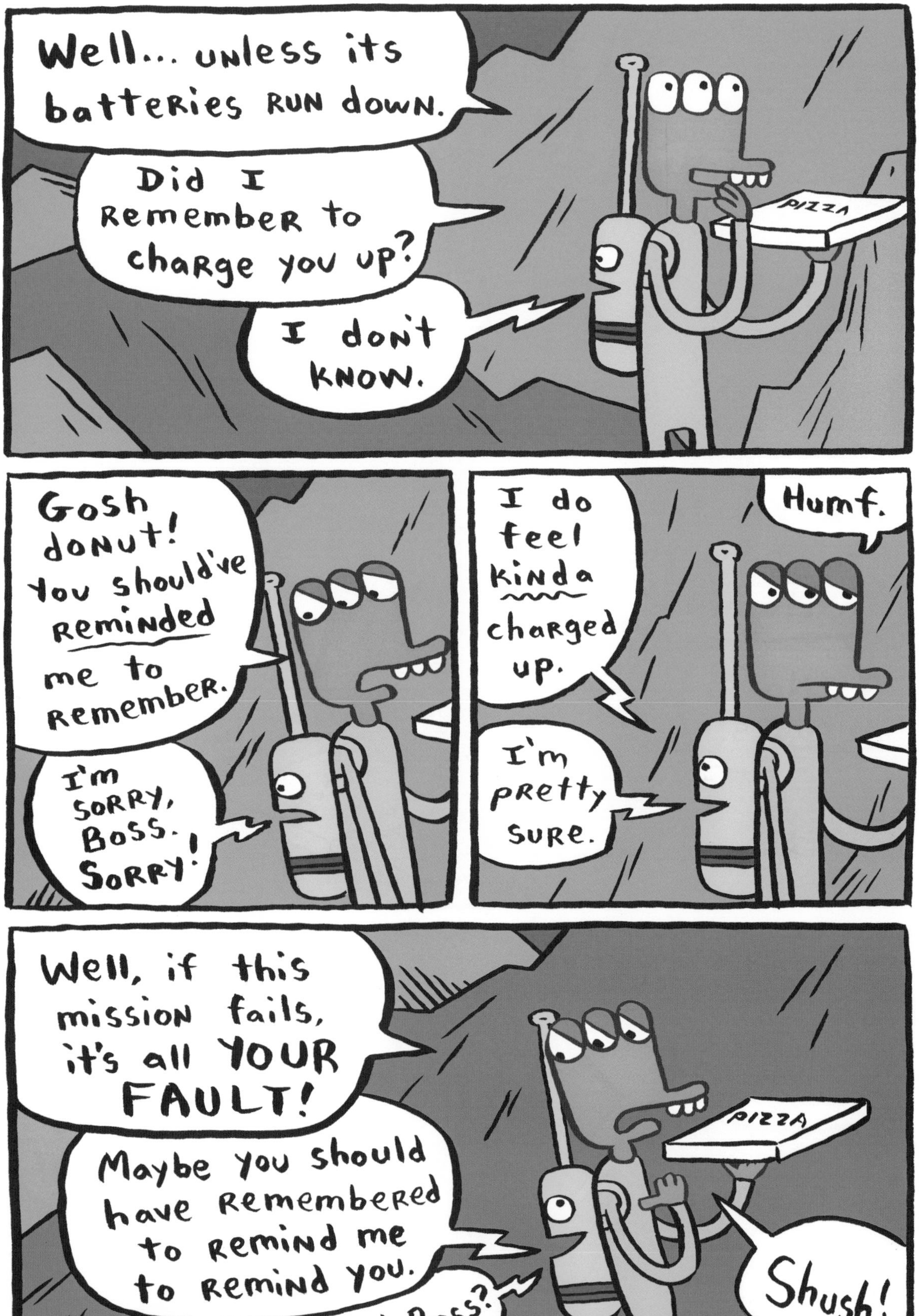

Well... unless its batteries RUN down.
Did I Remember to charge you up?
I don't KNOW.
Gosh donut! You should've Reminded me to Remember.
I'm SORRY, BOSS. SORRY!
I do feel kinda charged up.
Humf.
I'm pretty sure.
PIZZA
Well, if this mission fails, it's all YOUR FAULT!
Maybe you should have Remembered to Remind me to Remind you.
Right, Boss?
Shush!

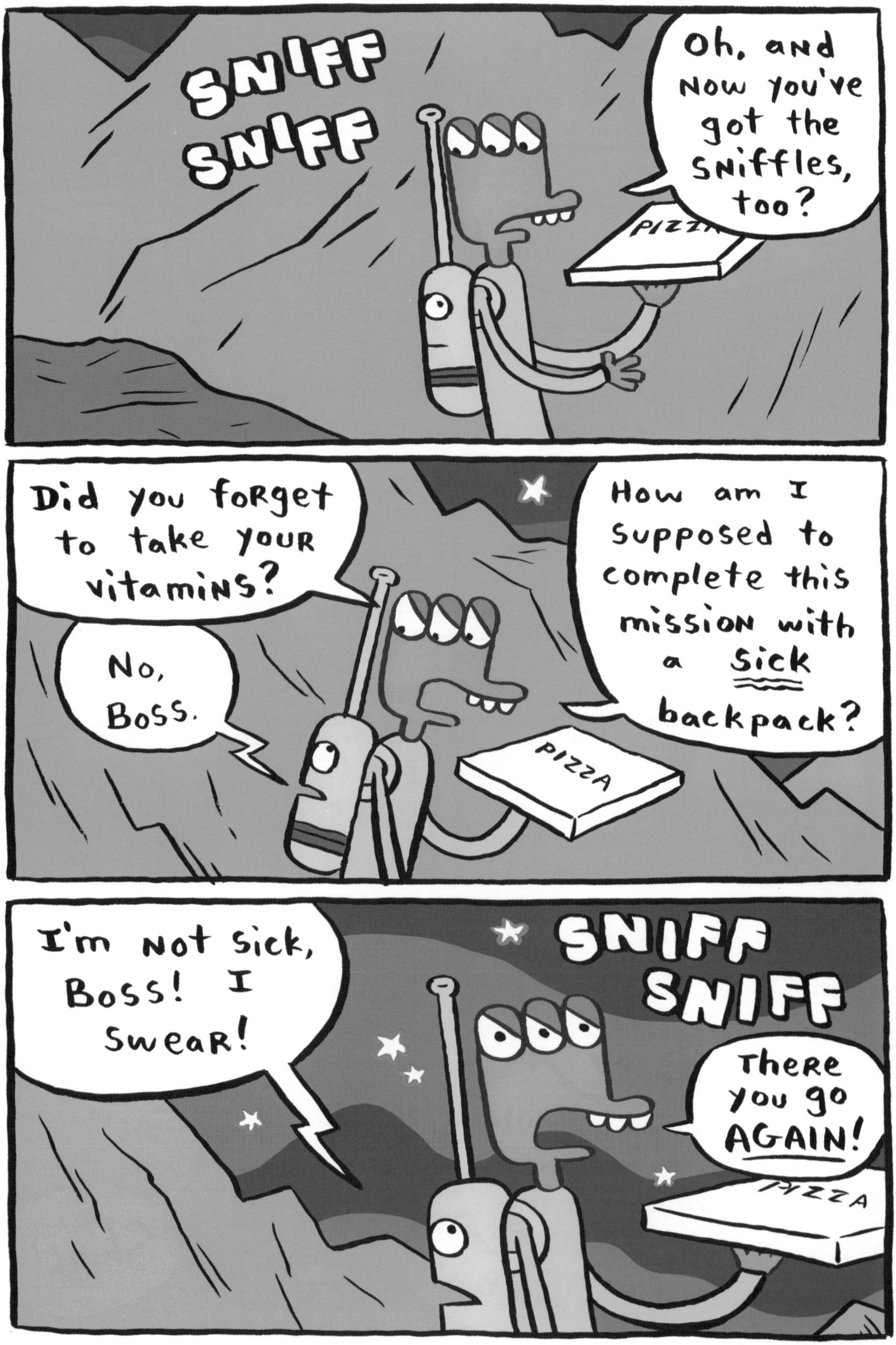
SNIFF
SNIFF
Oh, and now you've got the sniffles, too?
PIZZA
Did you forget to take your vitamins?
No, Boss.
How am I supposed to complete this mission with a sick backpack?
PIZZA
I'm not sick, Boss! I swear!
SNIFF
SNIFF
There you go AGAIN!
PIZZA

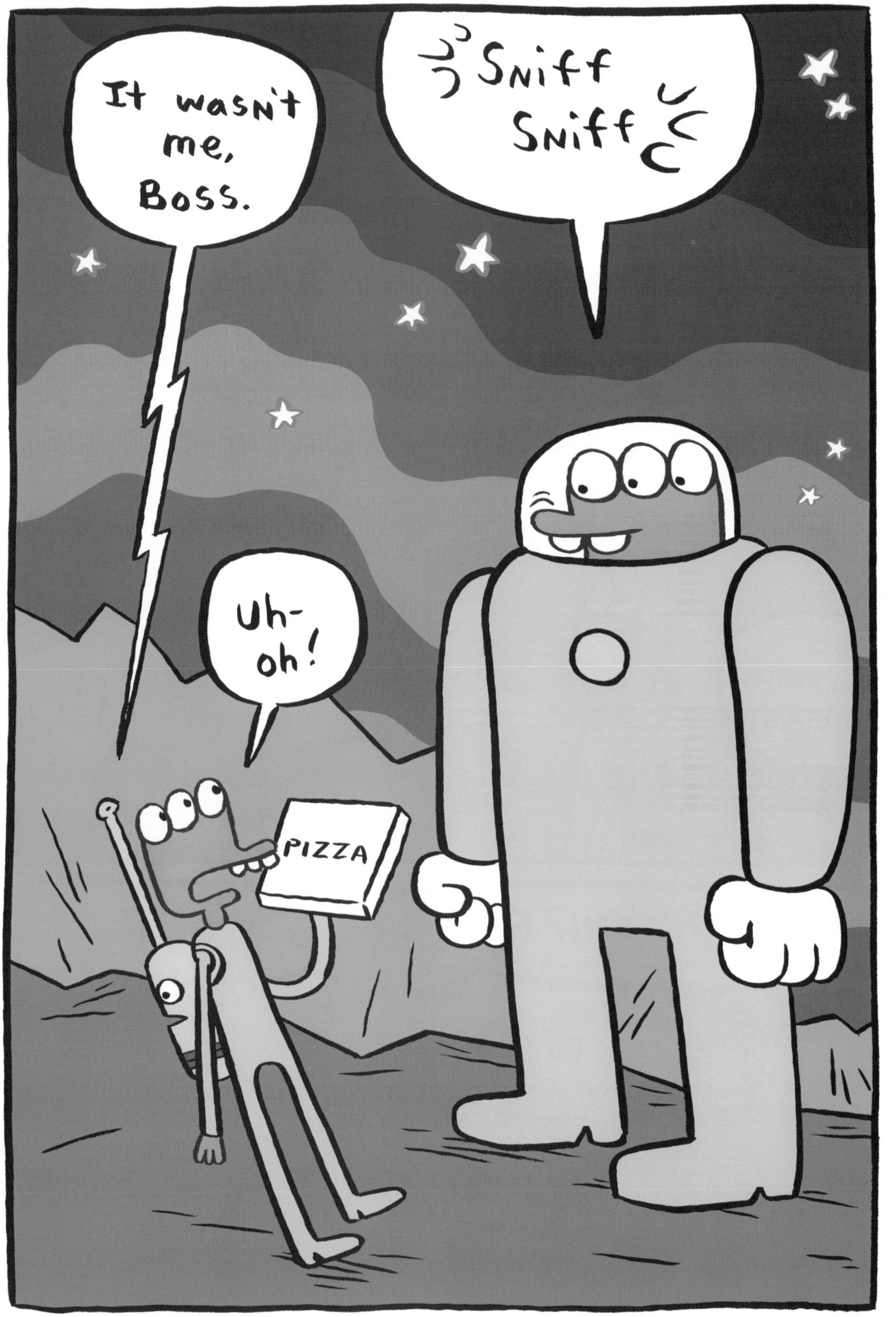
It wasn't me, Boss.
Sniff Sniff
Uh-oh!
PIZZA

CHAPTER SIX

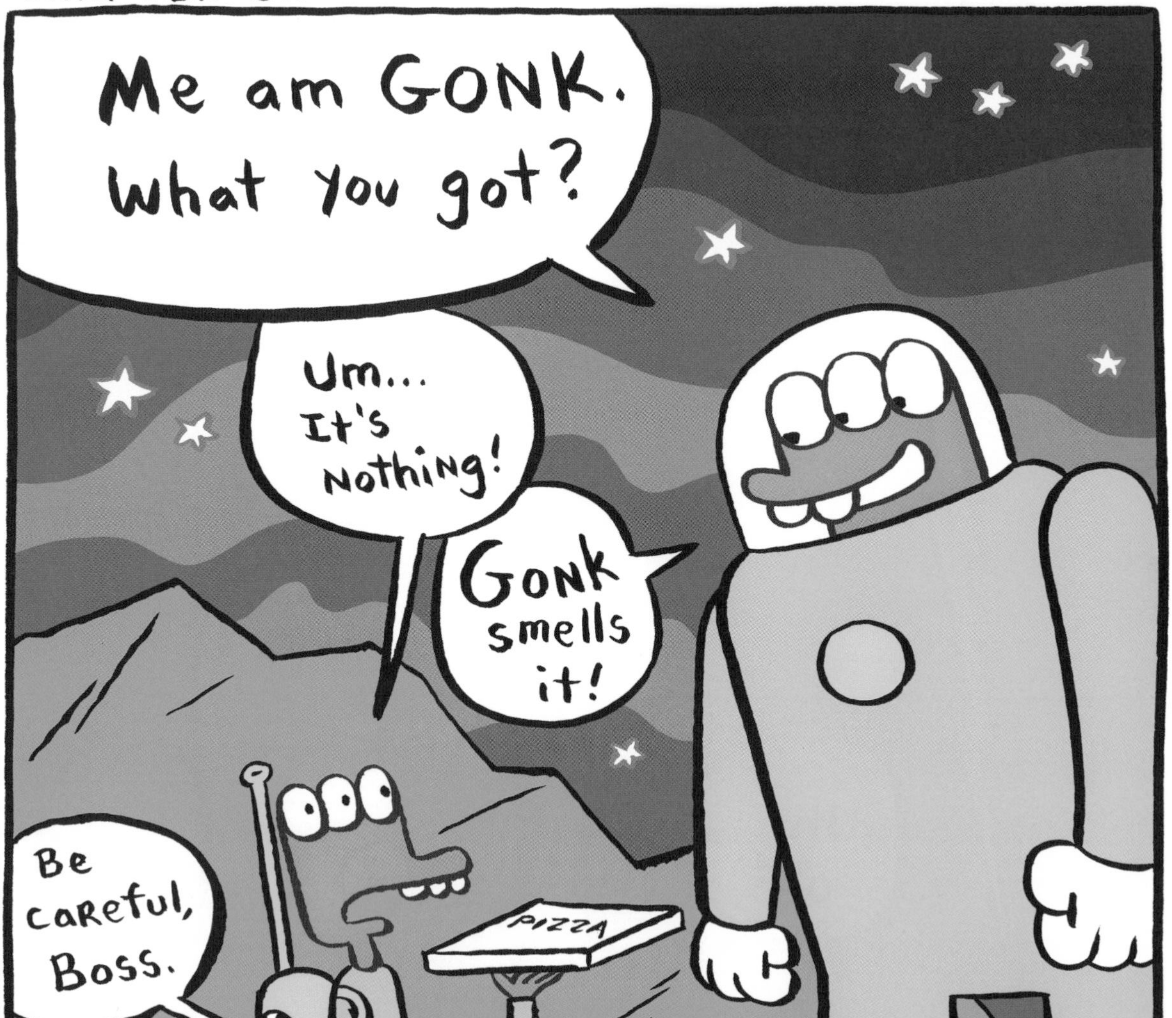
Me am GONK. What you got?
Um... It's nothing!
Gonk smells it!
Be careful, Boss.
PIZZA

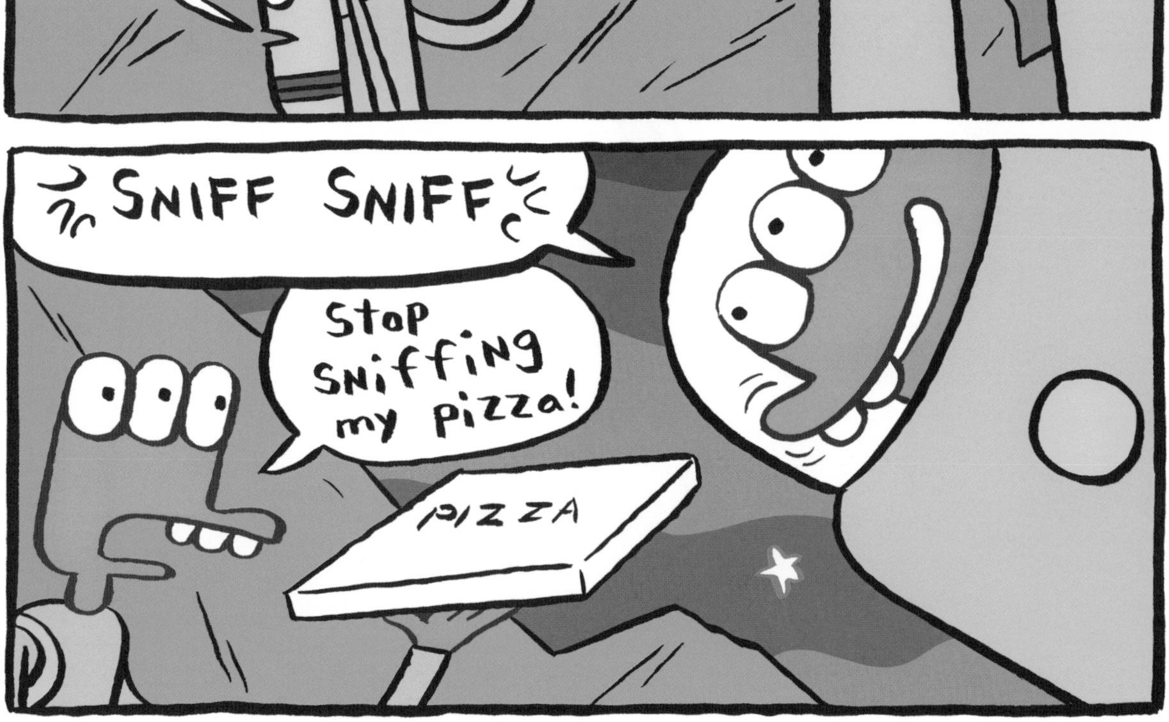
SNIFF SNIFF
Stop sniffing my pizza!
PIZZA

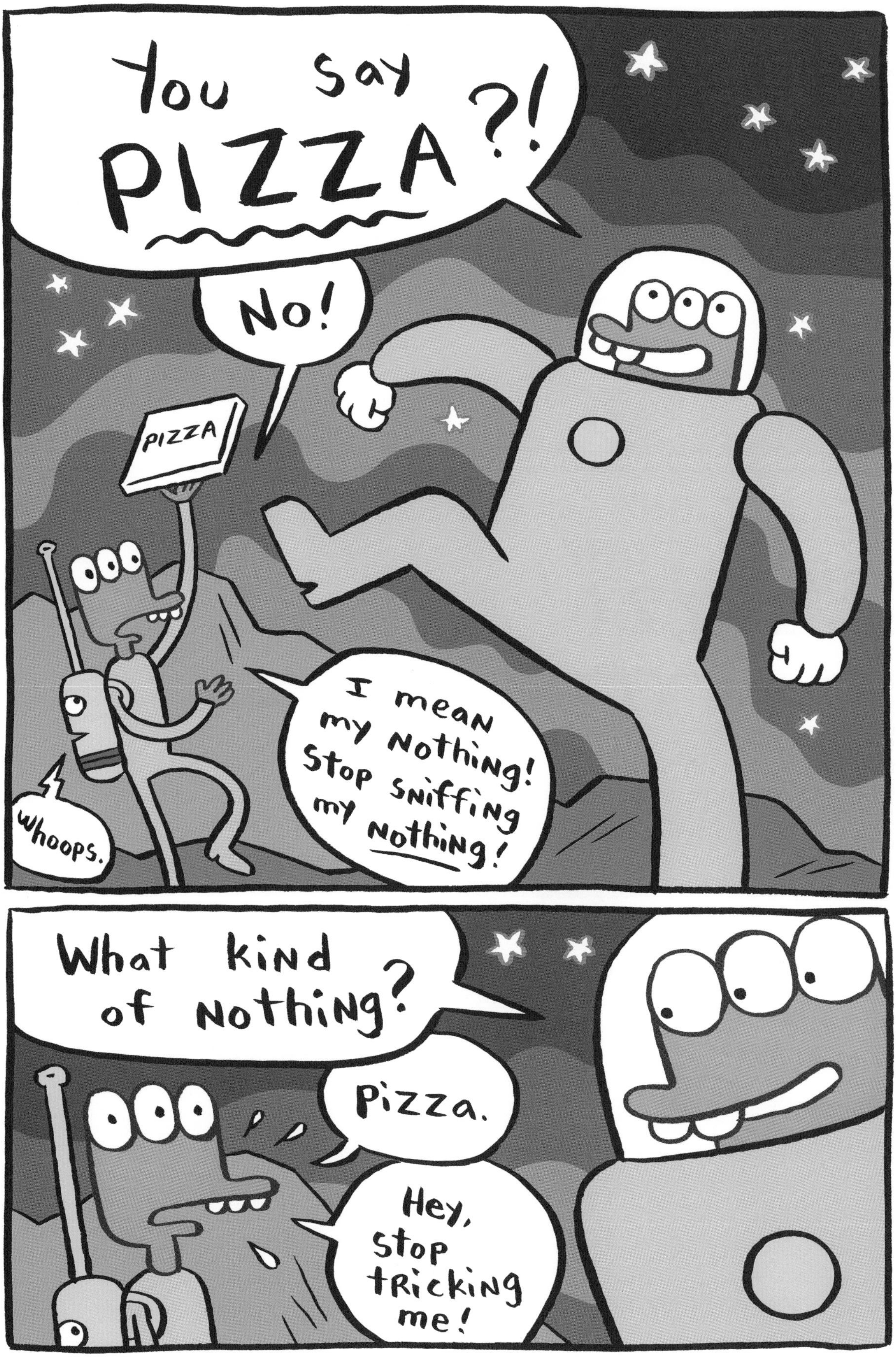
You say PIZZA?!
No!
PIZZA
I mean my Nothing! Stop sniffing my Nothing!
Whoops.
What kind of Nothing?
Pizza.
Hey, stop tricking me!

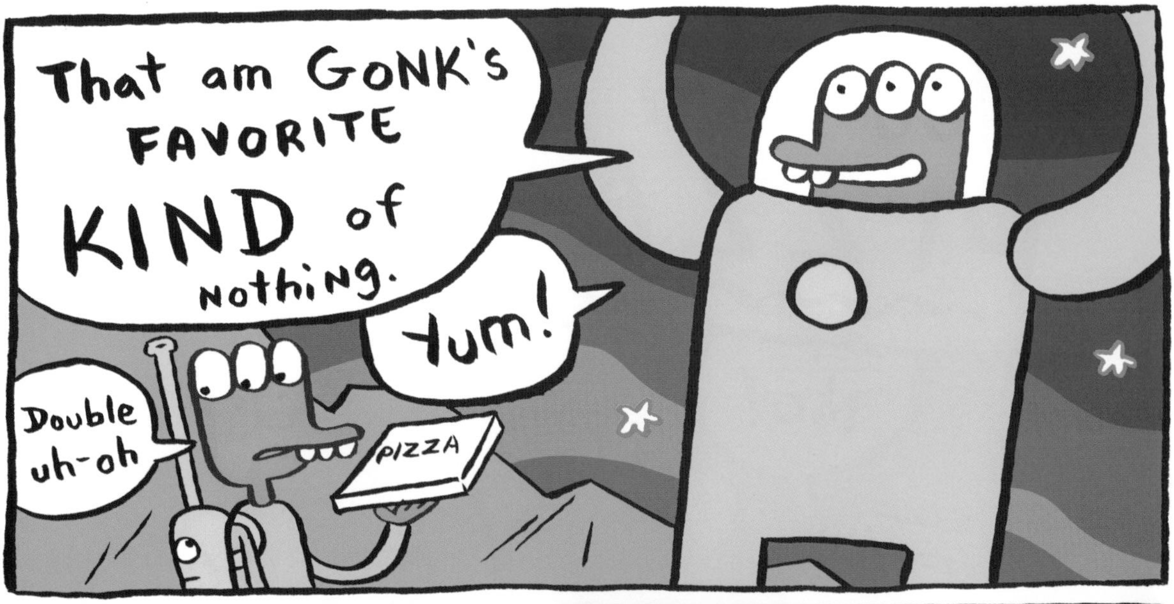
That am GONK's FAVORITE KIND of nothing.
Yum!
Double uh-oh
PIZZA

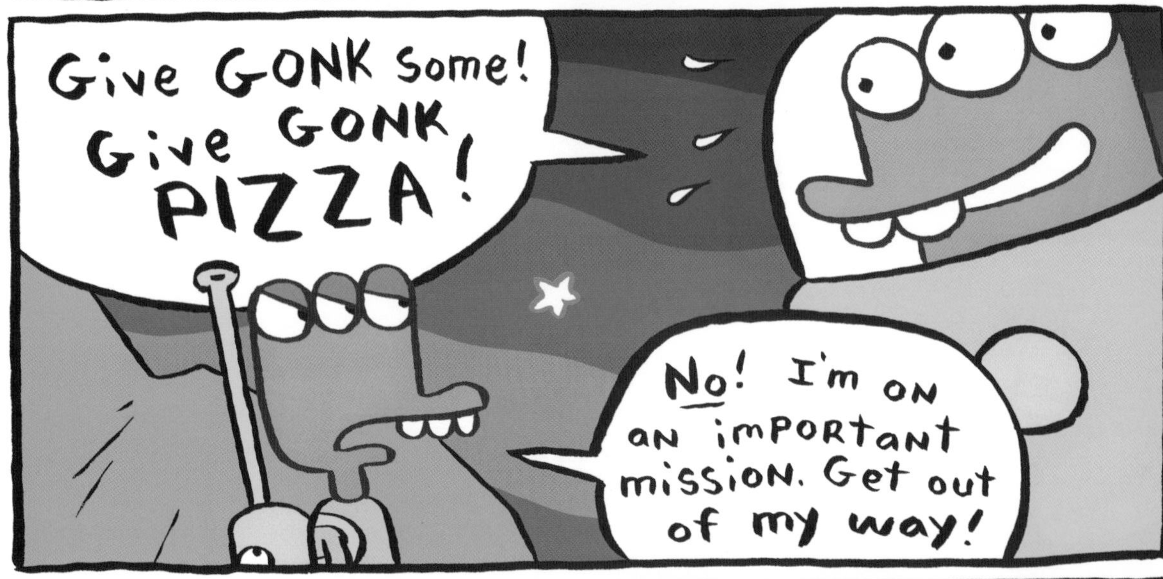
Give GONK some! Give GONK PIZZA!
No! I'm on an important mission. Get out of my way!

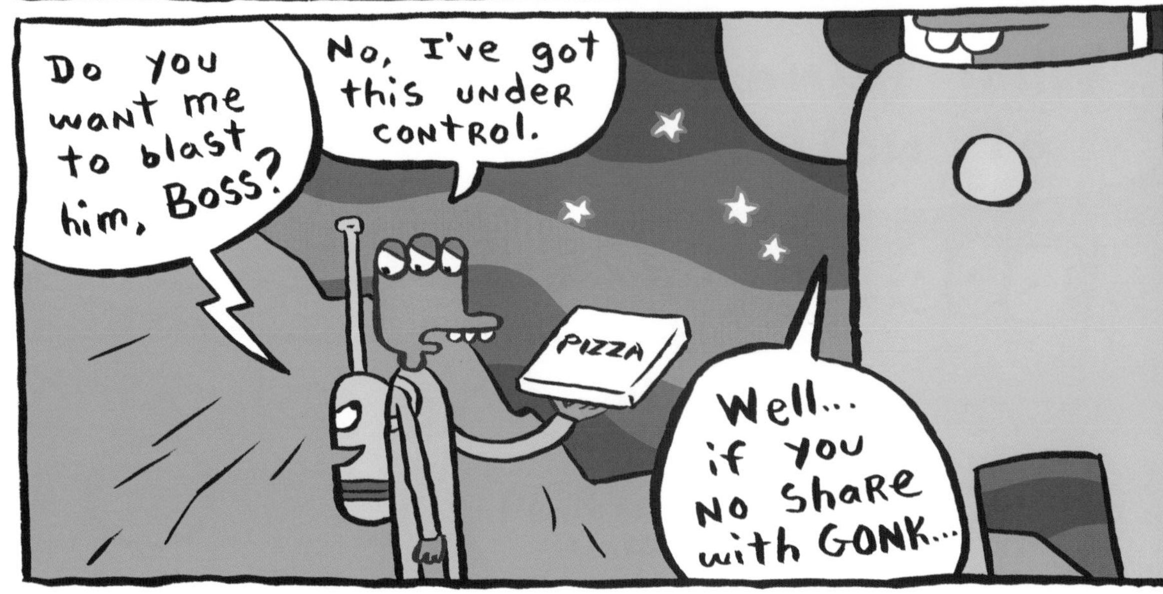
Do you want me to blast him, Boss?
No, I've got this under control.
PIZZA
Well... if you no share with GONK...

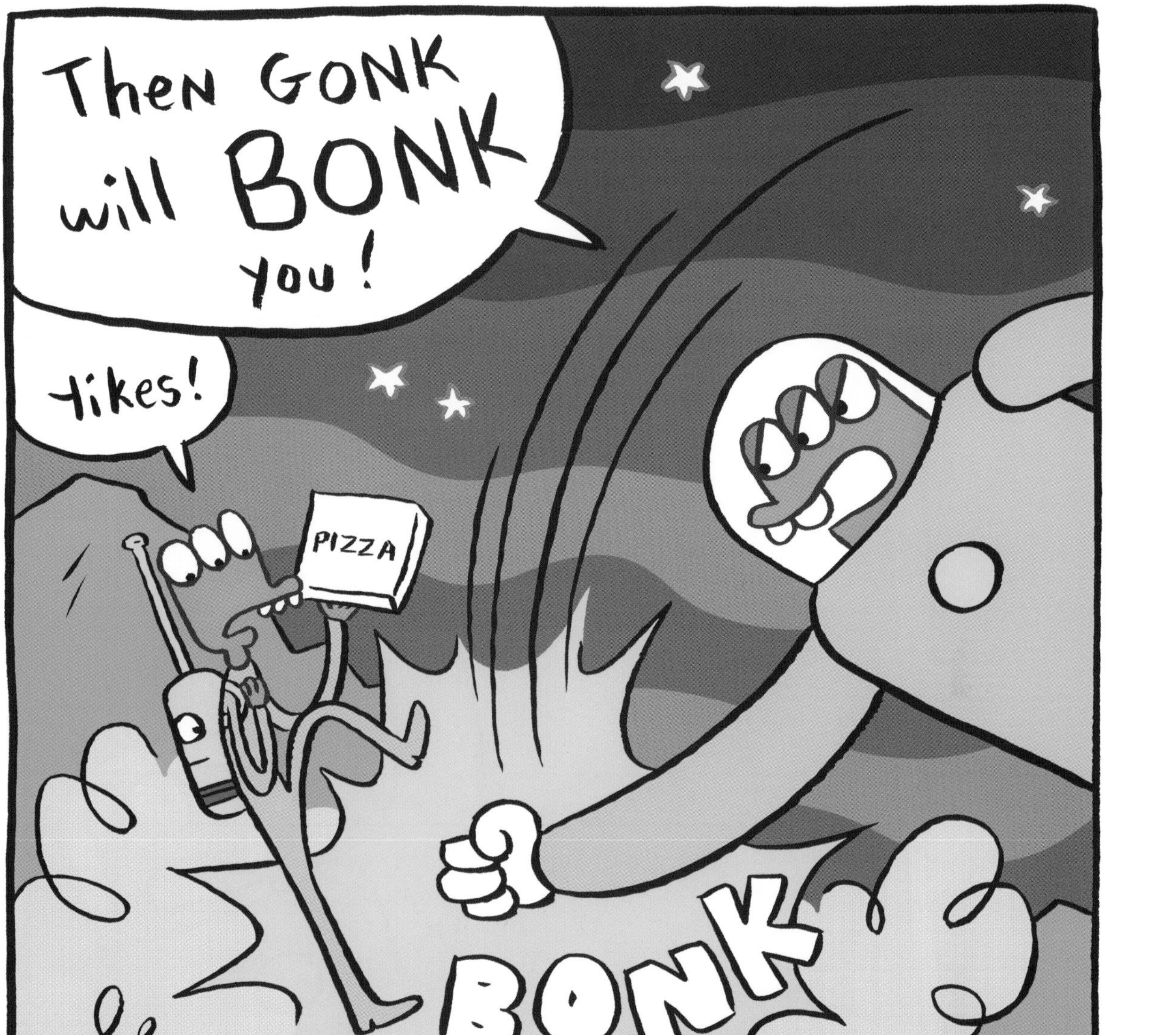
Then GONK will BONK you!
Yikes!
PIZZA
BONK

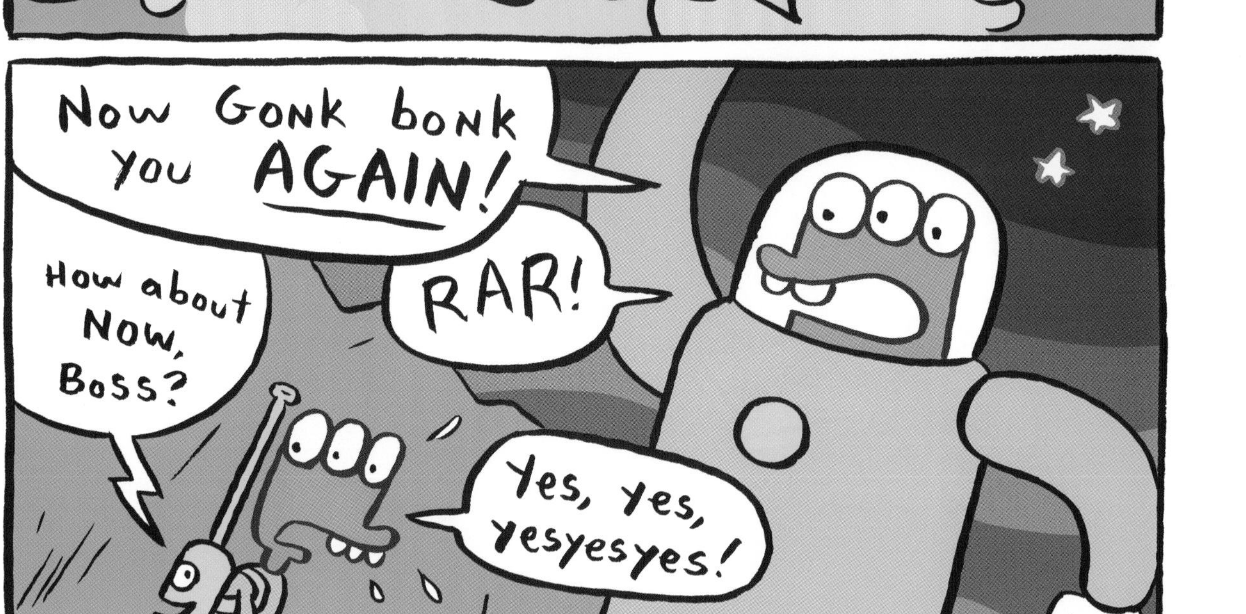
Now GONK bonk you AGAIN!
RAR!
How about NOW, Boss?
Yes, yes, yesyesyes!

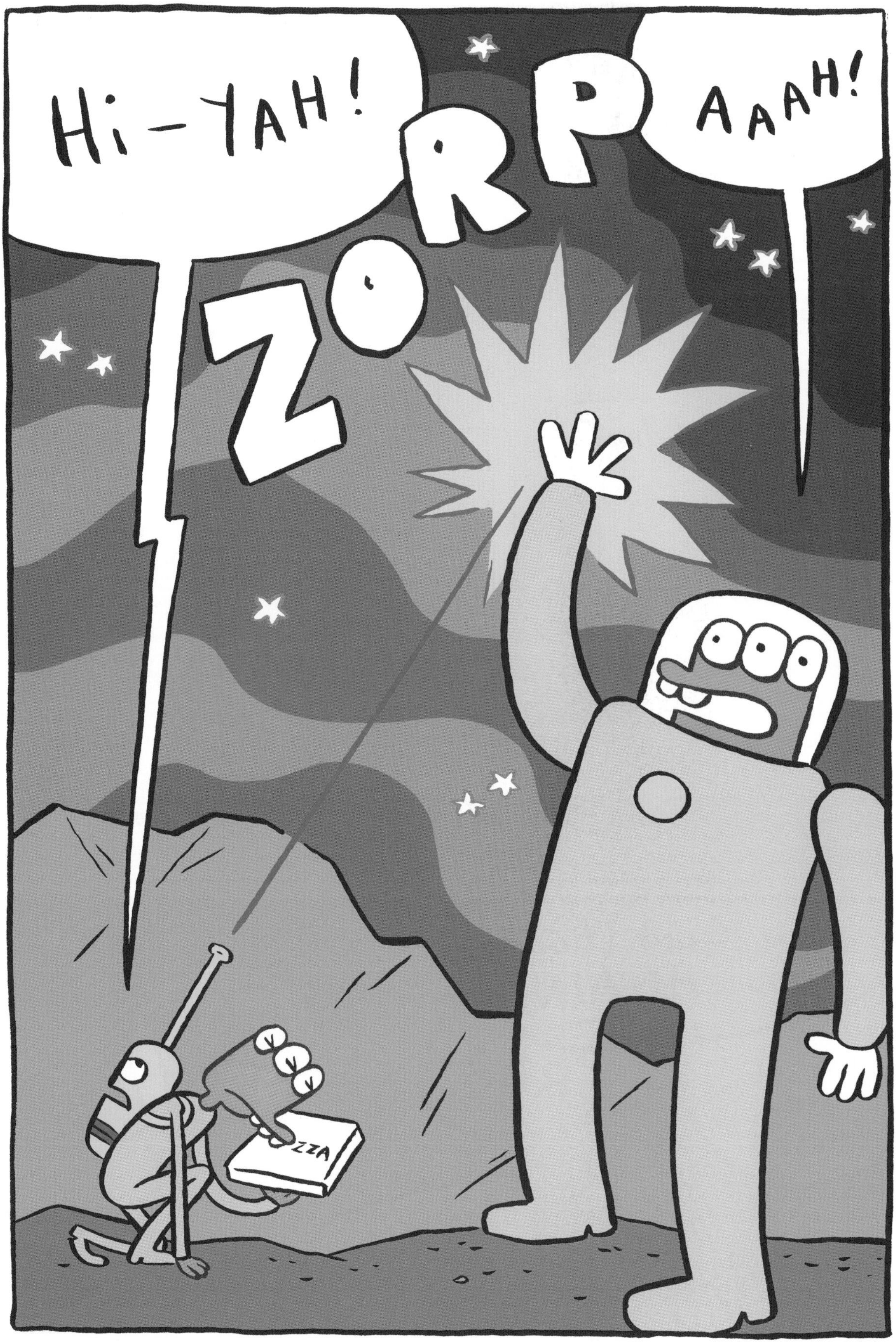
HI-YAH!
ZORP
AAAH!
ZZA

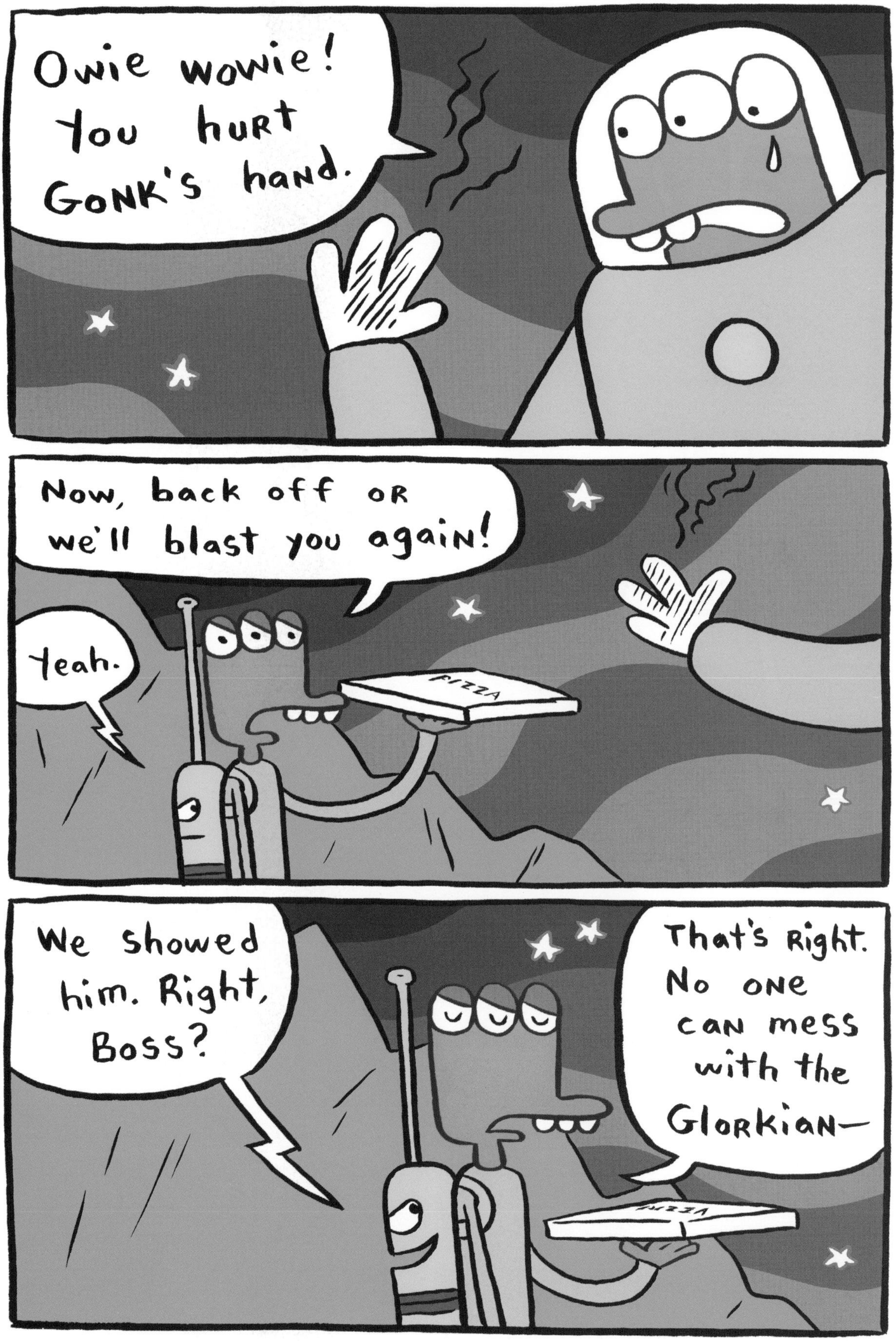
Owie wowie! You hurt GONK's hand.
Now, back off or we'll blast you again!
Yeah.
PIZZA
We showed him. Right, Boss?
That's Right. No one can mess with the Glorkian—
PIZZA

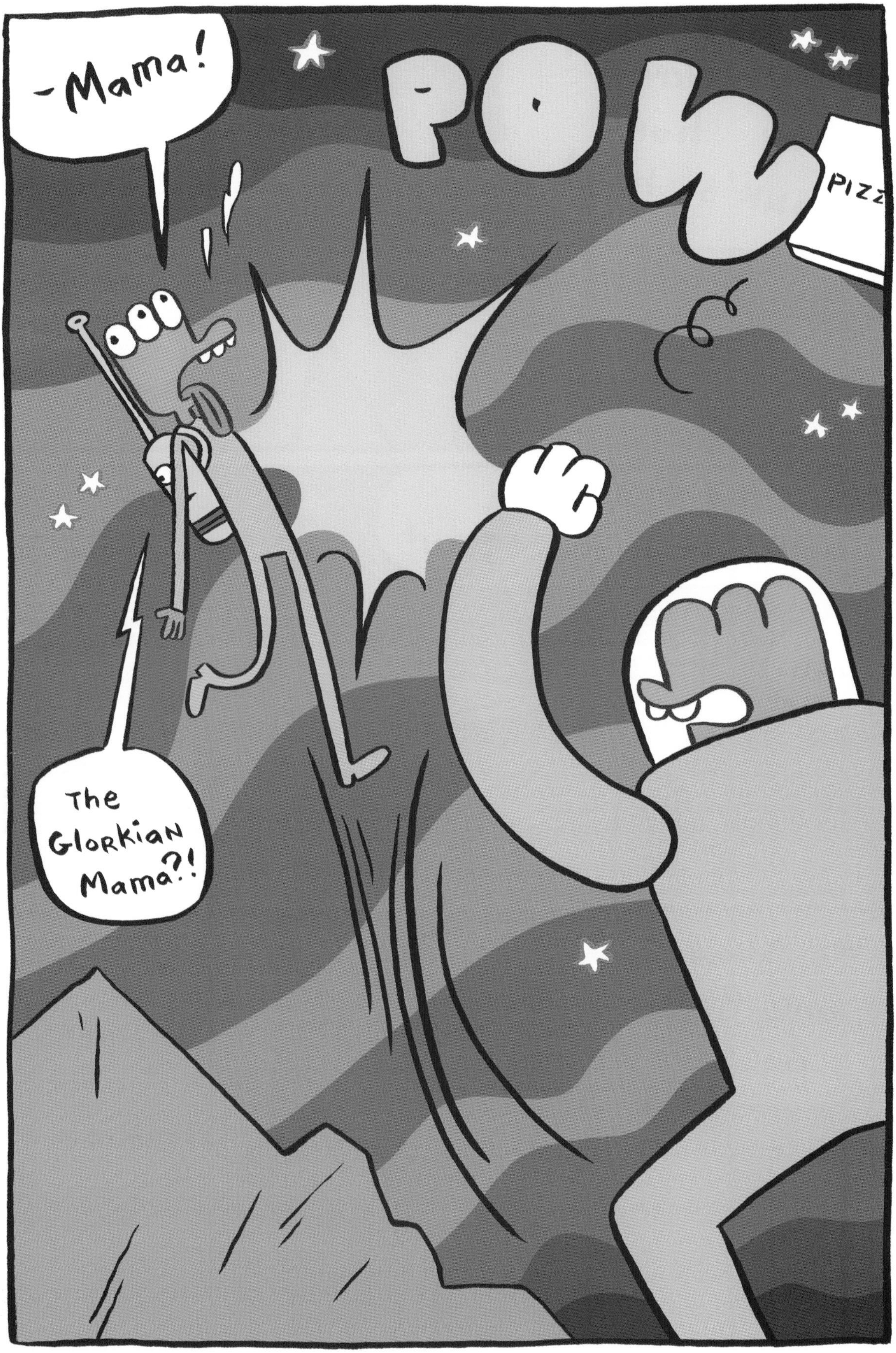
-Mama!
POW
PIZZ
The Glorkian Mama?!

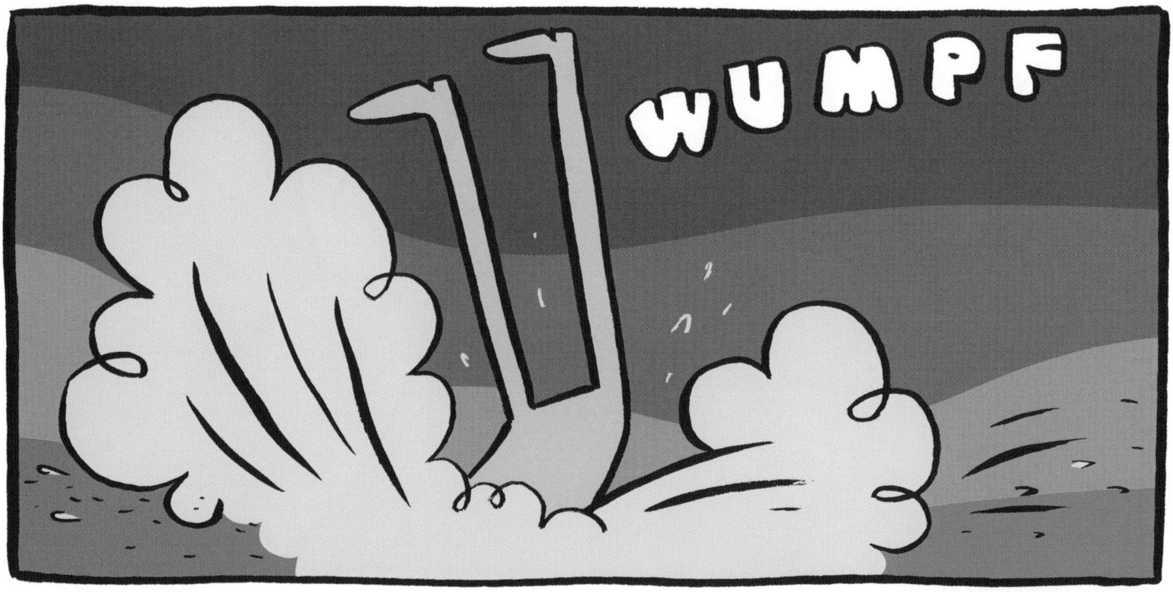
WUMPF

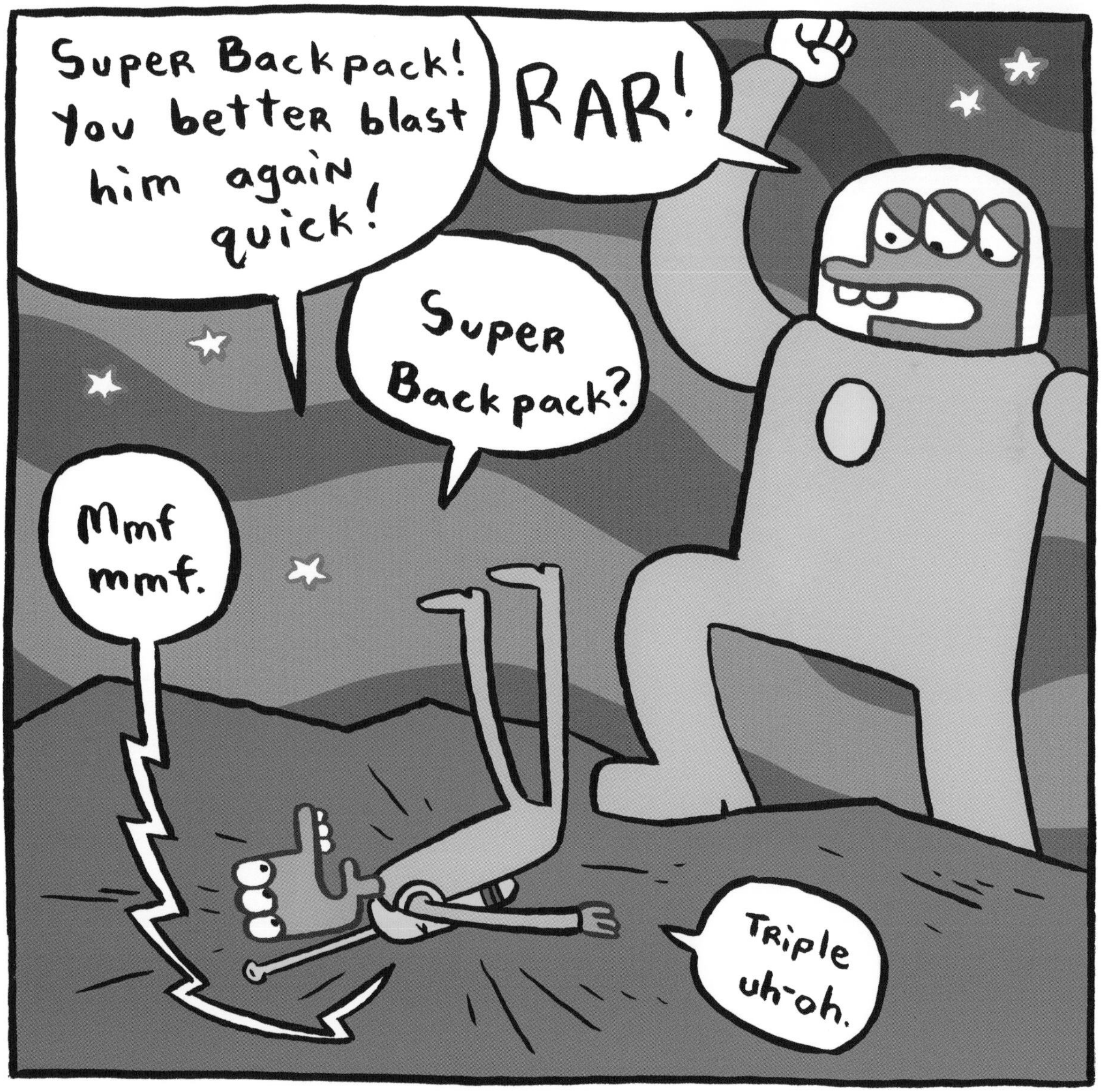
Super Backpack! You better blast him again quick!
RAR!
Super Backpack?
Mmf mmf.
Triple uh-oh.

CHAPTER SEVEN

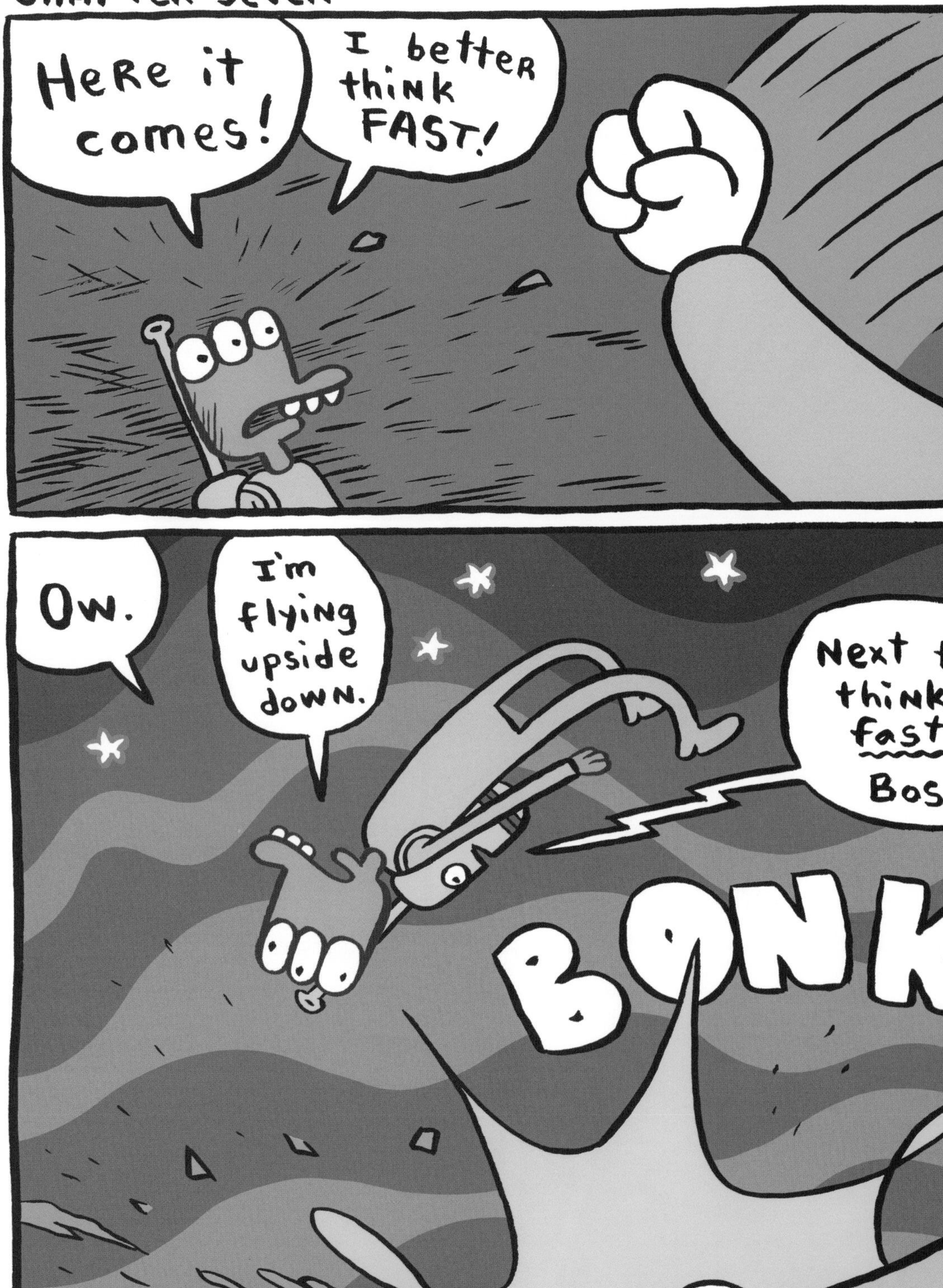

Here it comes!
I better think FAST!
Ow.
I'm flying upside down.
Next time think faster, Boss.
BONK

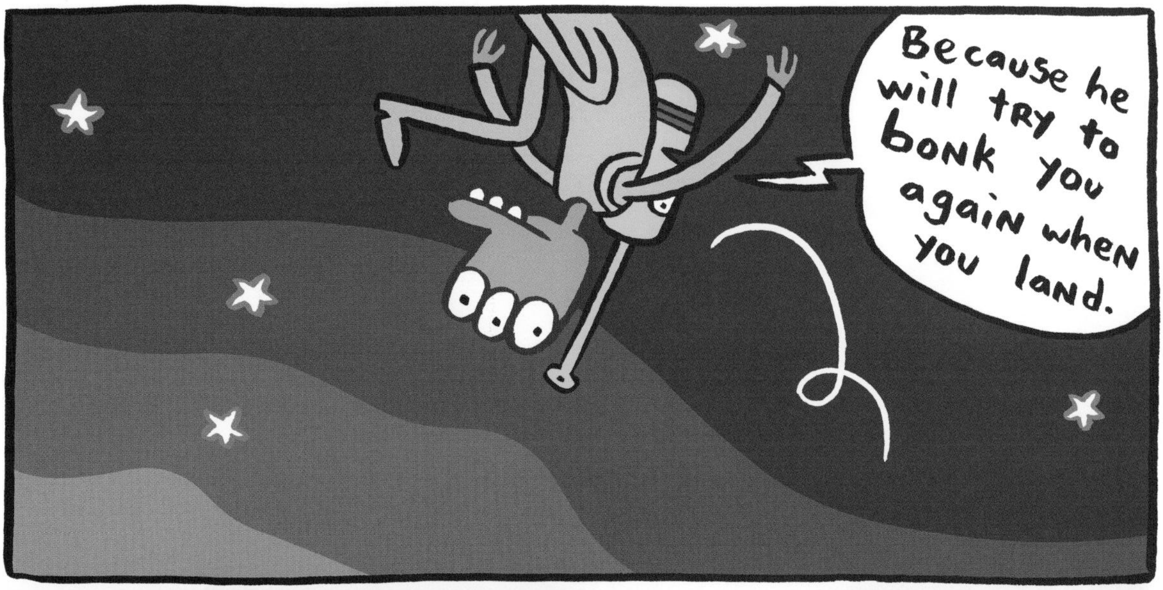
Because he will TRY to bonk you again when you land.

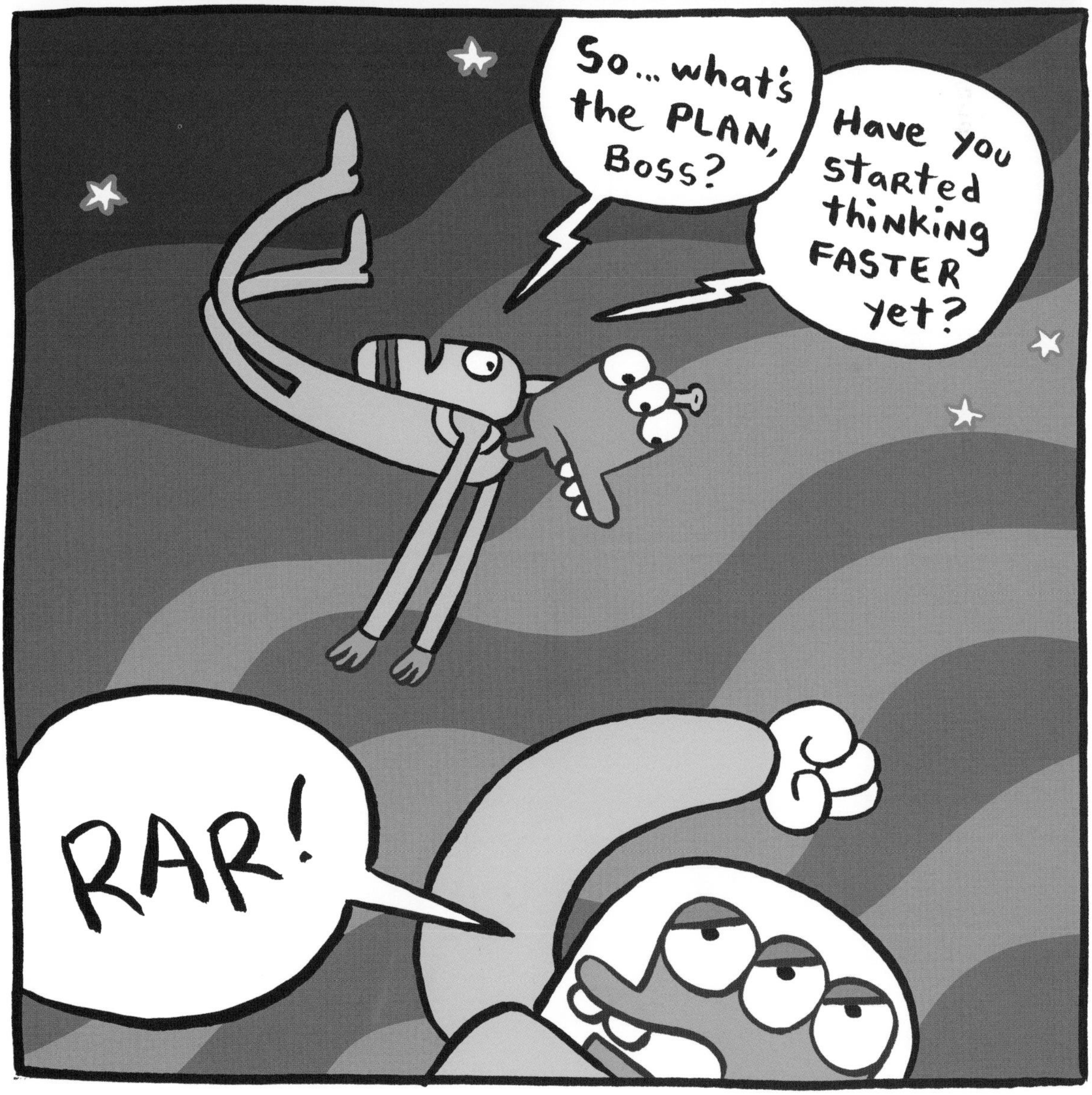
So... what's the PLAN, Boss?
Have you started thinking FASTER yet?
RAR!

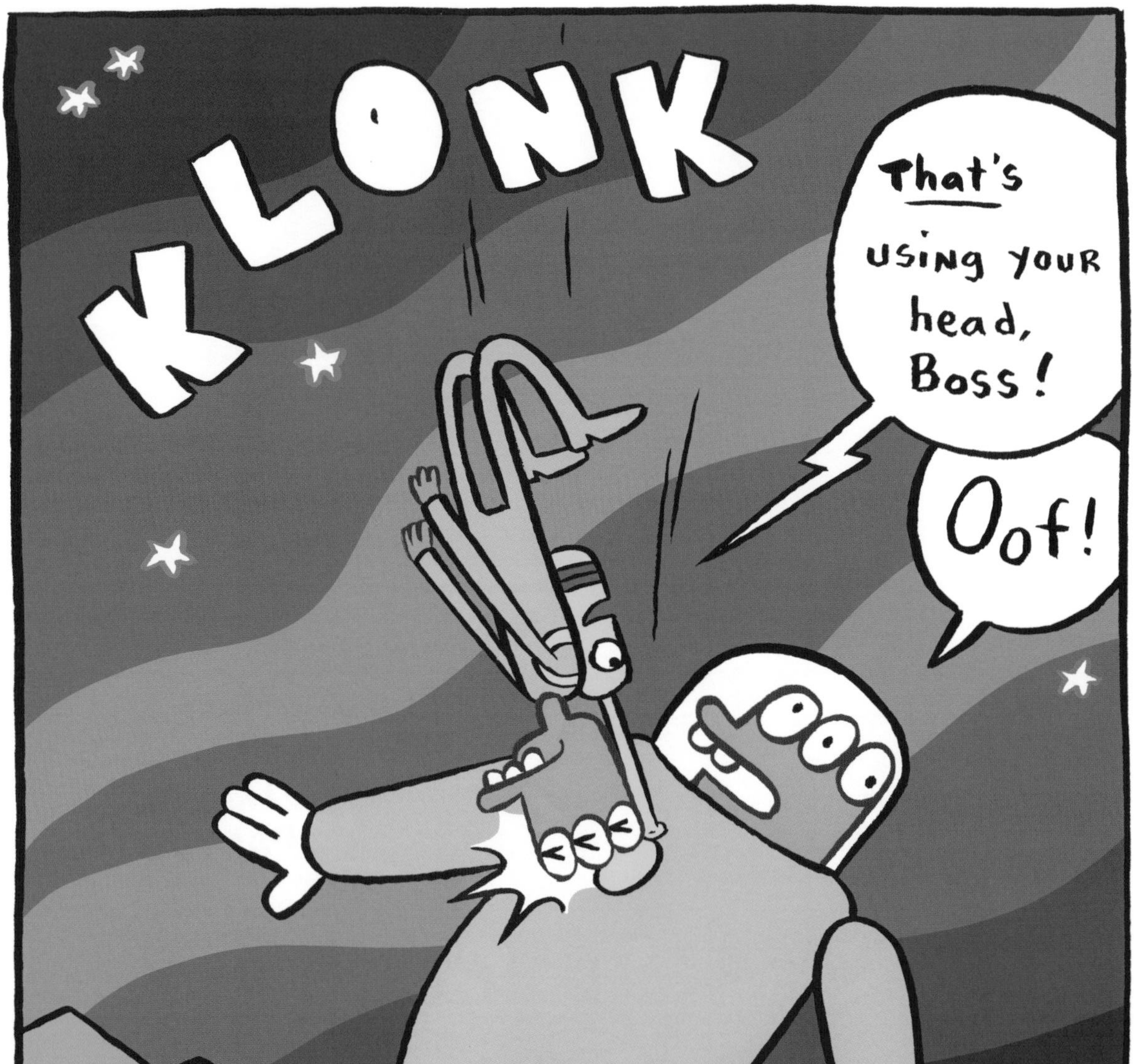
KLONK
That's using your head, Boss!
Oof!

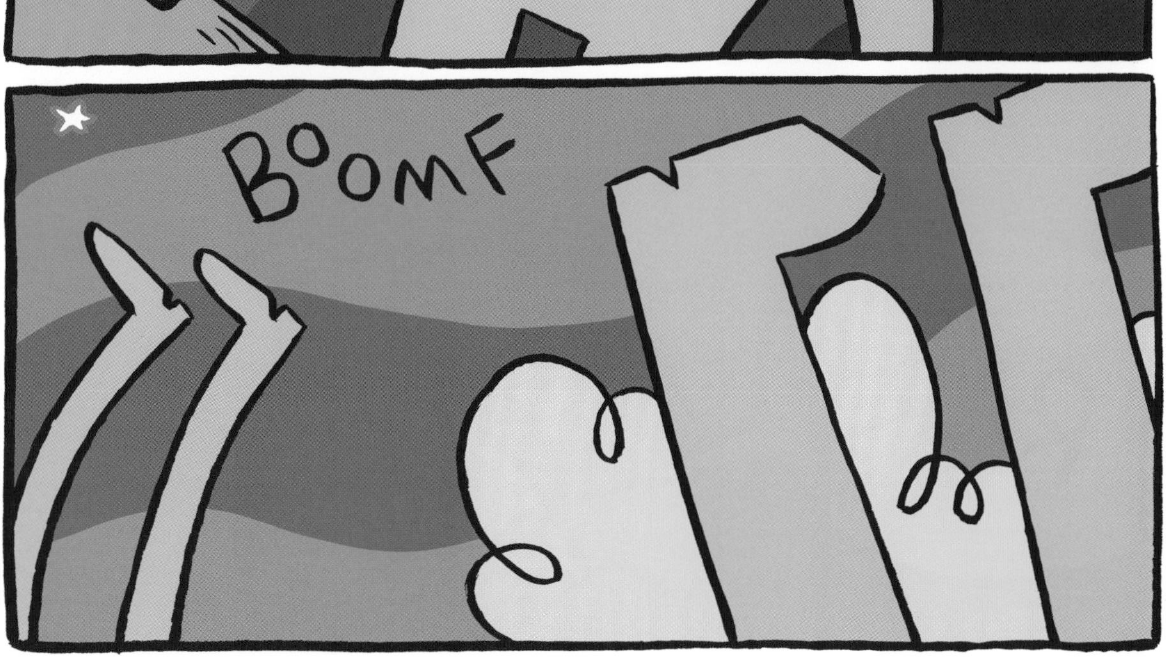
BOOMF

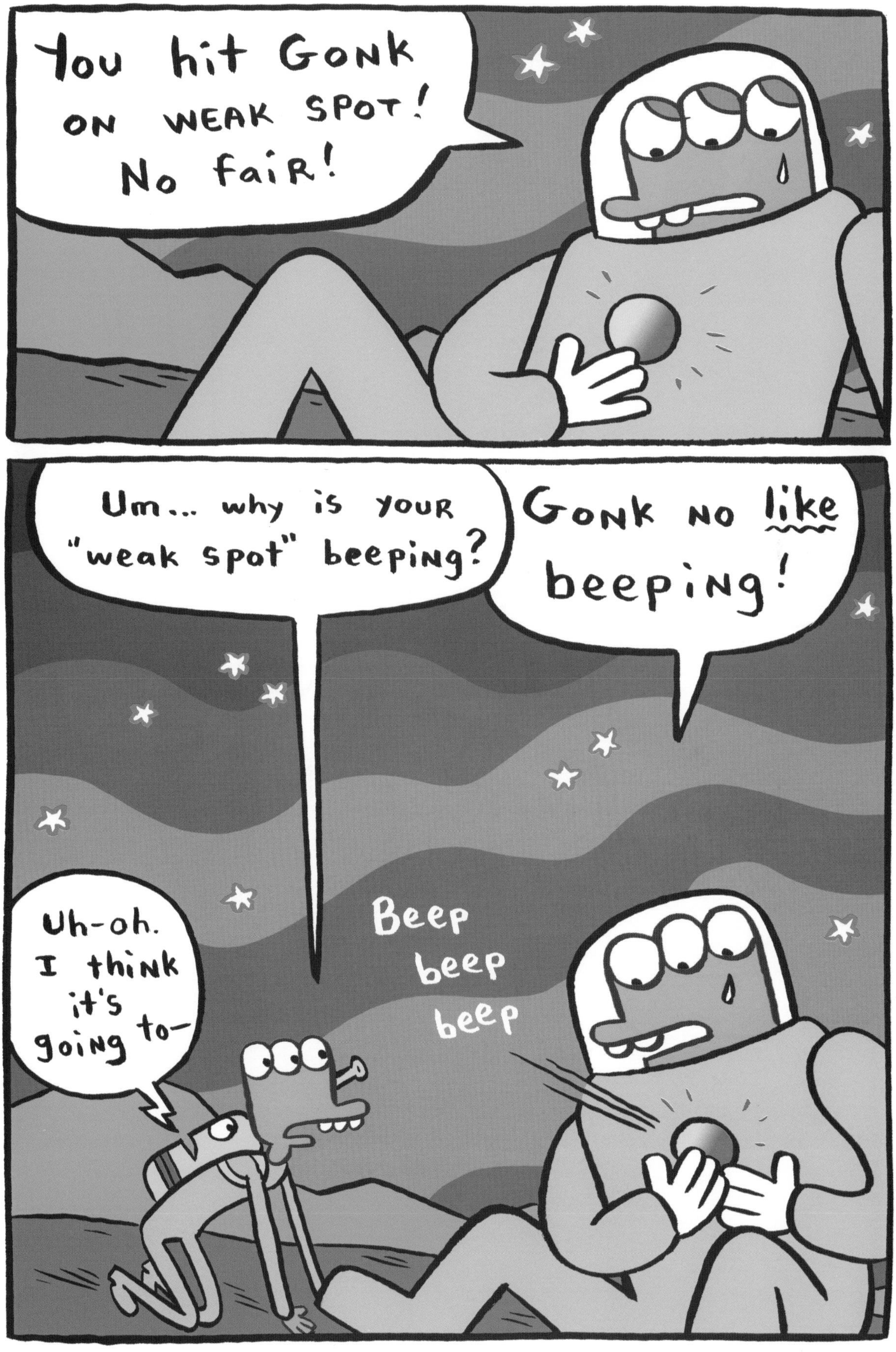
You hit Gonk ON WEAK SPOT! No fair!
Um... why is your "weak spot" beeping?
Gonk no like beeping!
Uh-oh. I think it's going to-
Beep beep beep

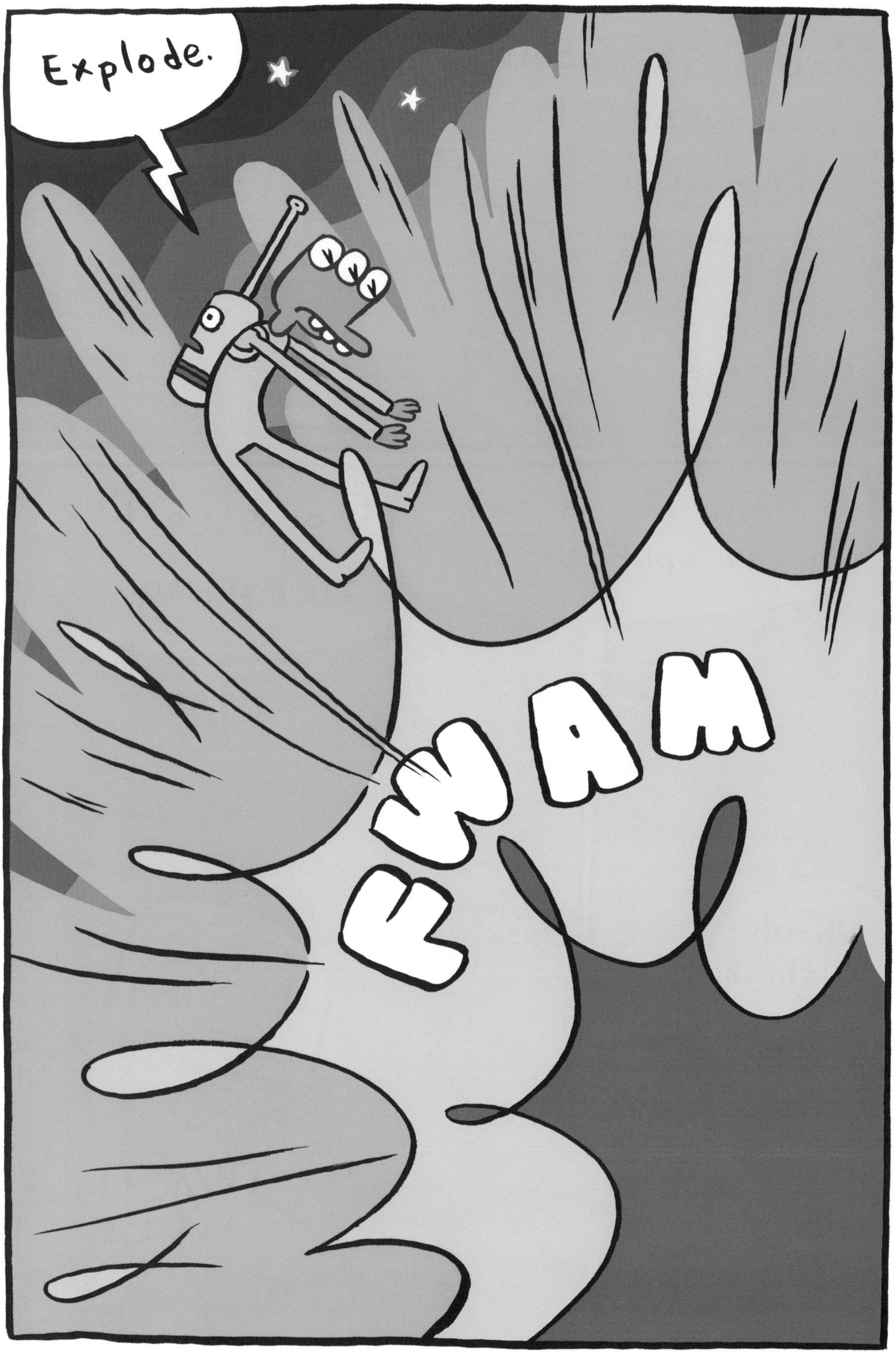
Explode.
FWAM

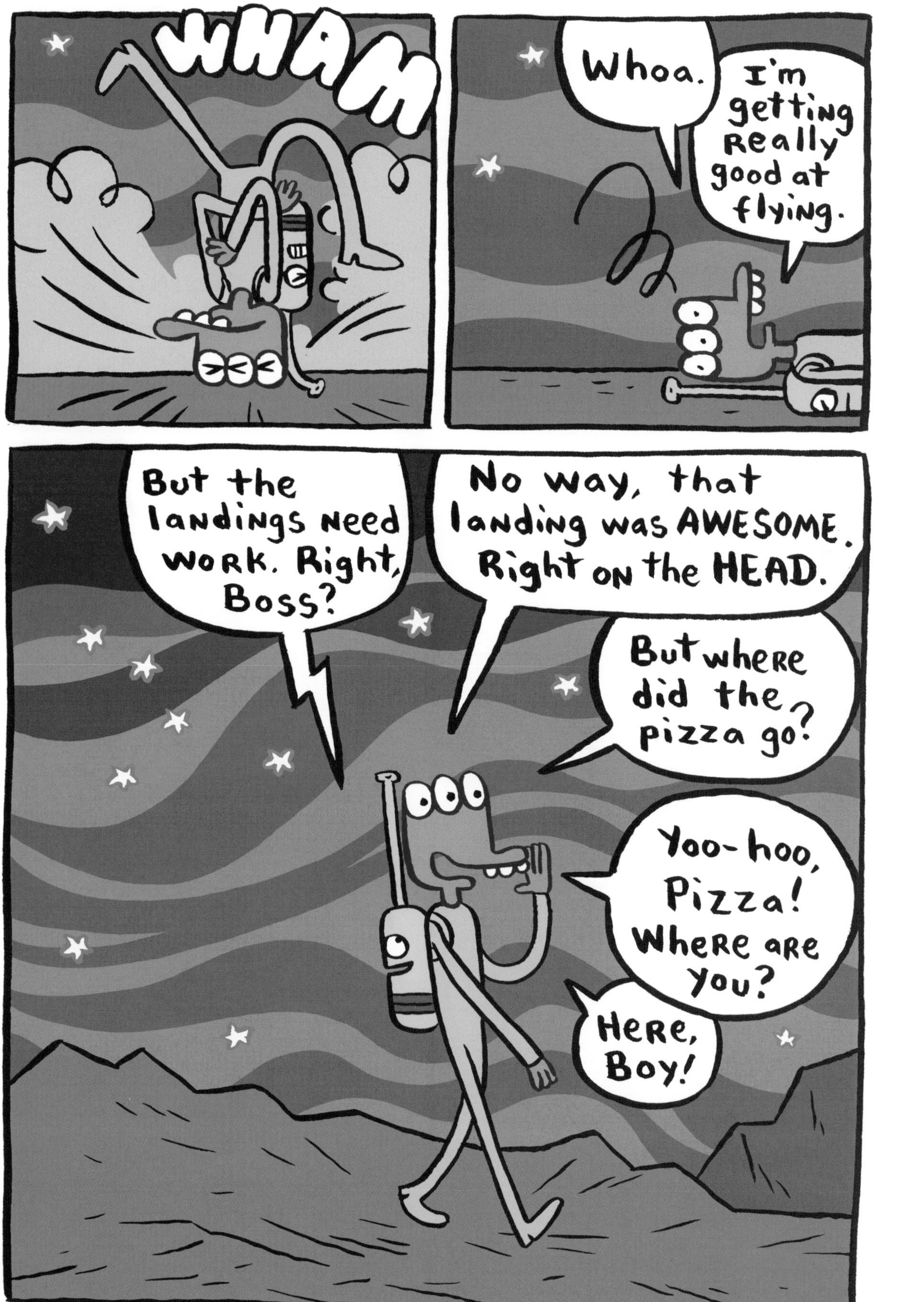
WHAM
Whoa.
I'm getting really good at flying.
But the landings need work. Right, Boss?
No way, that landing was AWESOME. Right on the HEAD.
But where did the pizza go?
Yoo-hoo, Pizza! Where are you?
Here, Boy!

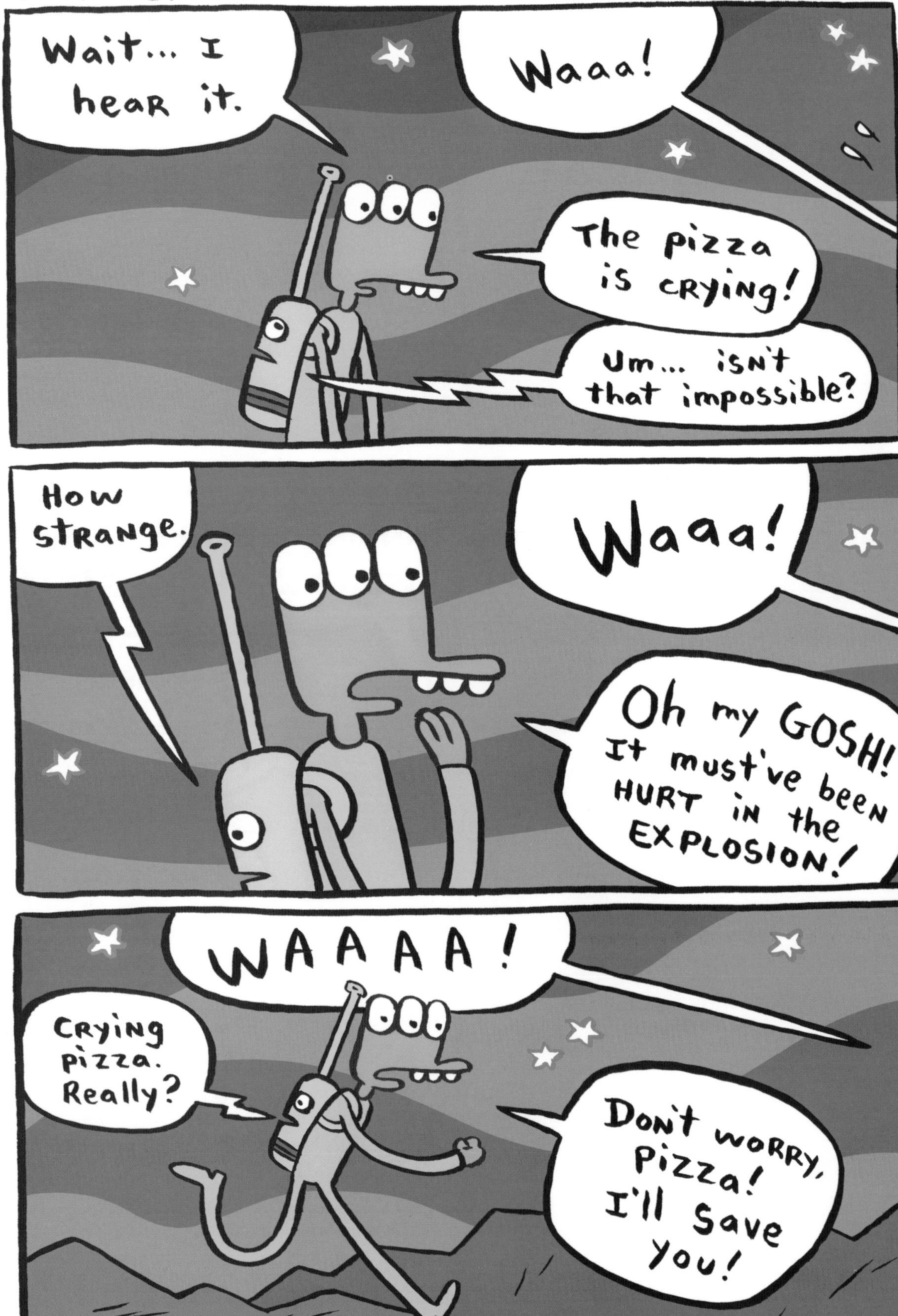
Wait... I hear it.
Waaa!
The pizza is crying!
Um... isn't that impossible?
How strange.
Waaa!
Oh my GOSH! It must've been HURT in the EXPLOSION!
WAAAA!
Crying pizza. Really?
Don't worry, Pizza! I'll save you!

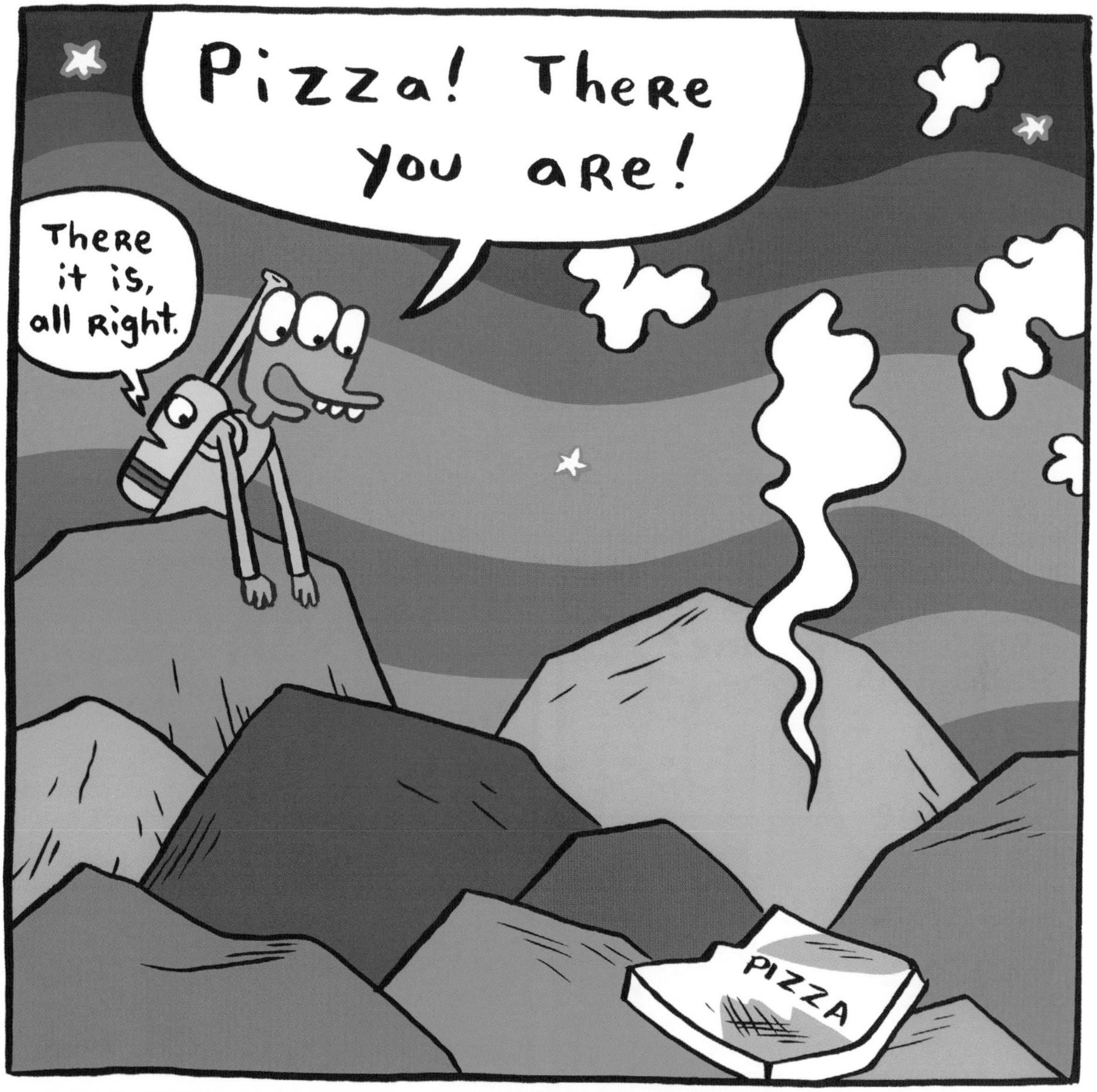
Pizza! There you are!
There it is, all right.
PIZZA

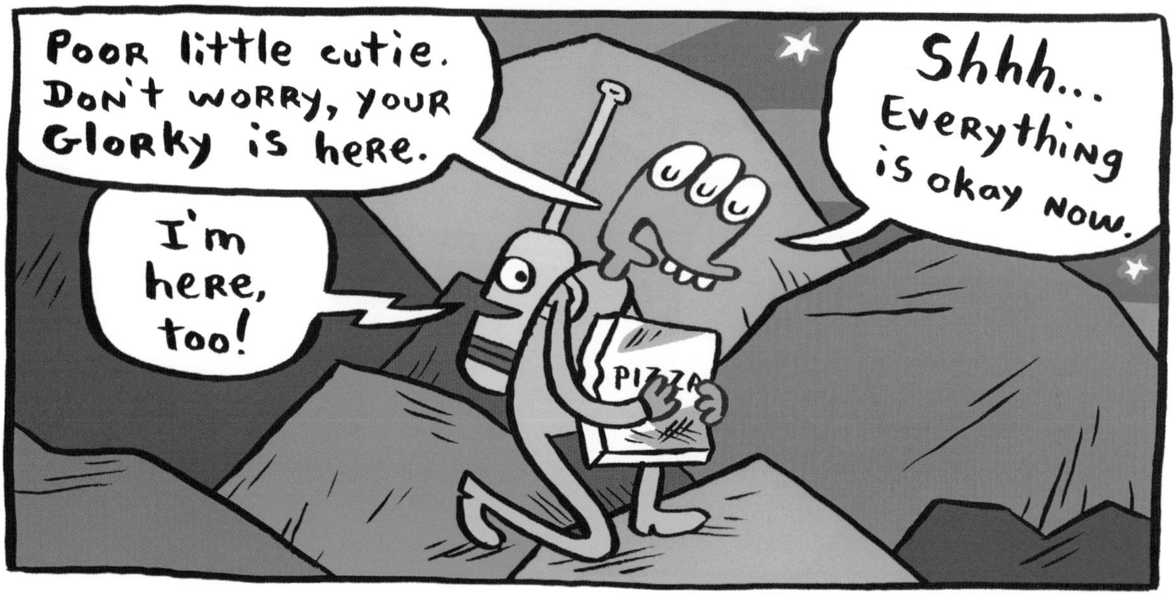
Poor little cutie. Don't worry, your Glorky is here.
I'm here, too!
Shhh... Everything is okay now.

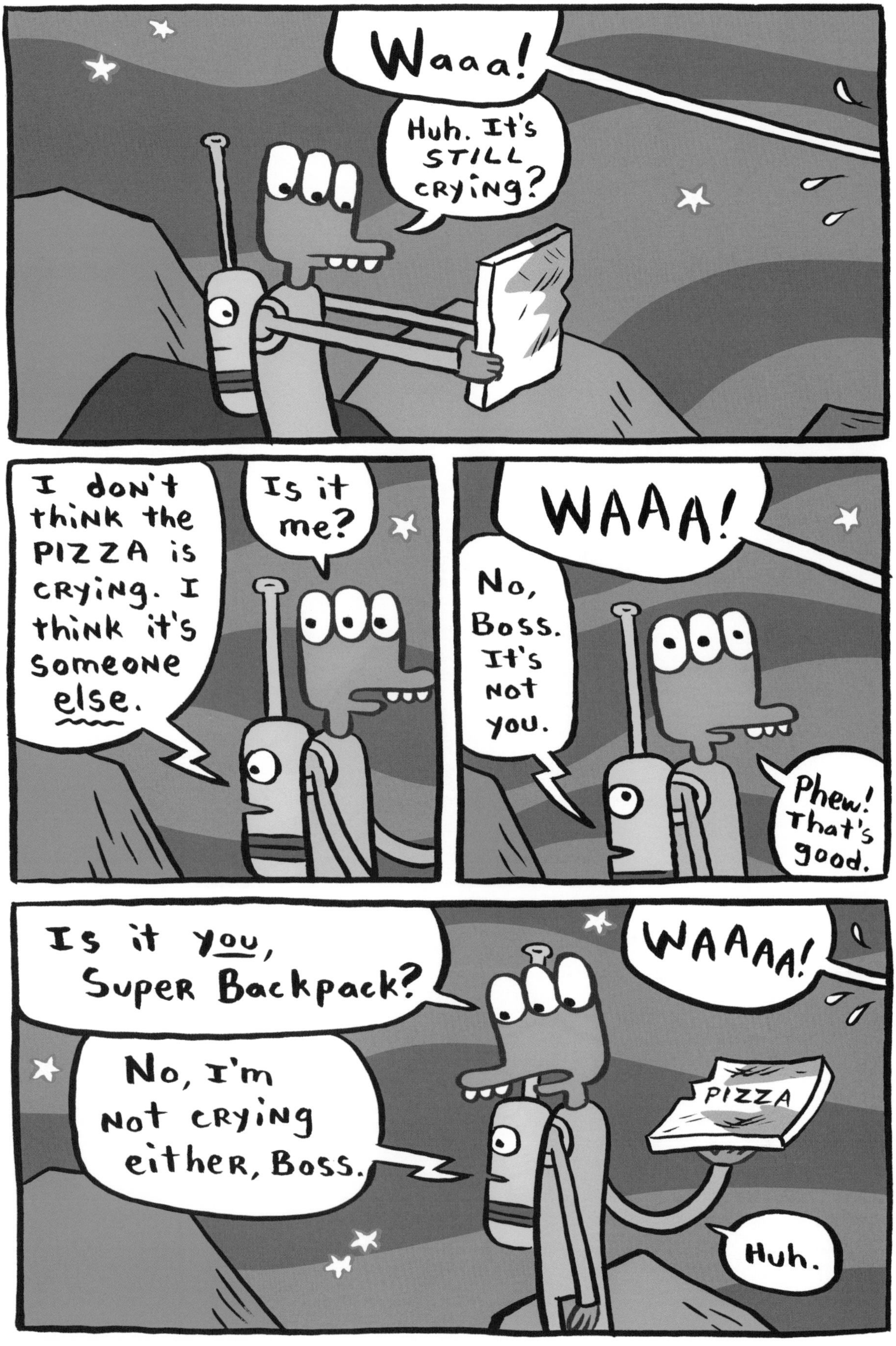
Waaa!
Huh. It's STILL crying?
I don't think the PIZZA is crying. I think it's someone else.
Is it me?
WAAA!
No, Boss. It's not you.
Phew! That's good.
Is it you, Super Backpack?
WAAAA!
No, I'm not crying either, Boss.
PIZZA
Huh.

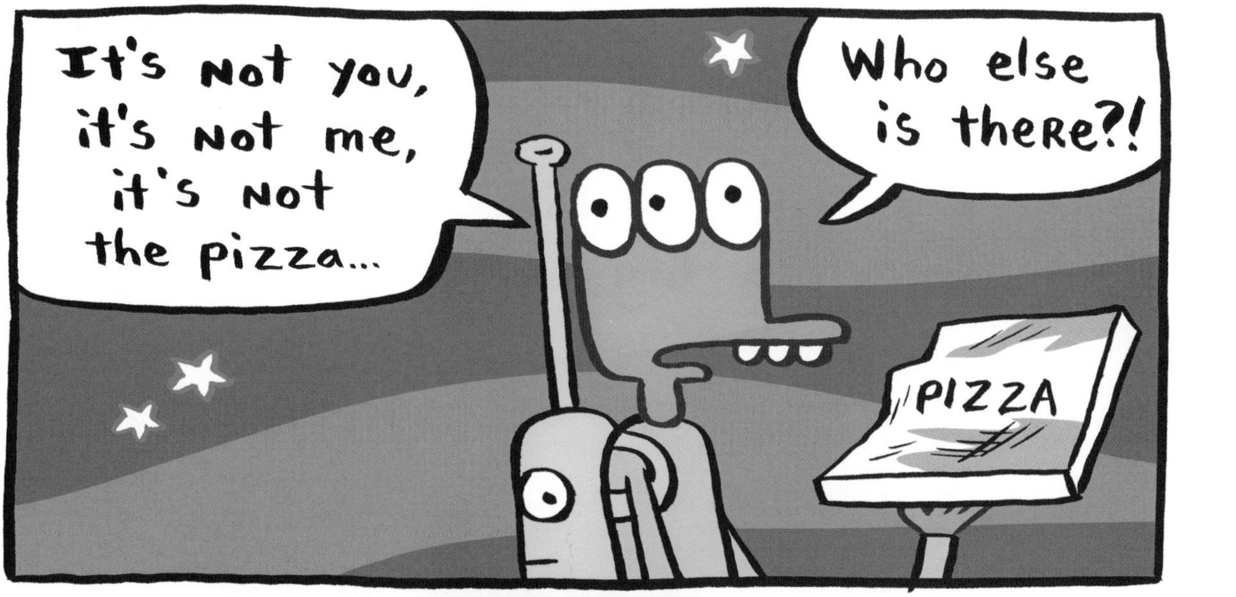
It's not you, it's not me, it's not the pizza...
Who else is there?!
PIZZA

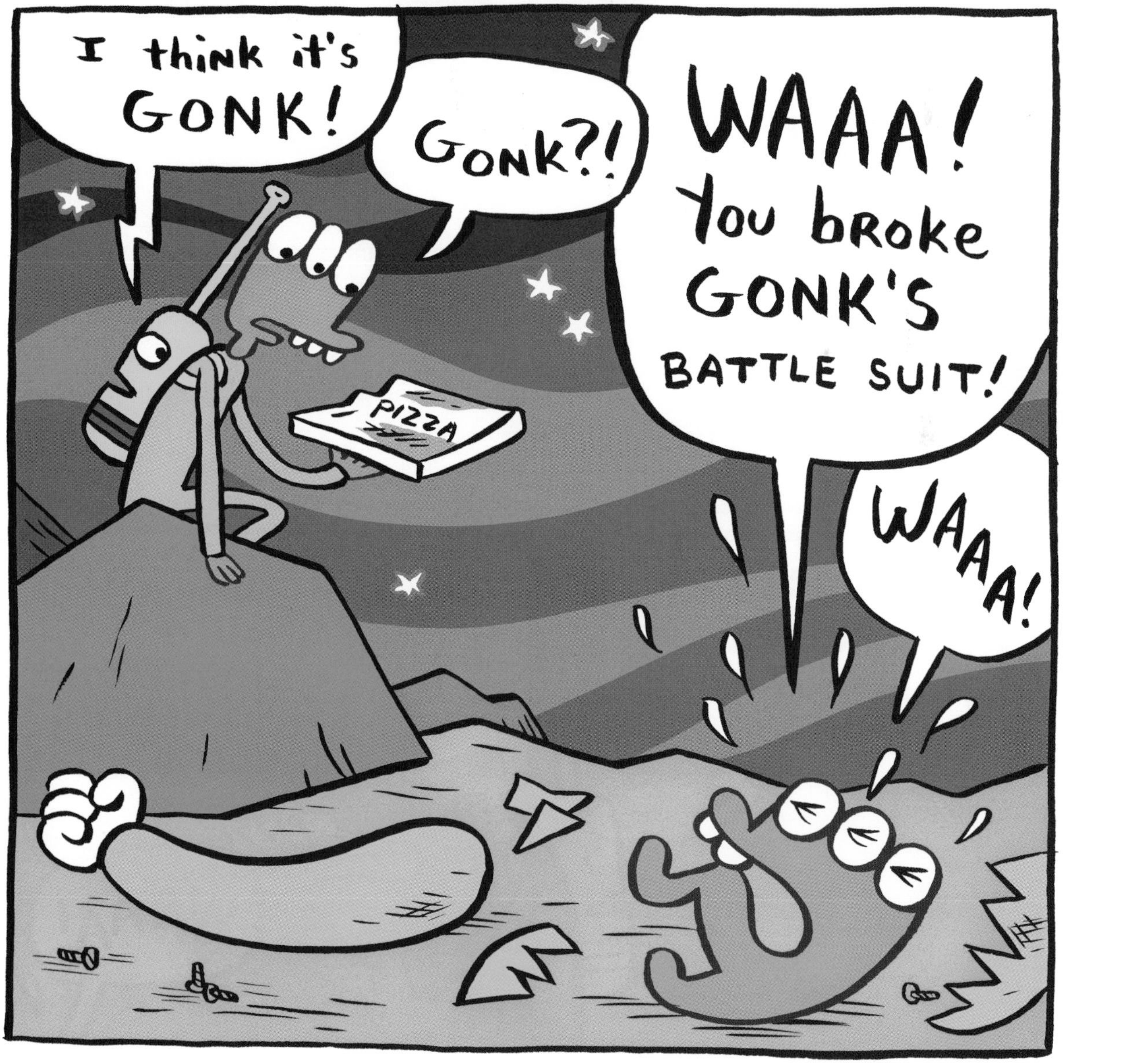
I think it's GONK!
GONK?!
WAAAA! You broke GONK'S BATTLE SUIT!
WAAAA!
PIZZA

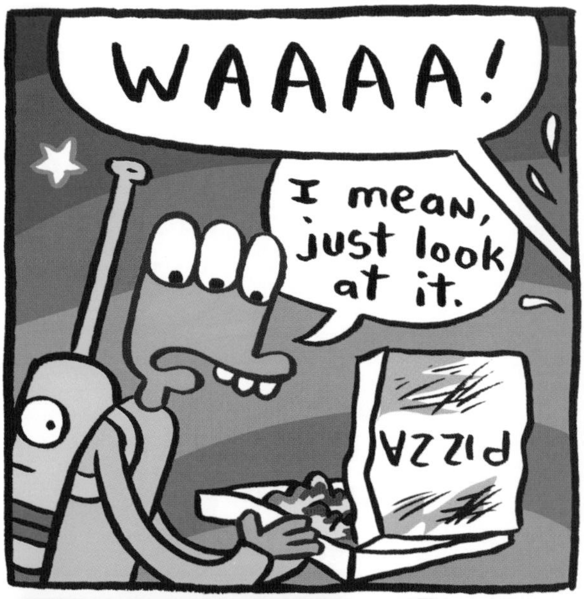
WAAAA!
I mean, just look at it.
PIZZA

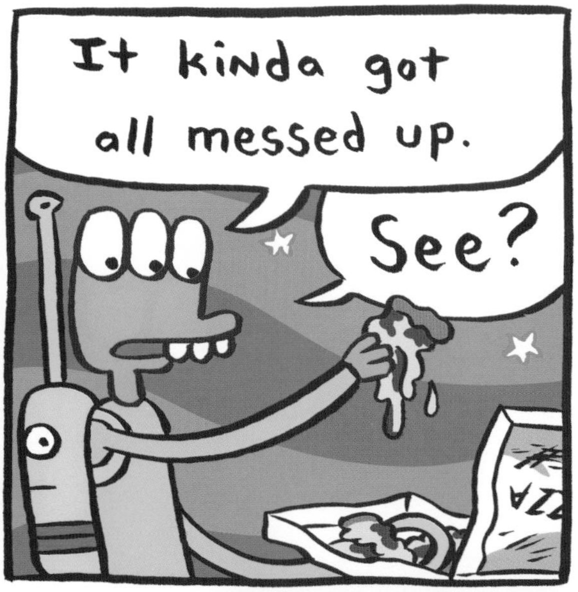
It kinda got all messed up.
See?

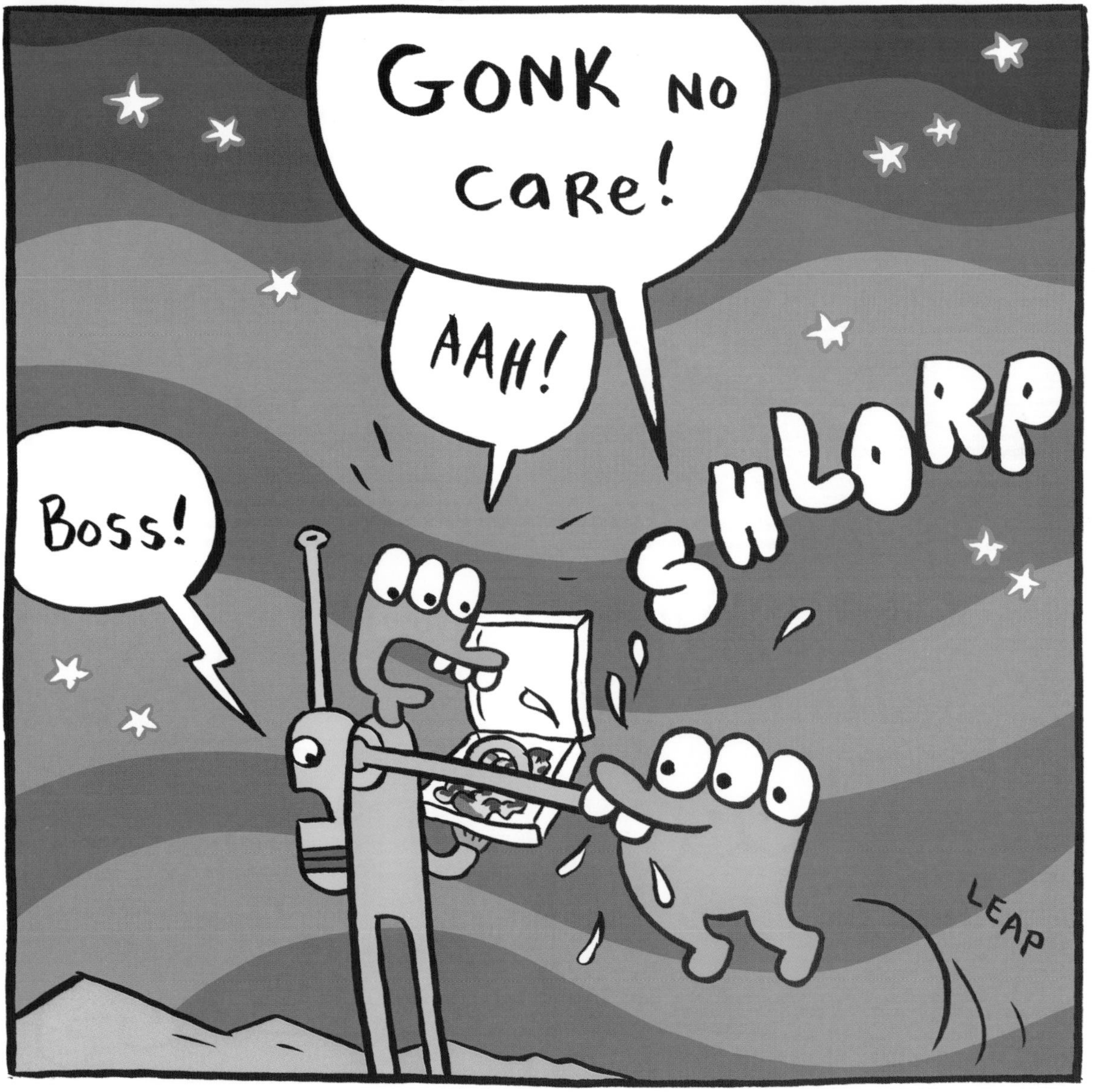
GONK NO CARE!
AAH!
Boss!
SHLORP
LEAP

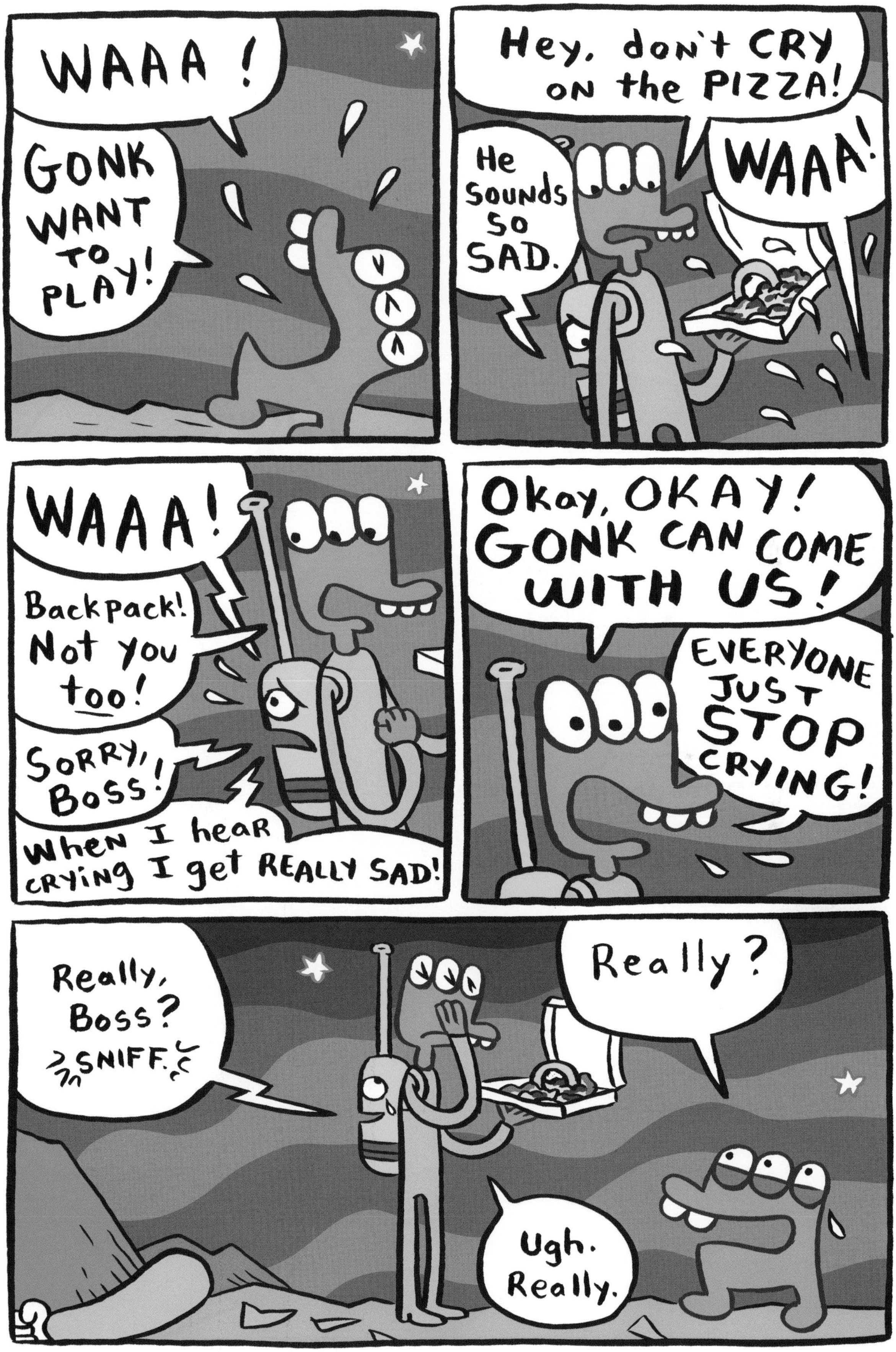
WAAA!
GONK WANT TO PLAY!
Hey, don't CRY on the PIZZA!
He sounds so SAD.
WAAA!
WAAA!
Backpack! Not you too!
SORRY, BOSS!
When I hear crying I get REALLY SAD!
Okay, OKAY! GONK CAN COME WITH US!
EVERYONE JUST STOP CRYING!
Really, Boss? SNIFF.
Really?
Ugh. Really.

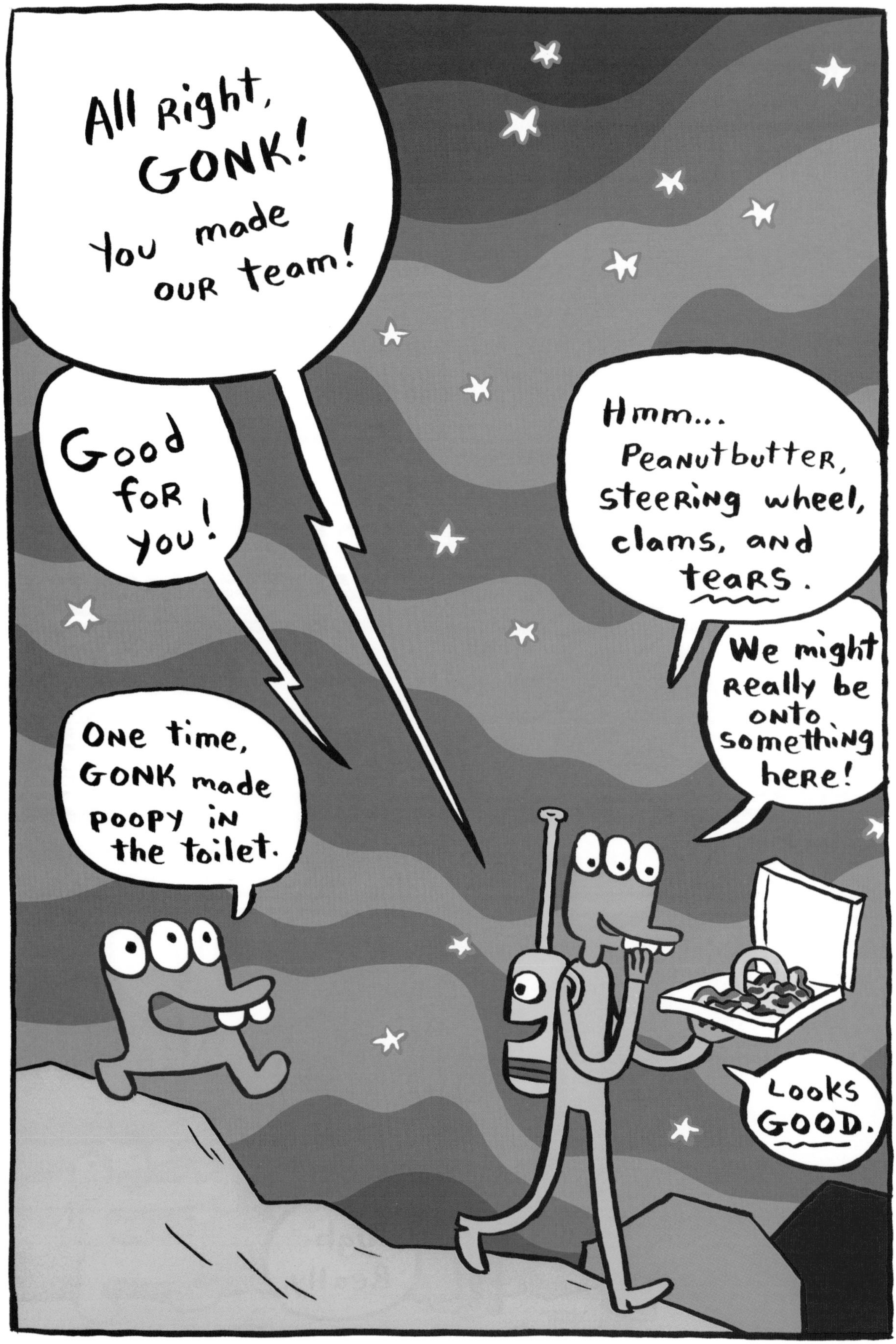
All Right, GONK! You made our team!
Good for you!
One time, GONK made poopy in the toilet.
Hmm... Peanutbutter, steering wheel, clams, and tears.
We might really be onto something here!
Looks GOOD.

51

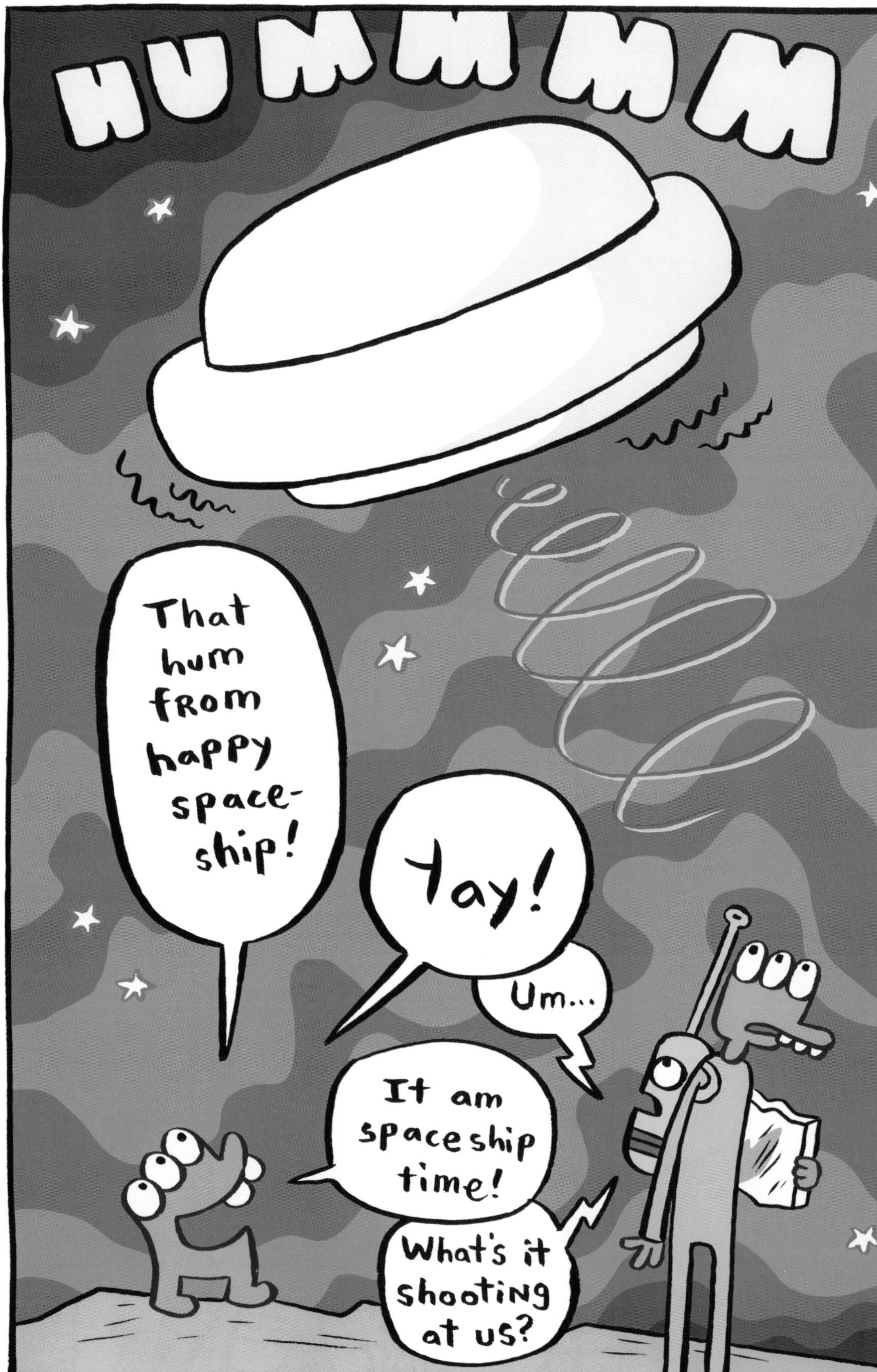
HUMMMM
That hum from happy space-ship!
Yay!
Um...
It am spaceship time!
What's it shooting at us?

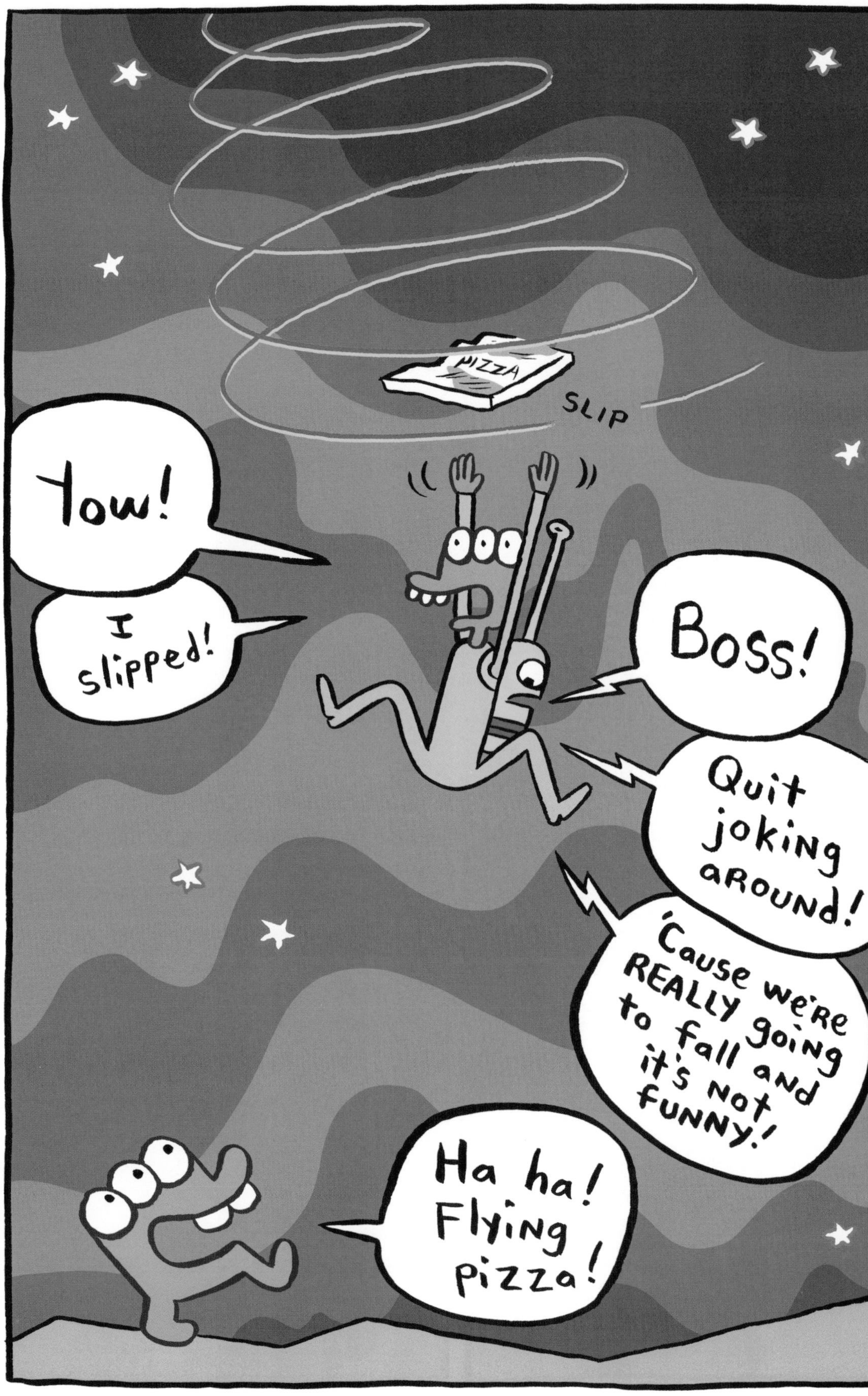
SLIP
Yow!
I slipped!
Boss!
Quit joking around!
'Cause we're REALLY going to fall and it's not FUNNY!
Ha ha! Flying pizza!

CHAPTER ELEVEN

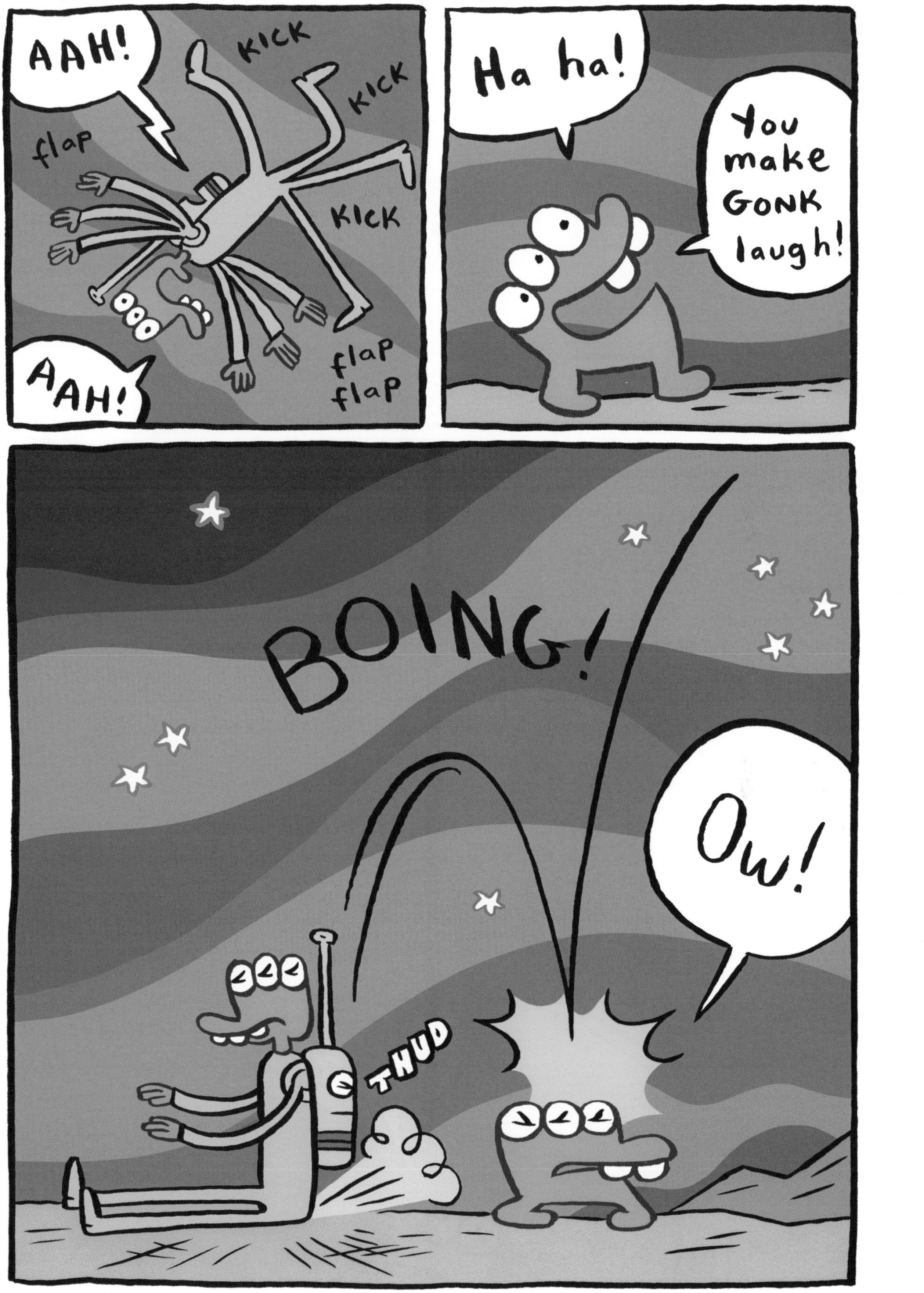
AAH!
KICK
KICK
flap
KICK
AAH!
flap flap
Ha ha!
You make GONK laugh!
BOING!
THUD
Ow!

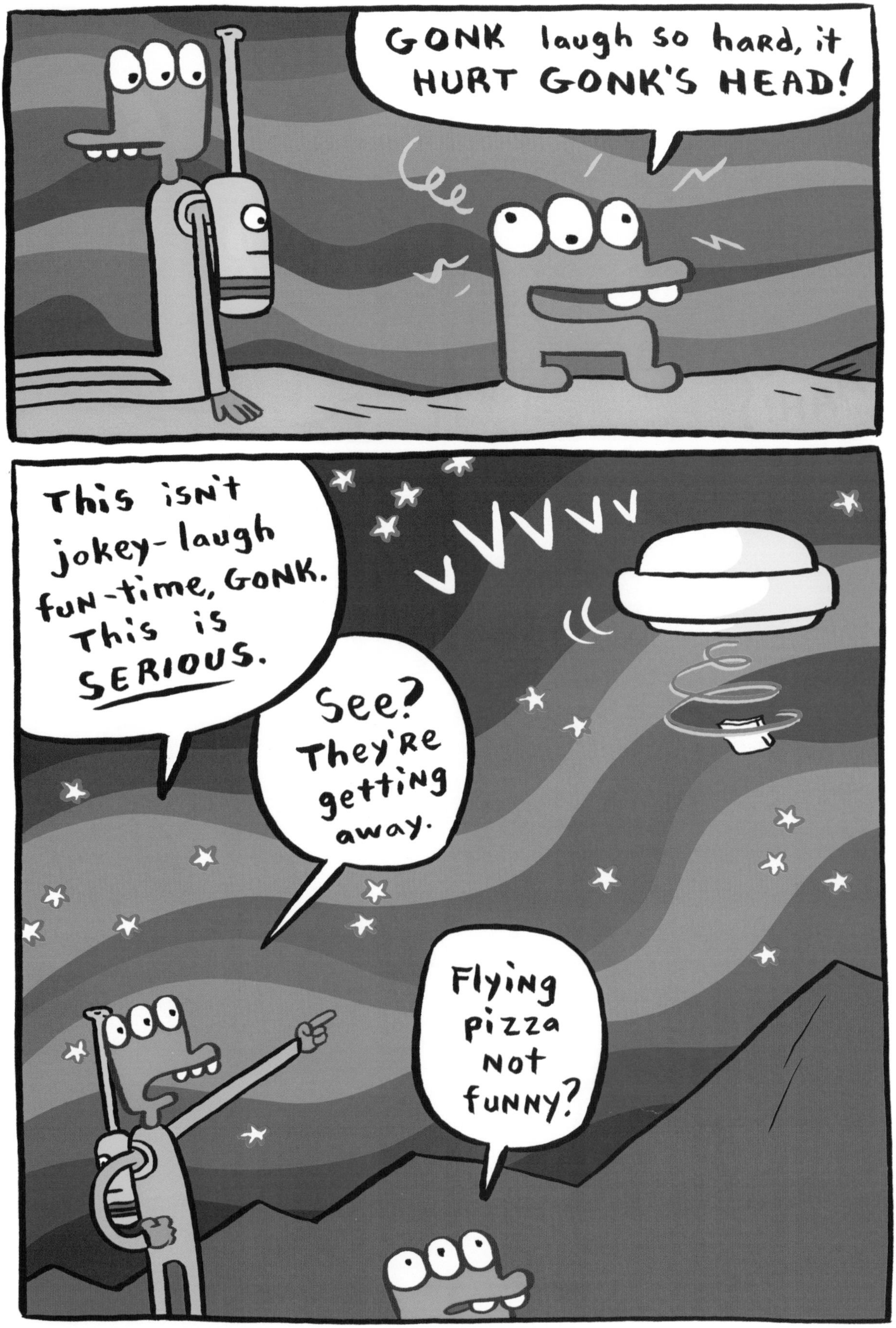
GONK laugh so hard, it HURT GONK'S HEAD!
This isn't jokey-laugh fun-time, GONK. This is SERIOUS.
VVVVVV
See? They're getting away.
Flying pizza not funny?

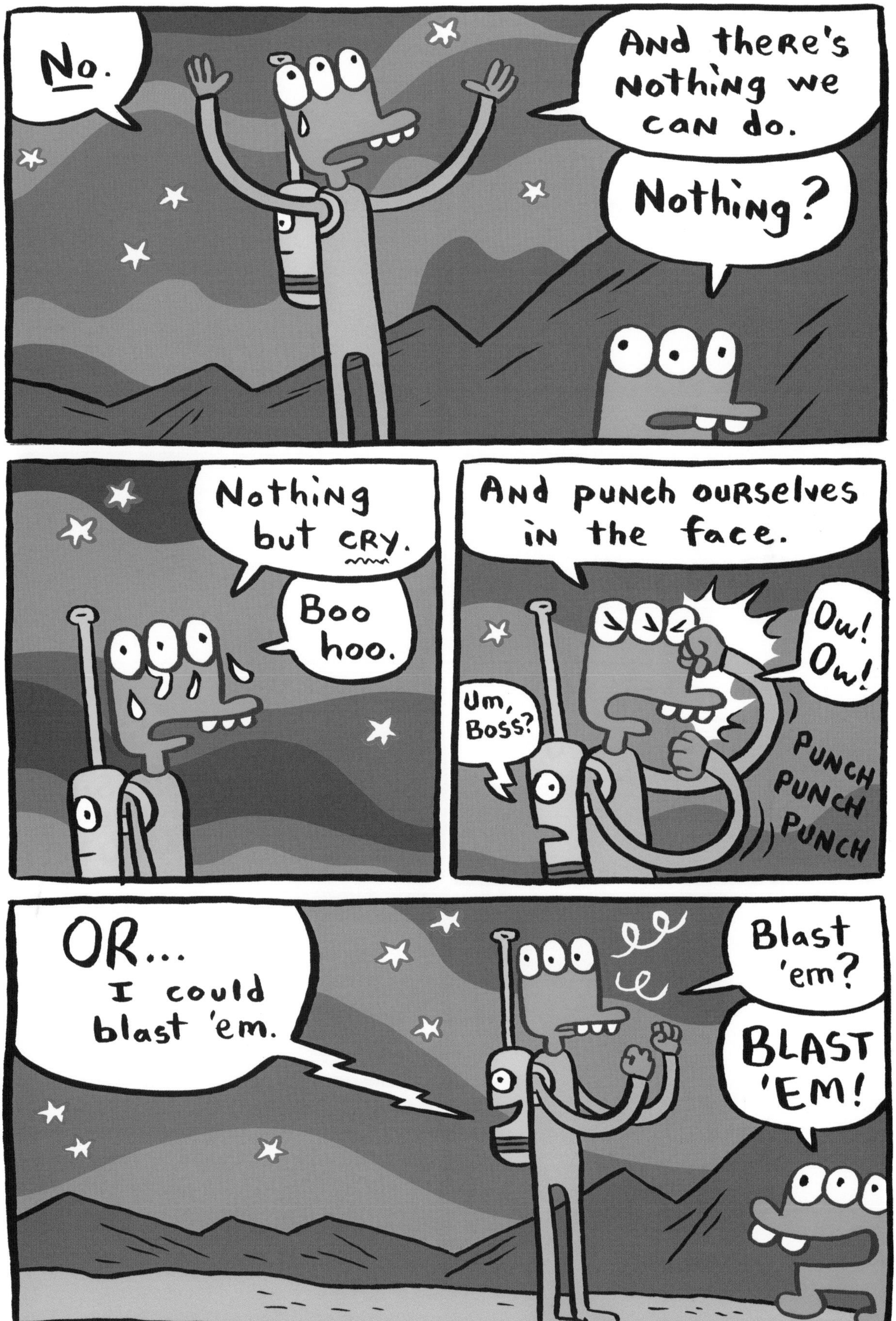
No.
And there's Nothing we can do.
Nothing?
Nothing but CRY.
Boo hoo.
And punch ourselves in the face.
Ow! Ow!
Um, Boss?
PUNCH PUNCH PUNCH
OR... I could blast 'em.
Blast 'em?
BLAST 'EM!

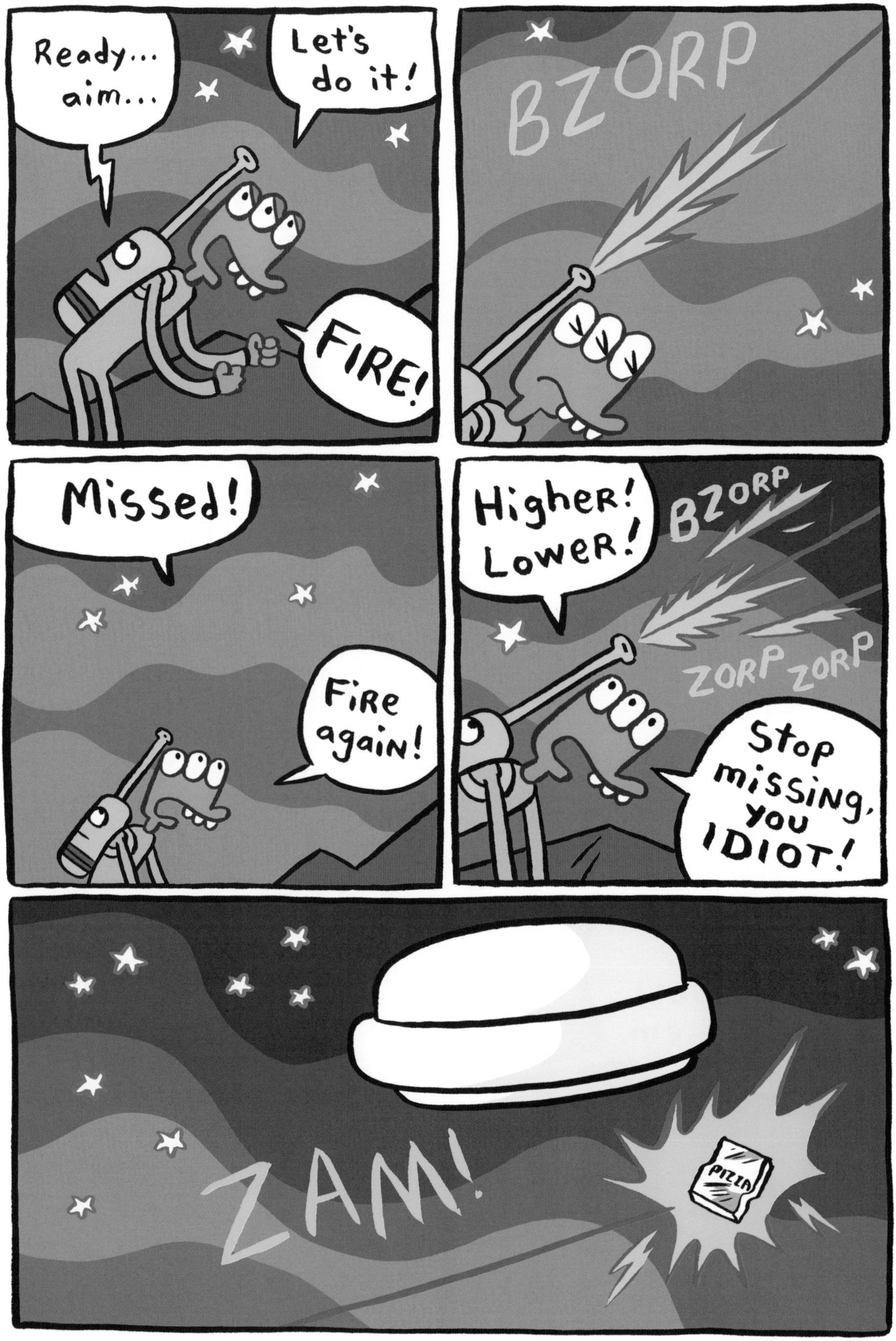
Ready... aim...
Let's do it!
FIRE!
BZORP
Missed!
Fire again!
Higher! Lower!
BZORP
ZORP ZORP
Stop missing, you IDIOT!
ZAM!
PIZZA

CHAPTER TWELVE

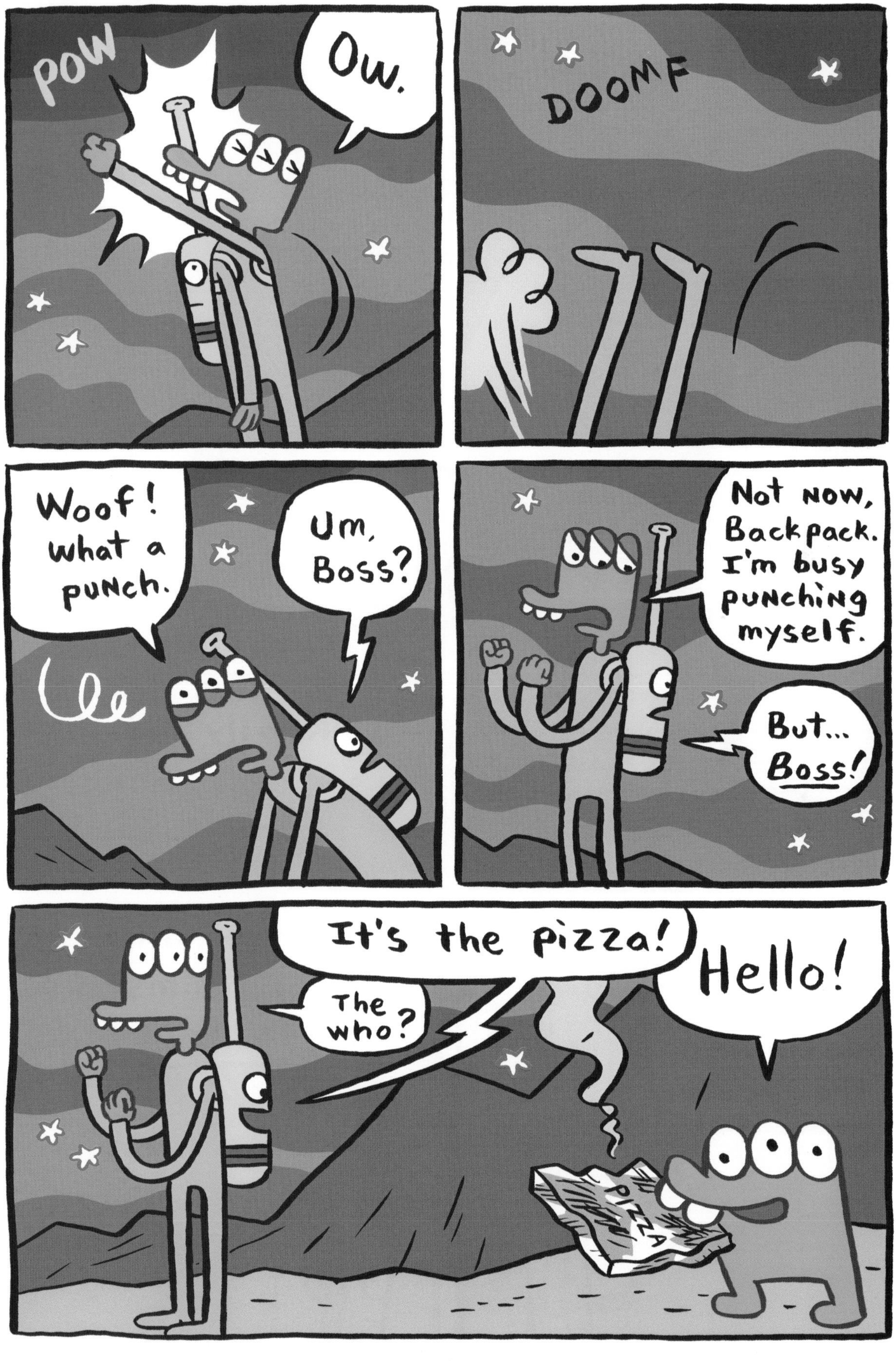
POW
Ow.
DOOMF
Woof! what a punch.
Um, Boss?
Not now, Backpack. I'm busy punching myself.
But... Boss!
It's the pizza!
The who?
Hello!
PIZZA

63

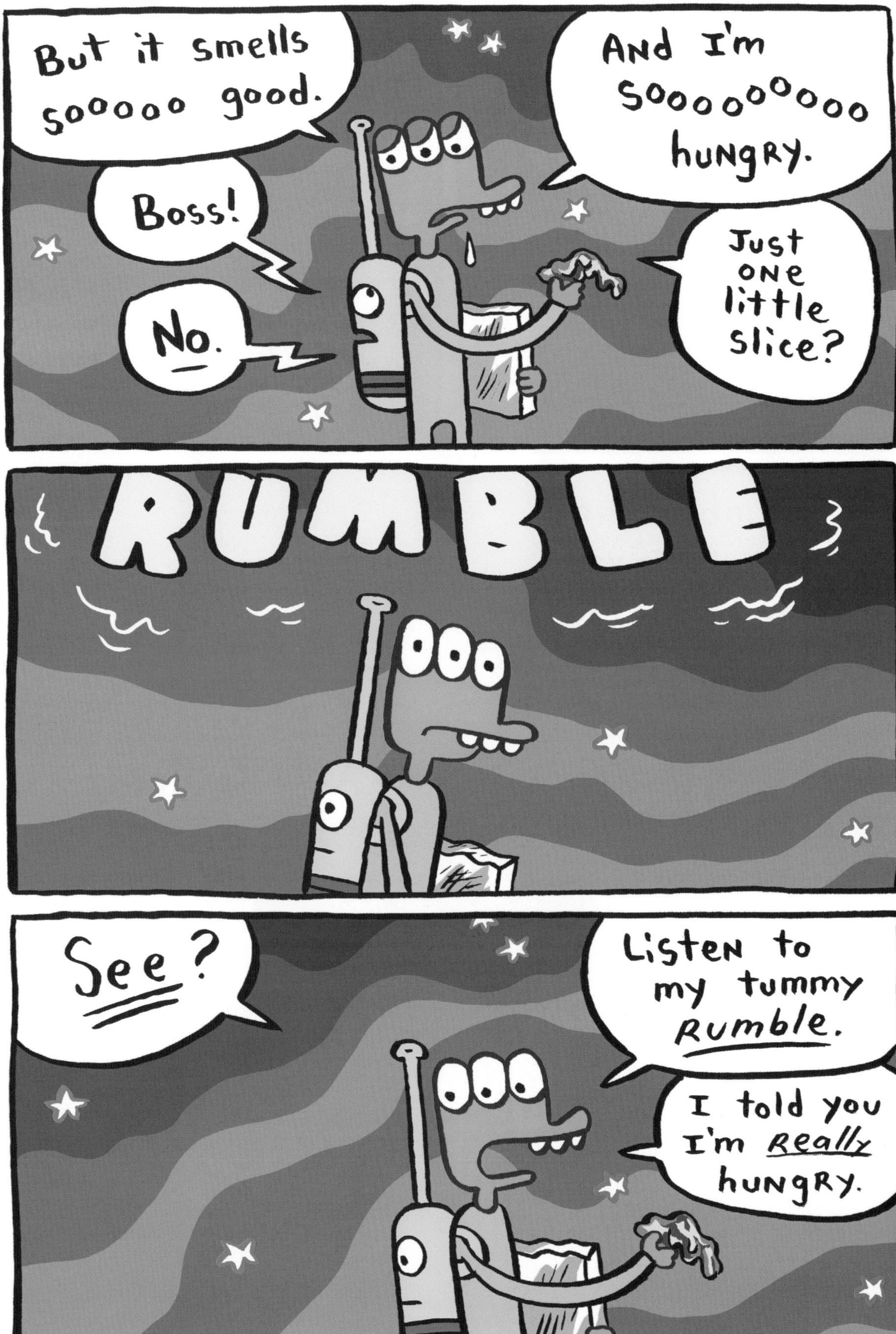

But it smells sooooo good.
And I'm sooooooooo hungry.
Boss!
No.
Just one little slice?
RUMBLE
See?
Listen to my tummy Rumble.
I told you I'm Really hungry.

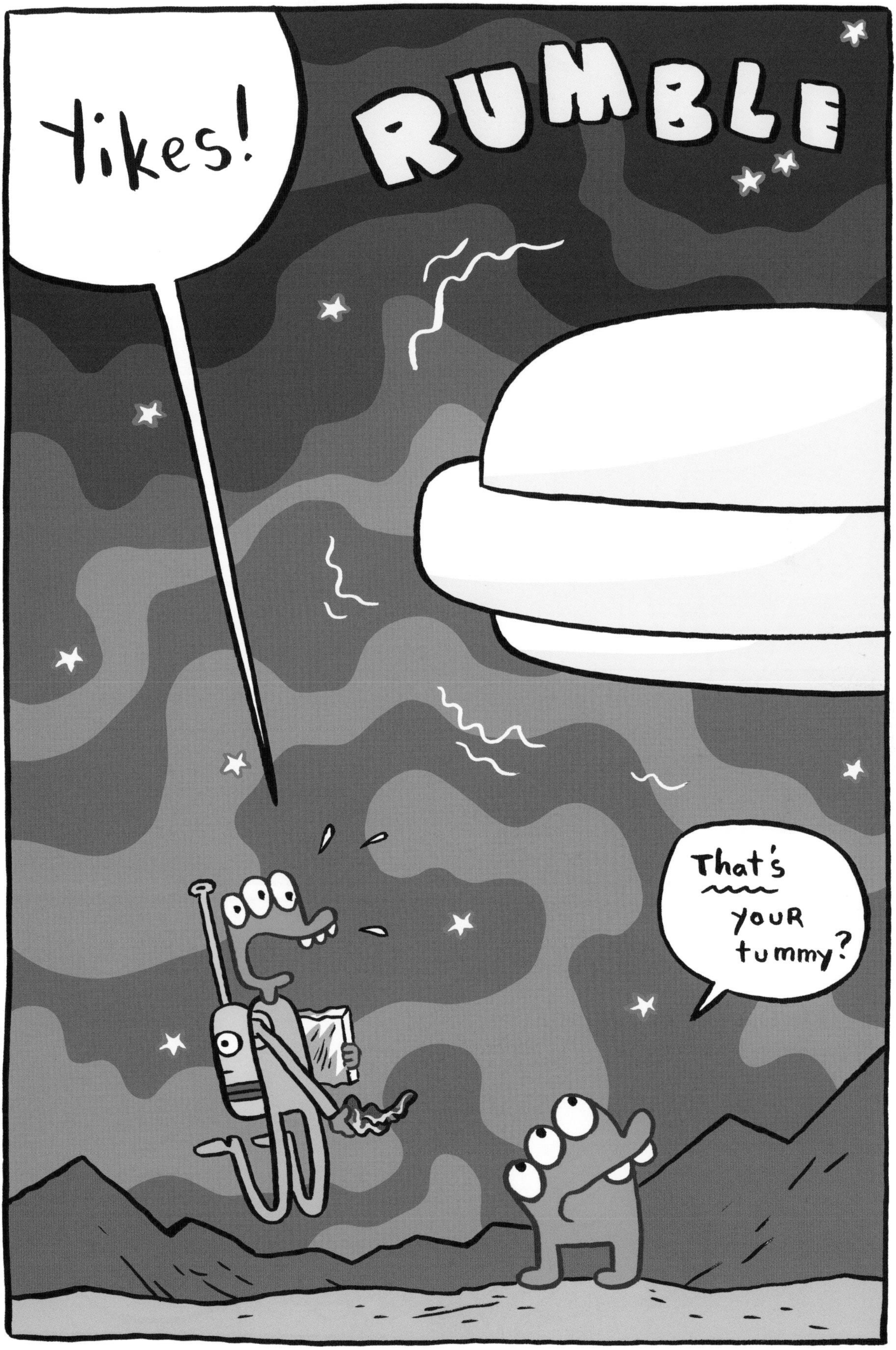
Yikes!
RUMBLE
That's your tummy?

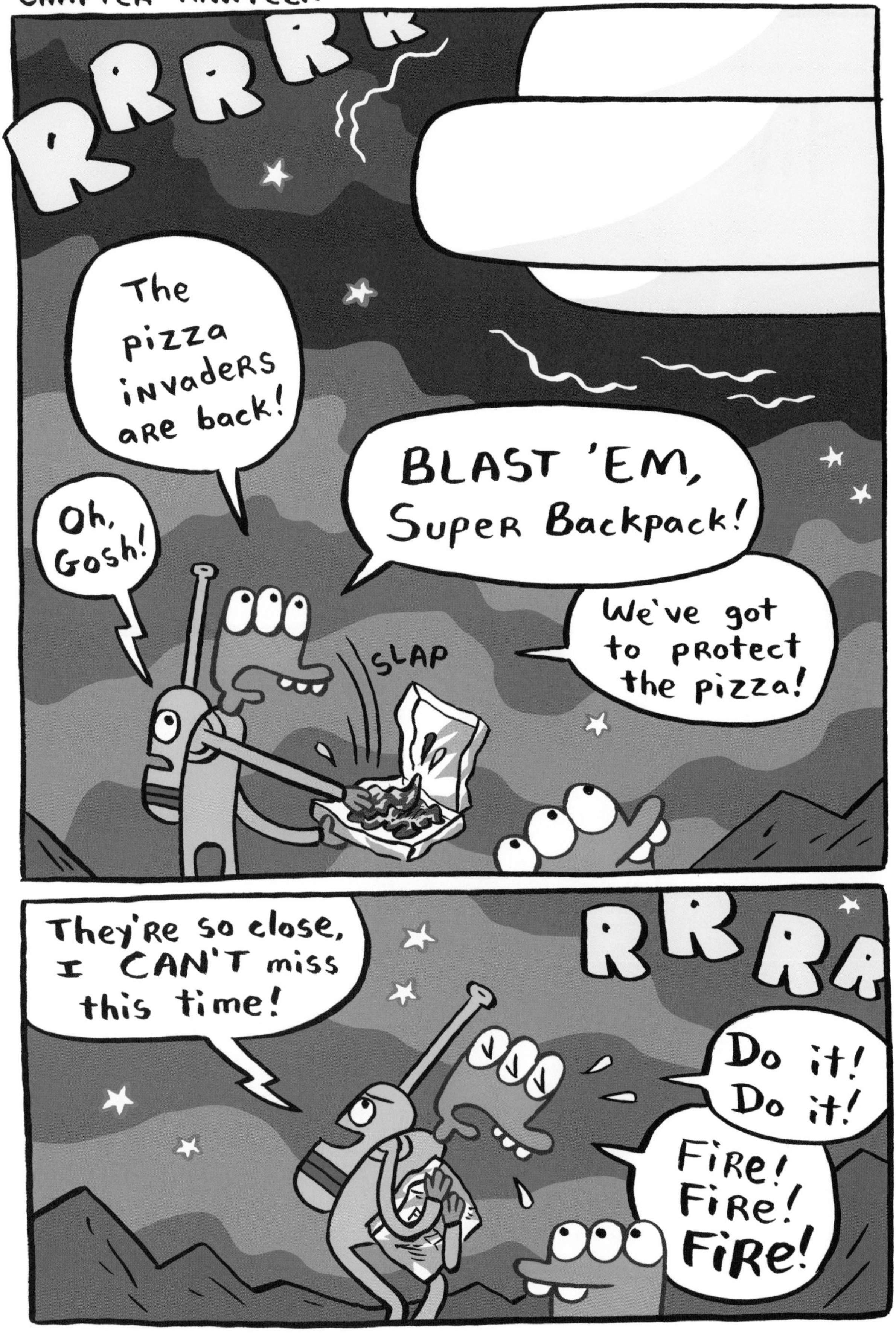
RRRRR
The pizza invaders are back!
BLAST 'EM, Super Backpack!
Oh, Gosh!
SLAP
We've got to protect the pizza!
They're so close, I CAN'T miss this time!
RRRR
Do it! Do it!
Fire! Fire! FiRE!

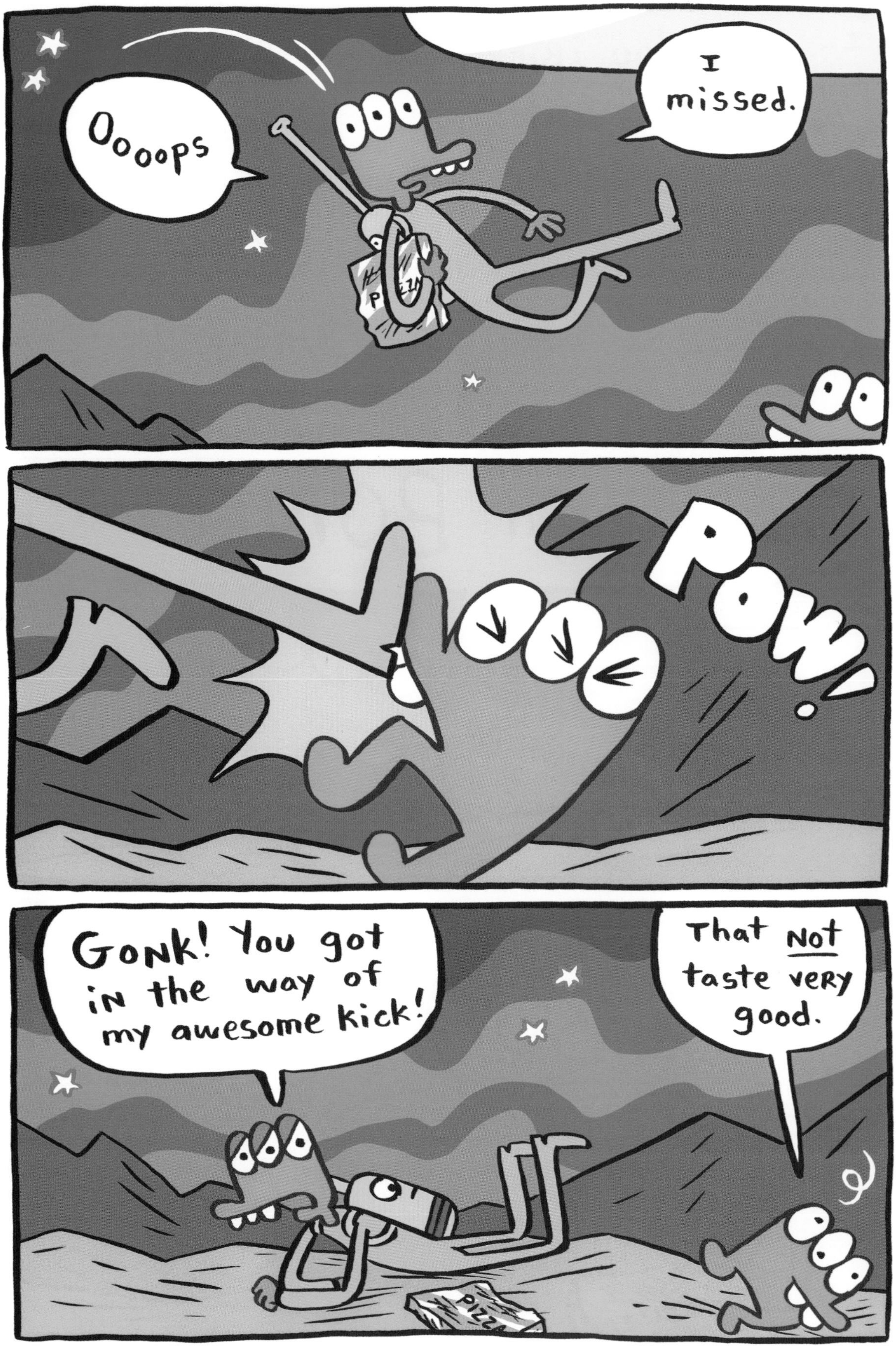
Oooops
I missed.
POW!
GONK! You got in the way of my awesome kick!
That NOT taste very good.

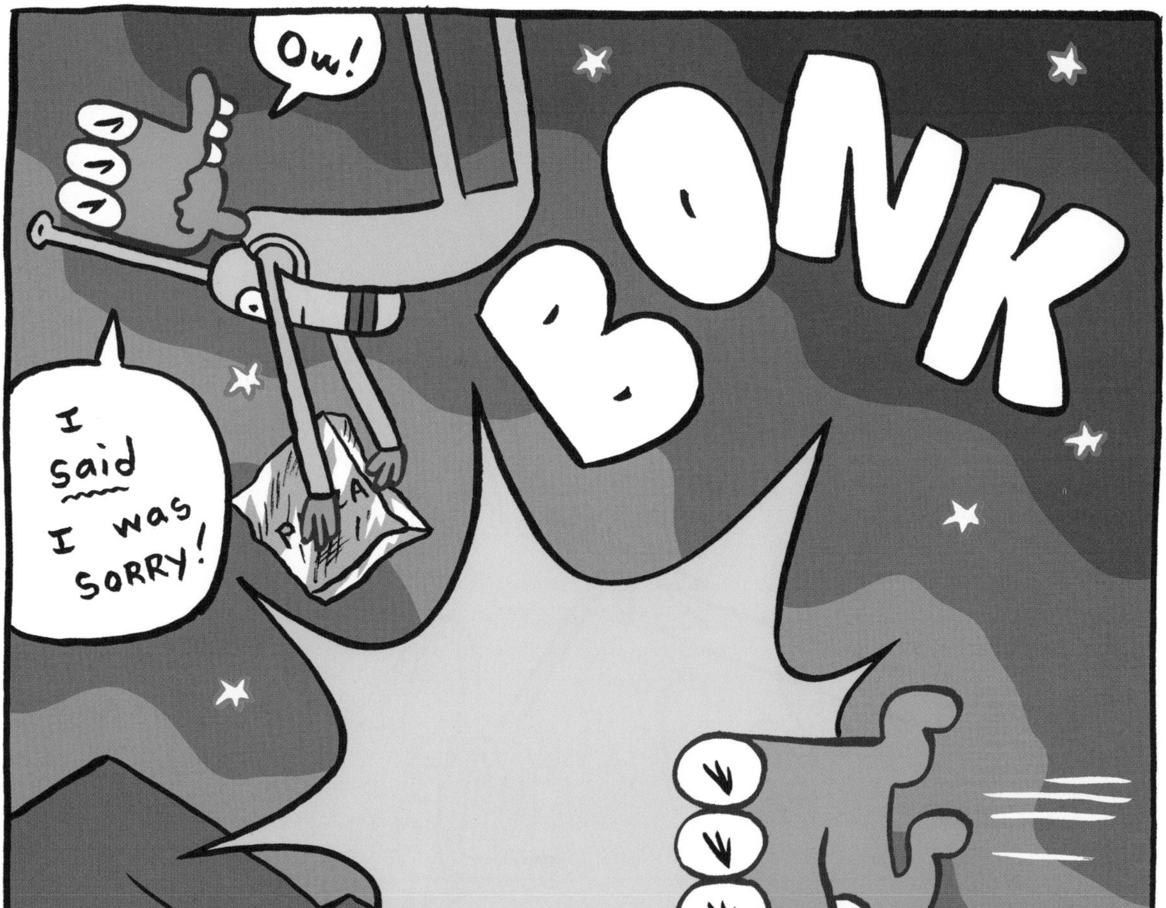
Ow!
BONK
I said I was SORRY!

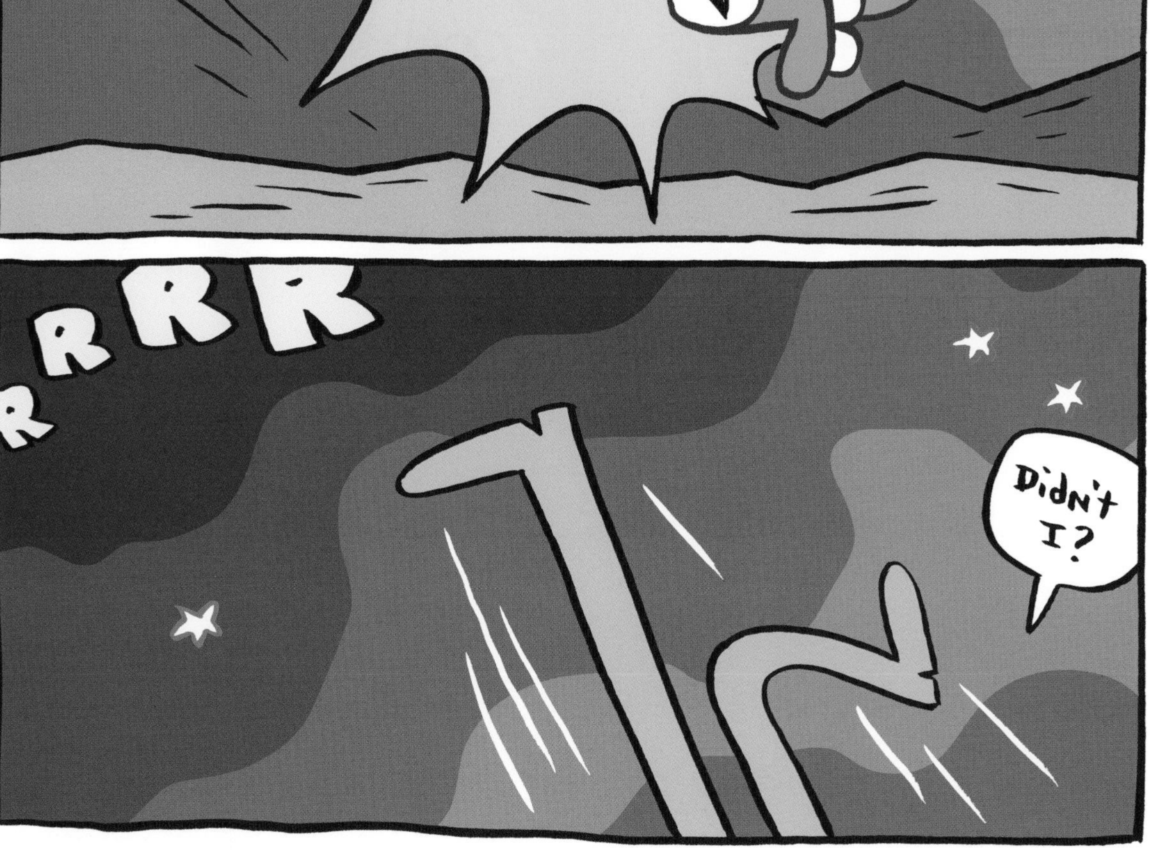
RRRR
Didn't I?

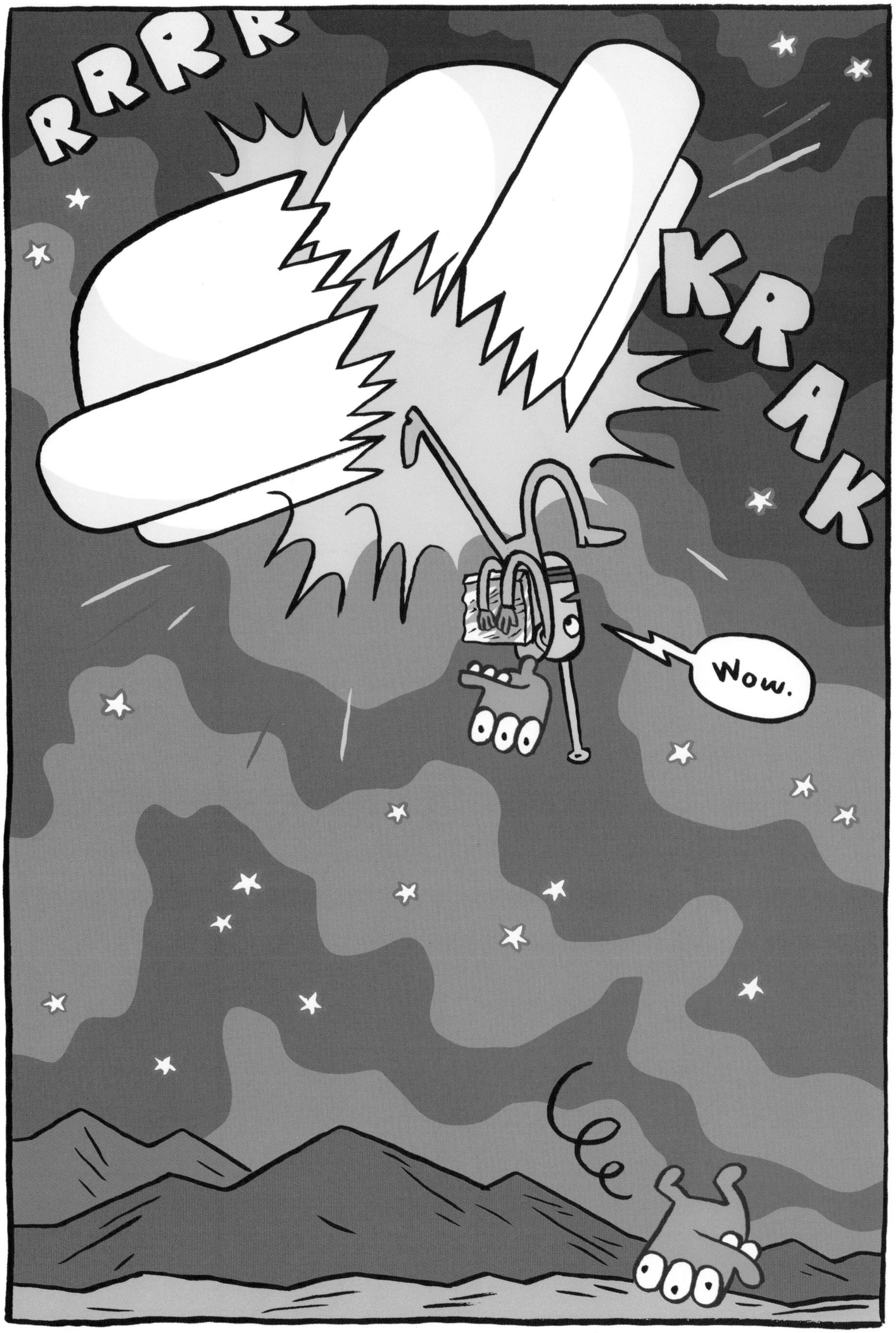
RRRR
KRAK
Wow.

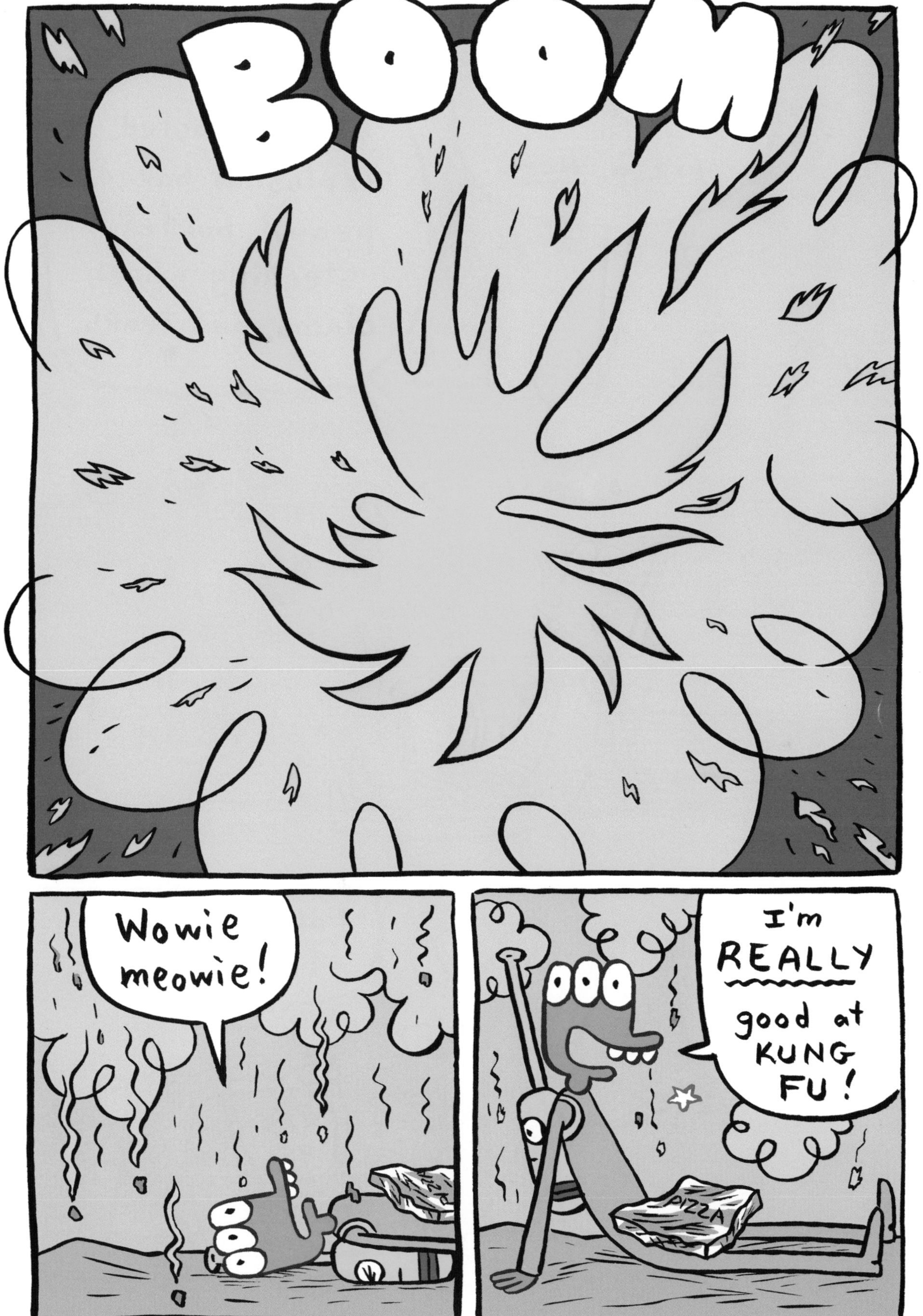
BOOM
Wowie meowie!
I'm REALLY good at KUNG FU!
PIZZA

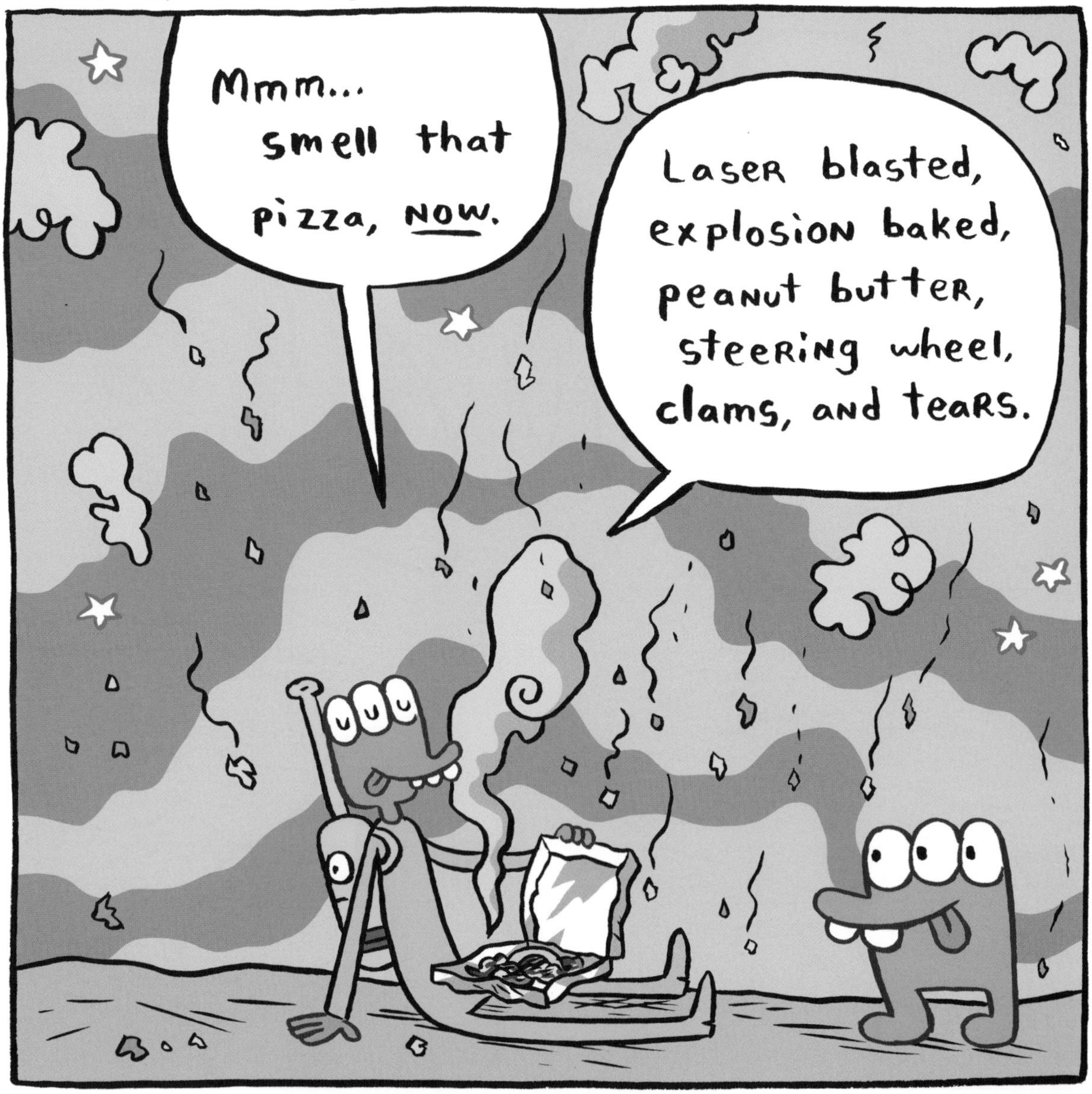
Mmm... smell that pizza, NOW.
Laser blasted, explosion baked, peanut butter, steering wheel, clams, and tears.

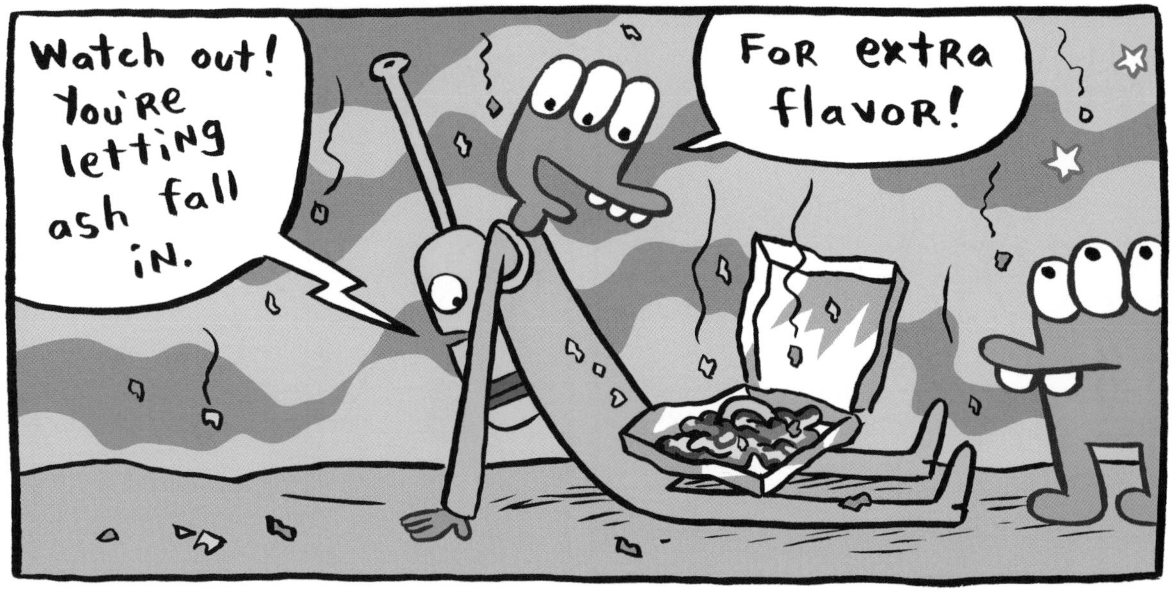
Watch out! You're letting ash fall in.
For extra flavor!

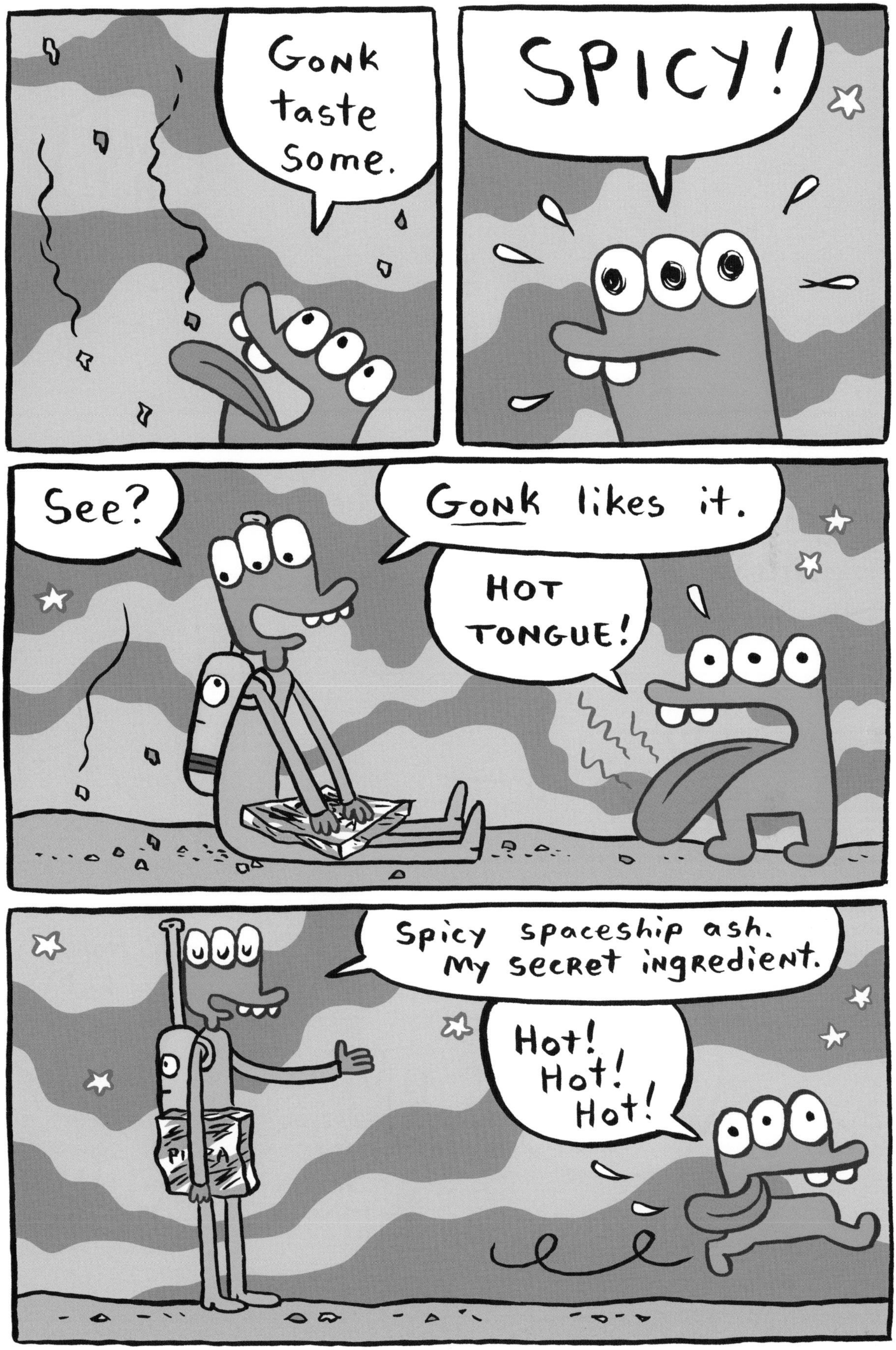
Gonk taste some.
SPICY!
See?
GONK likes it.
HOT TONGUE!
Spicy spaceship ash. My secret ingredient.
Hot! Hot! Hot!
PIZZA

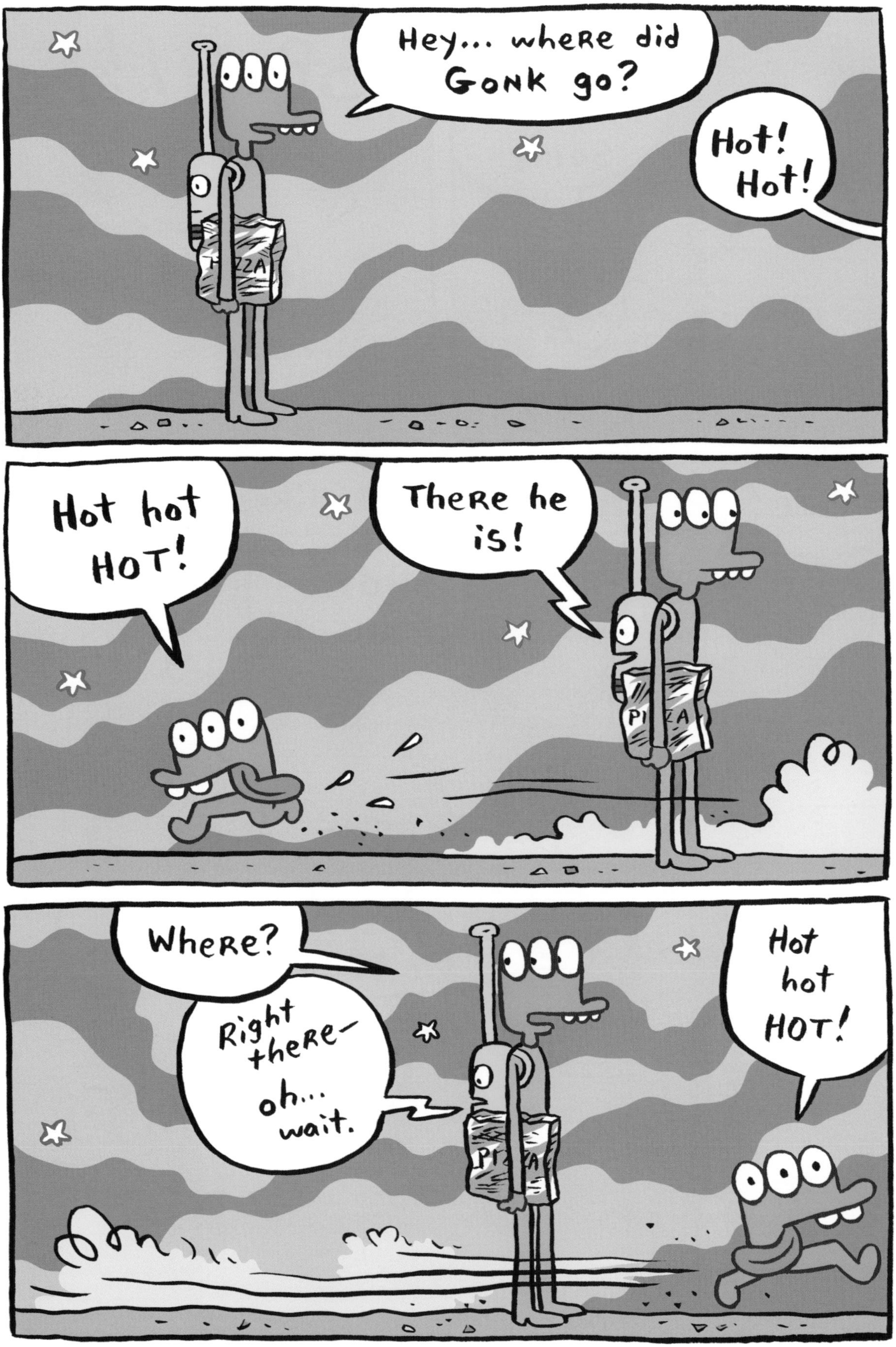
Hey... where did Gonk go?
Hot! Hot!
Hot hot HOT!
There he is!
Where?
Right there-
oh... wait.
Hot hot HOT!

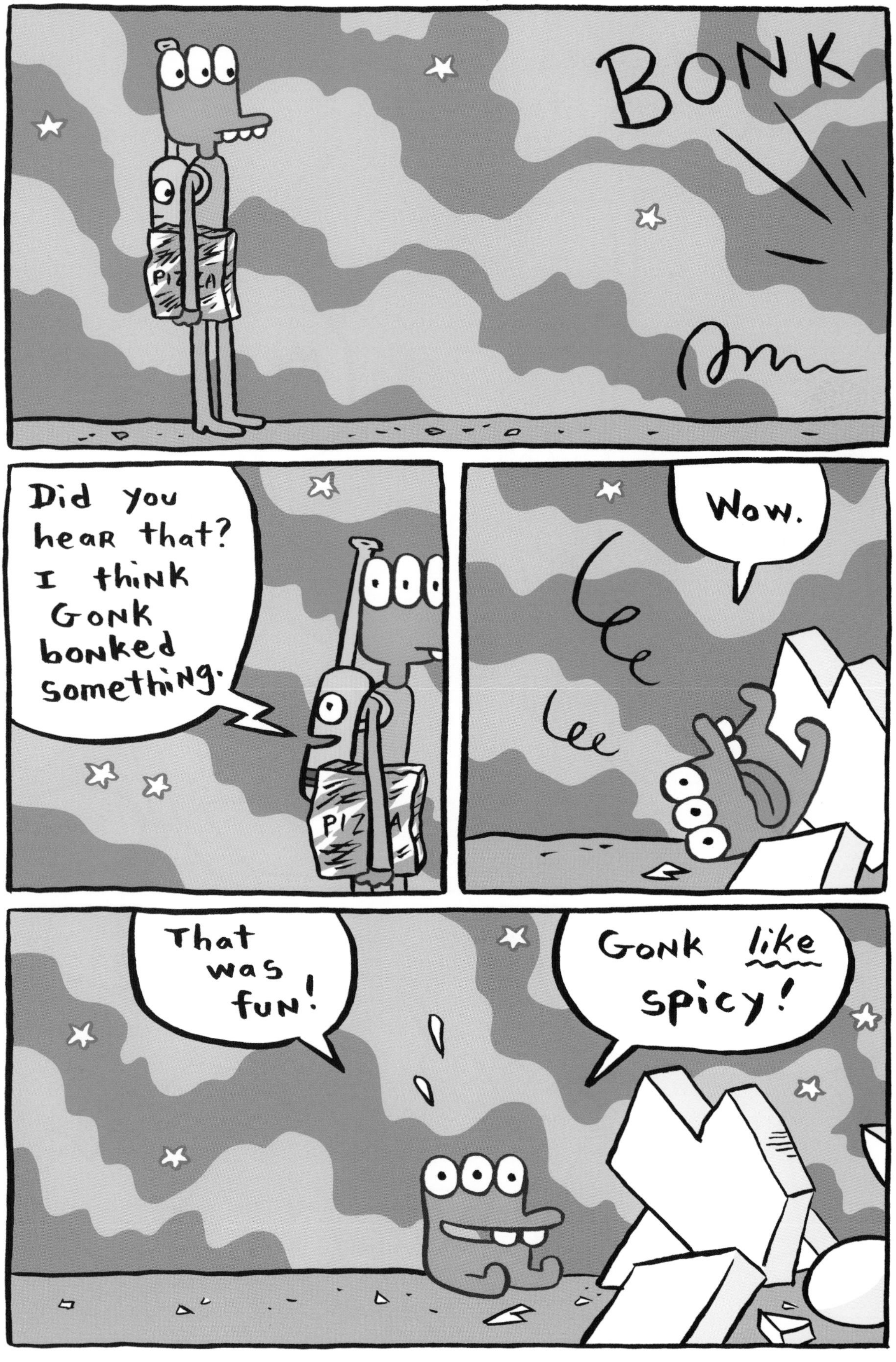
BONK
Bmm
Did you hear that? I think GONK bonked something.
Wow.
Wee
wee
That was fun!
GONK like spicy!

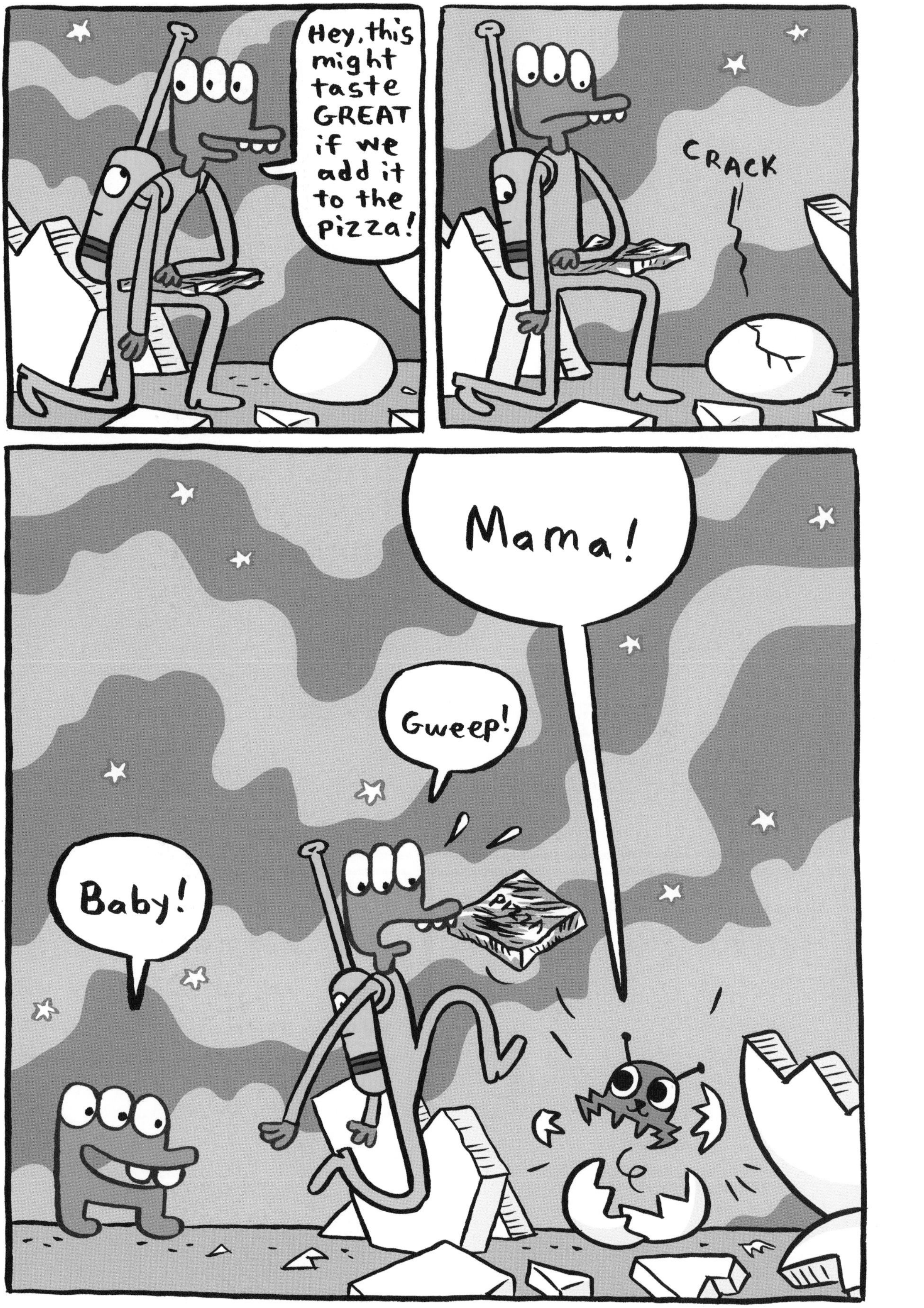
Hey, this might taste GREAT if we add it to the pizza!
CRACK
Mama!
Gweep!
Baby!

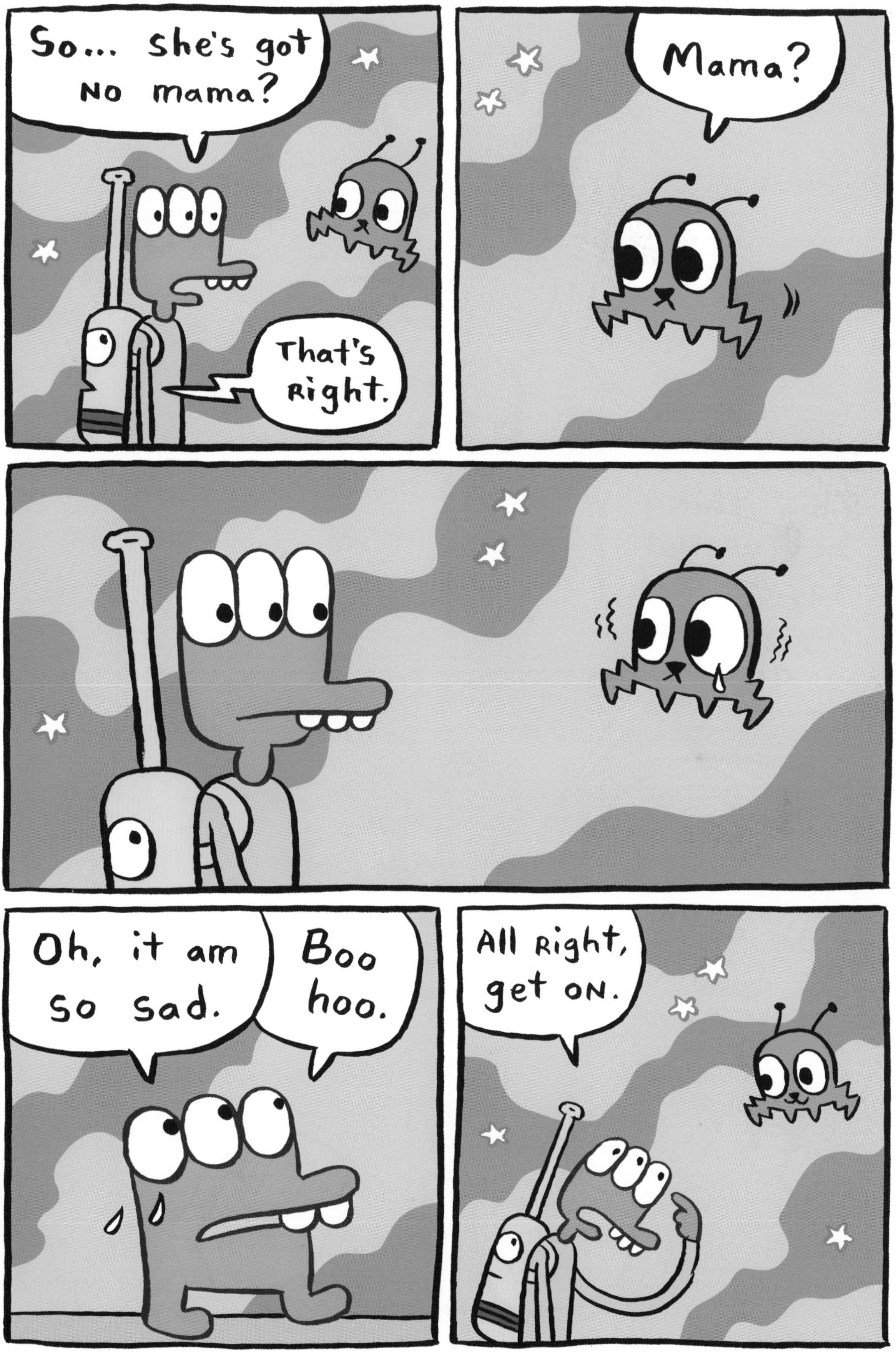
So... she's got no mama?
That's right.
Mama?
Oh, it am so sad.
Boo hoo.
All right, get on.

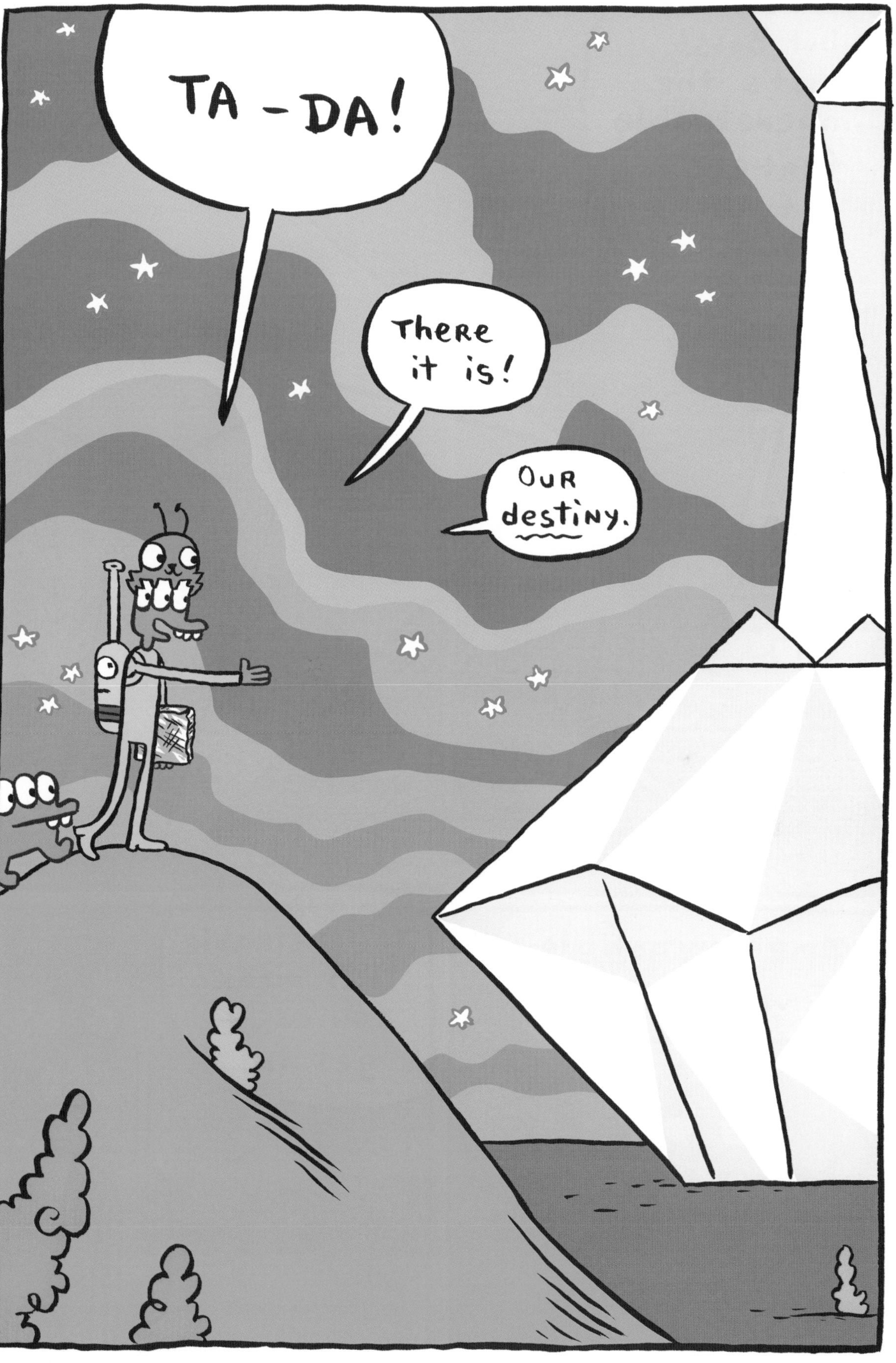
TA-DA!
There it is!
Our destiny.

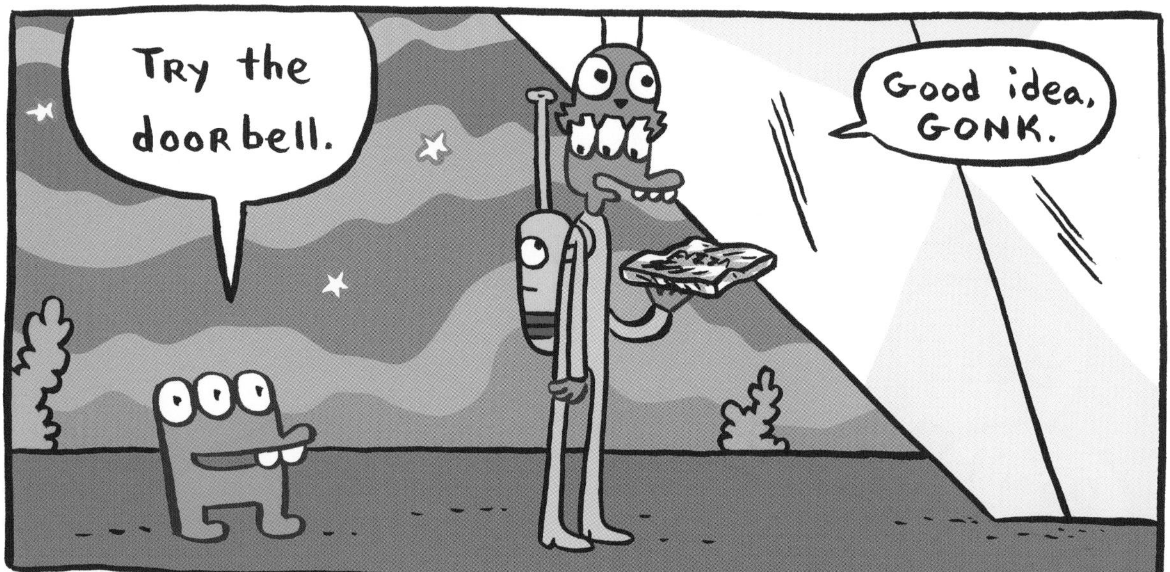
Try the doorbell.
Good idea, GONK.

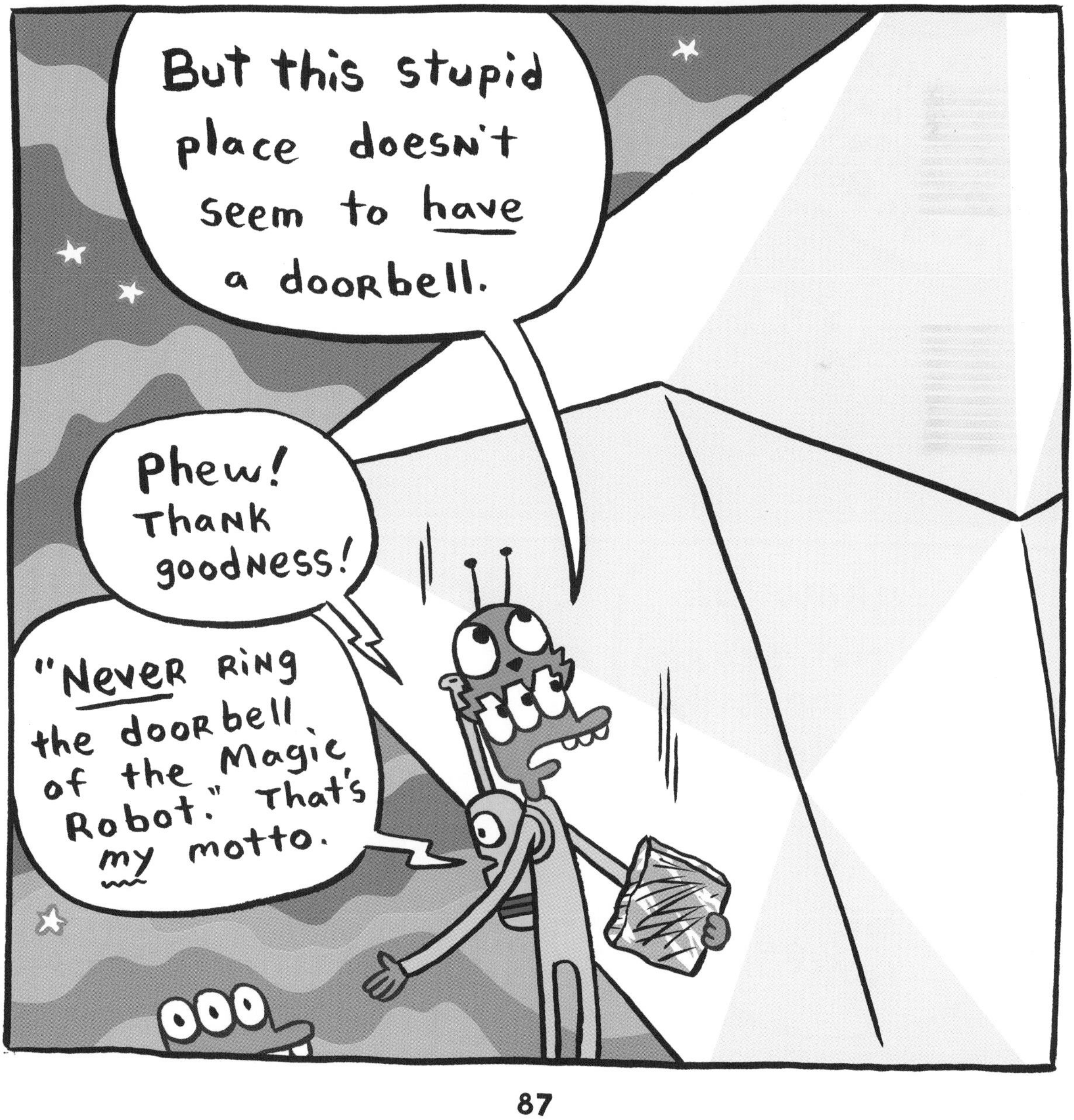
But this stupid place doesn't seem to have a doorbell.
Phew! Thank goodness!
"Never ring the doorbell of the Magic Robot." That's my motto.

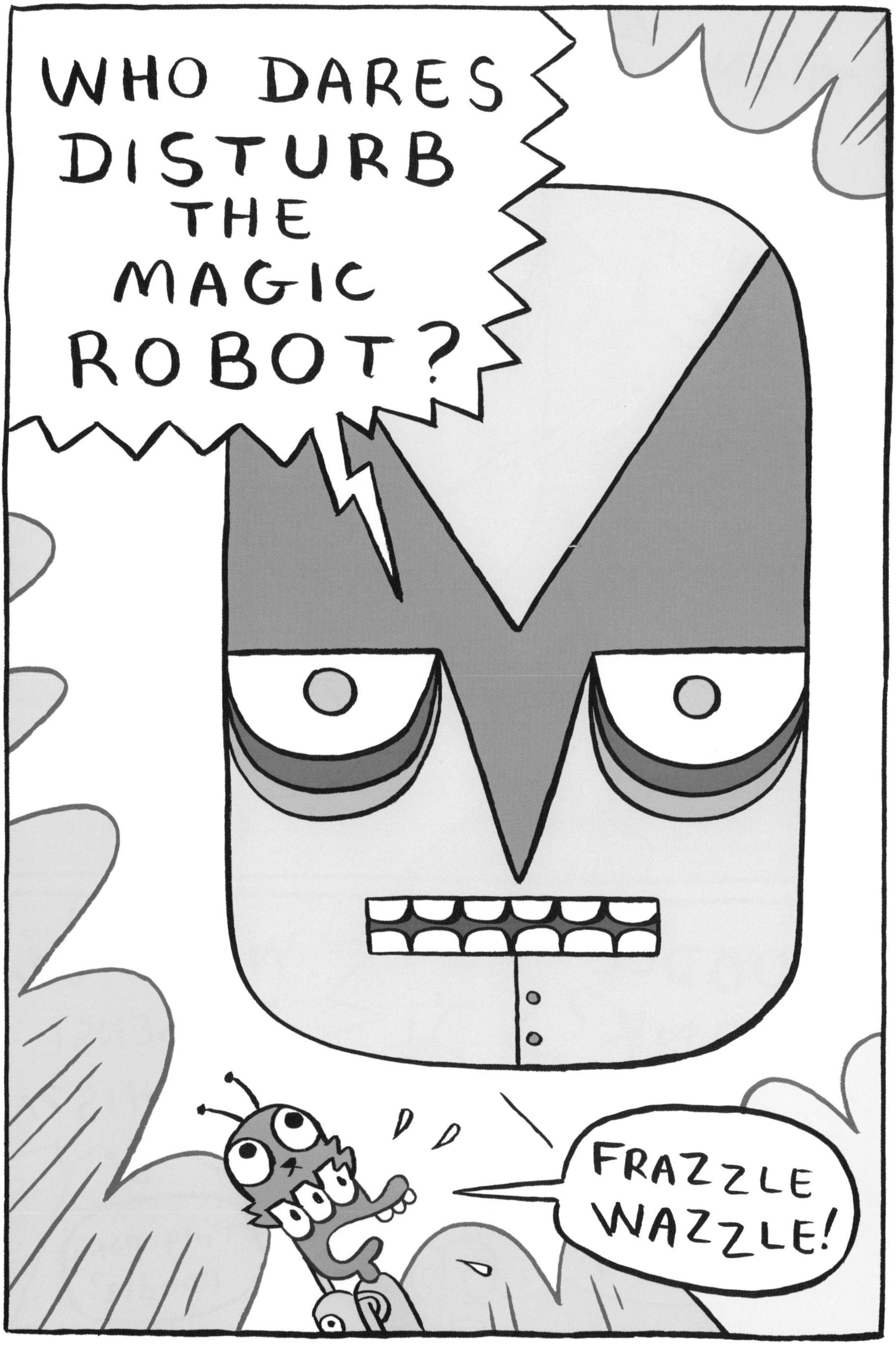
WHO DARES DISTURB THE MAGIC ROBOT?
FRAZZLE WAZZLE!

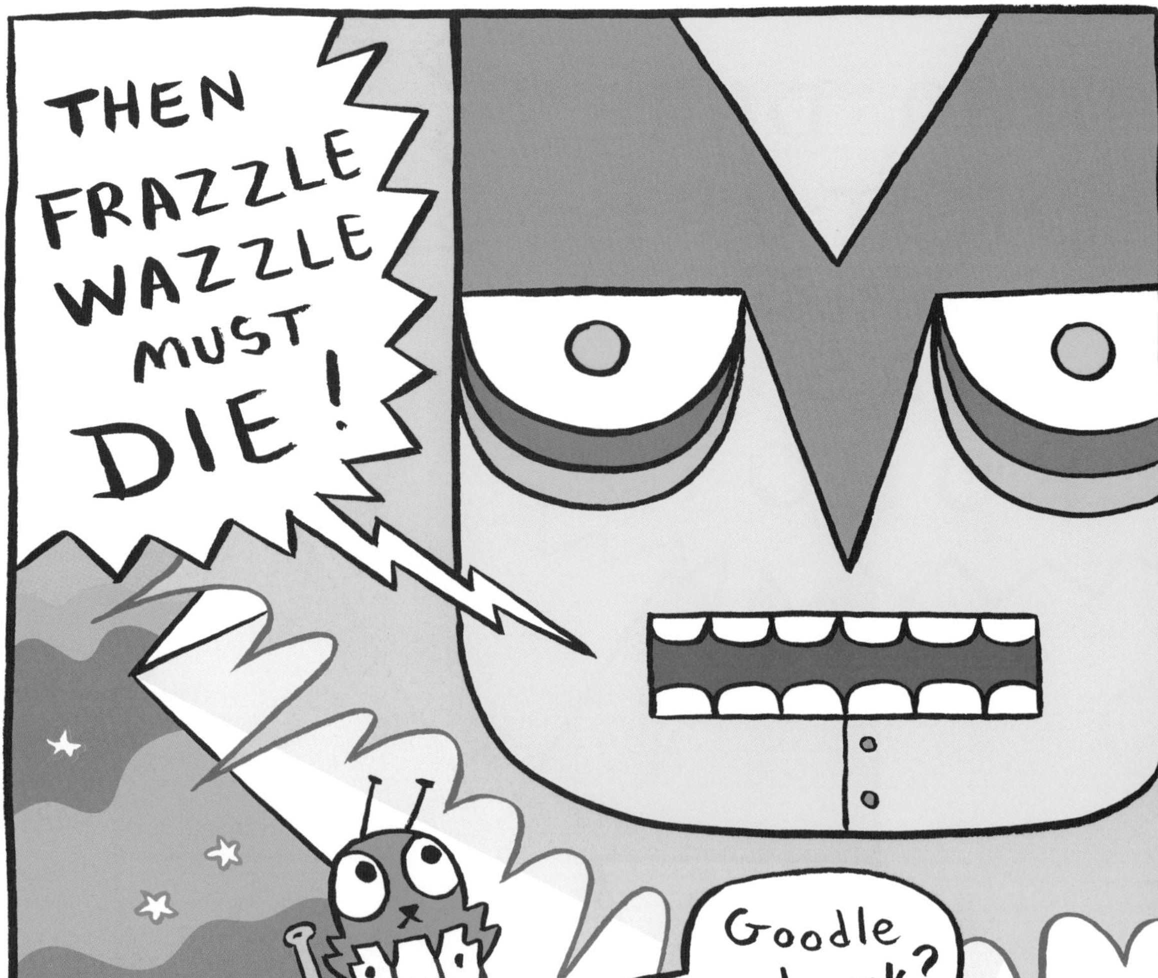
THEN FRAZZLE WAZZLE MUST DIE!
Goodle doonk?

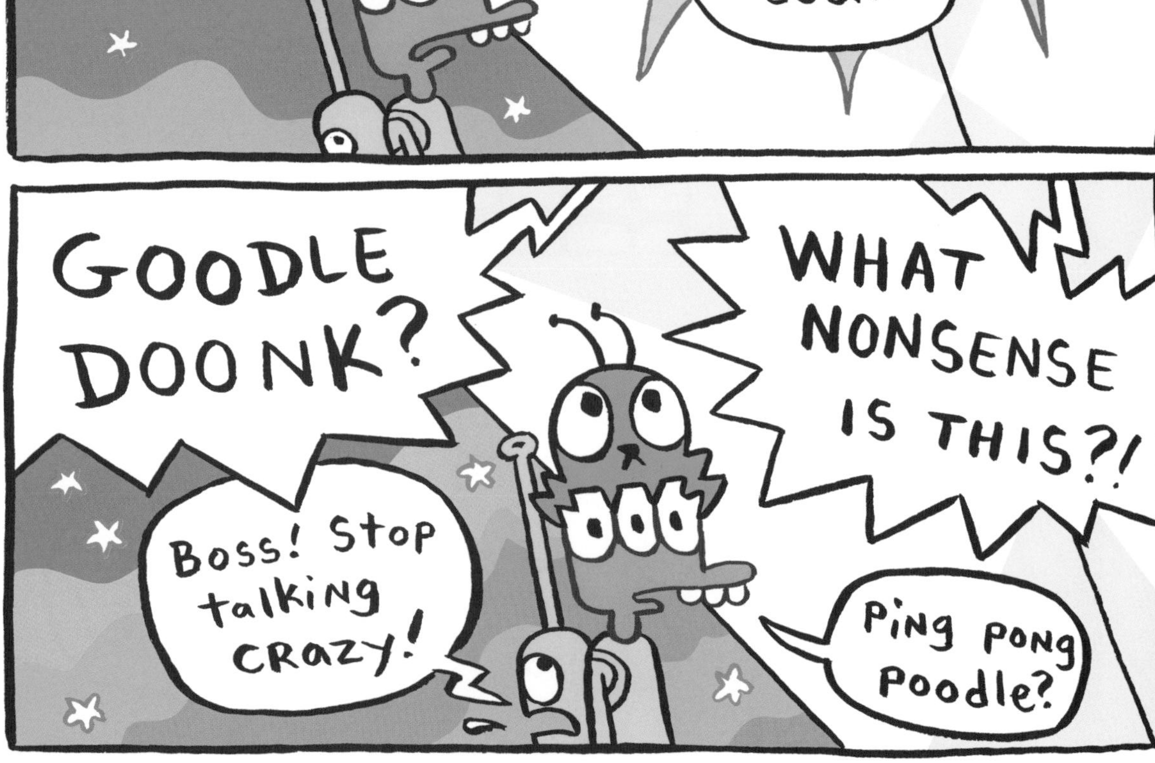
GOODLE DOONK?
WHAT NONSENSE IS THIS?!
Boss! Stop talking crazy!
Ping pong poodle?

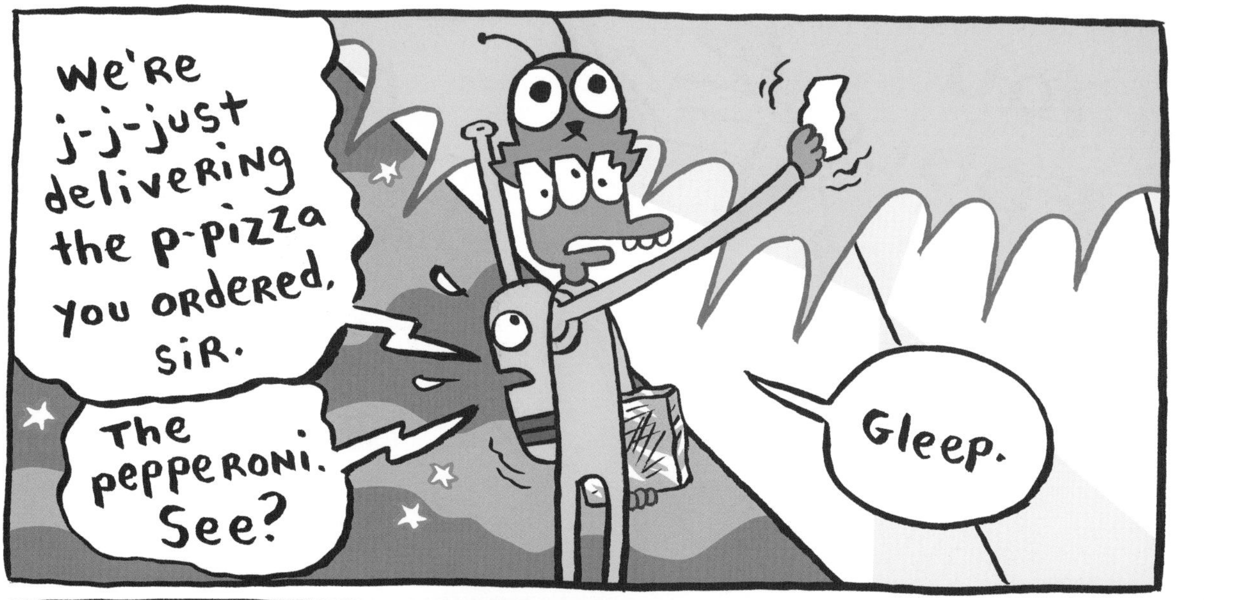
We're j-j-just delivering the p-pizza you ordered, sir.
The pepperoni. See?
Gleep.

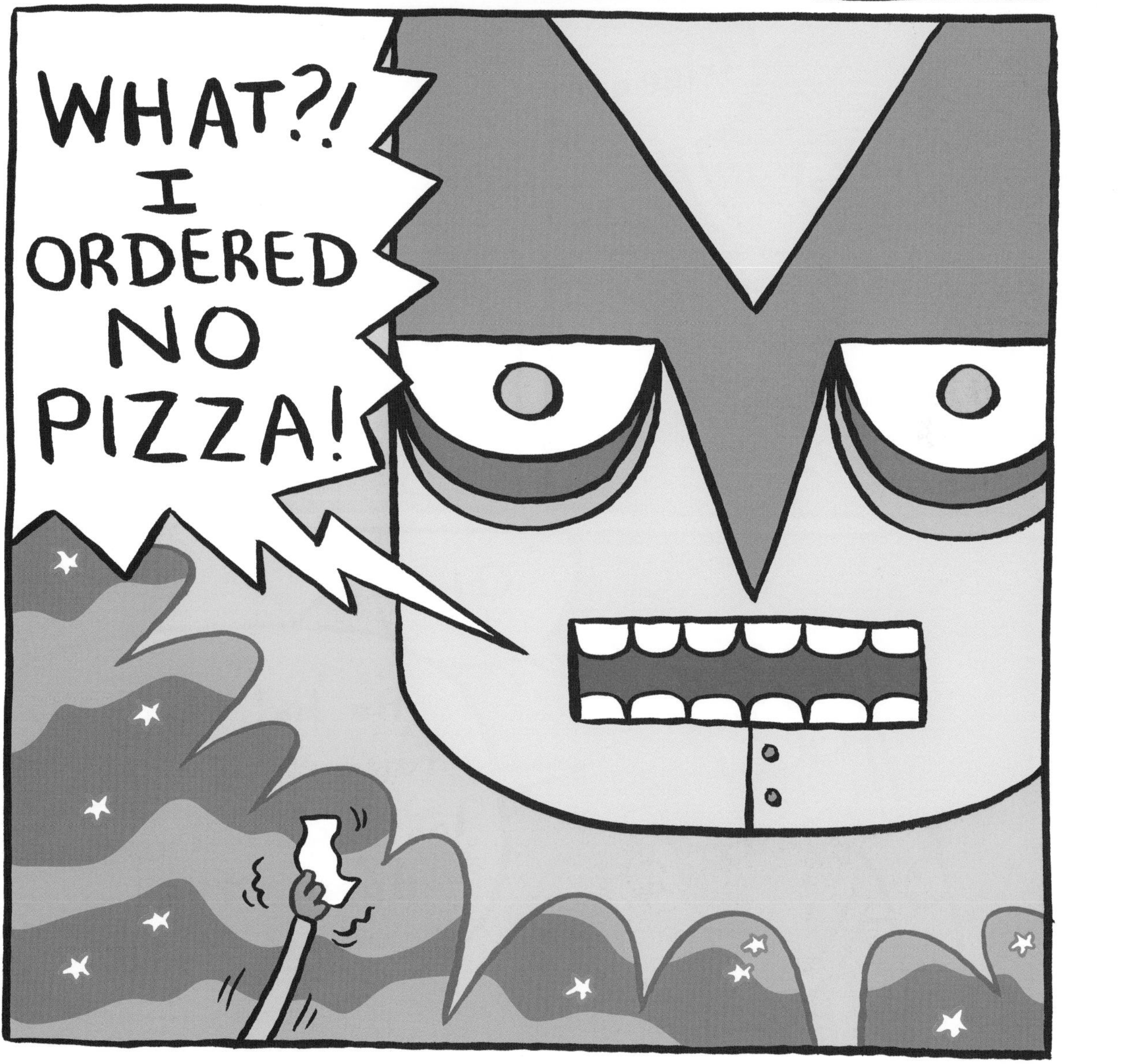
WHAT?! I ORDERED NO PIZZA!

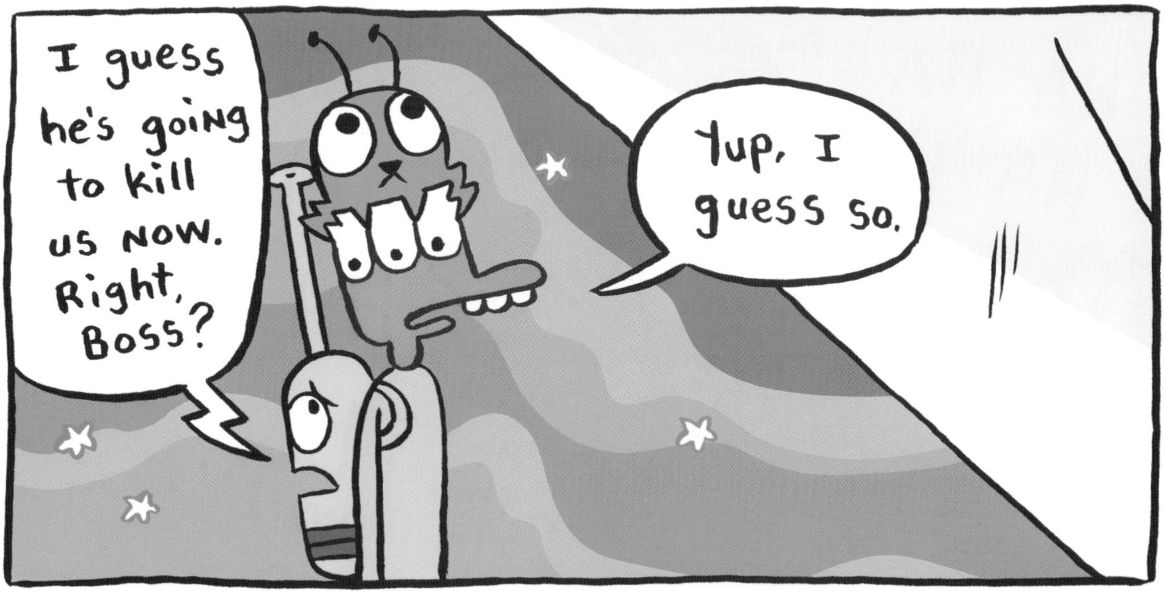
I guess he's going to kill us now. Right, Boss?
Yup, I guess so.

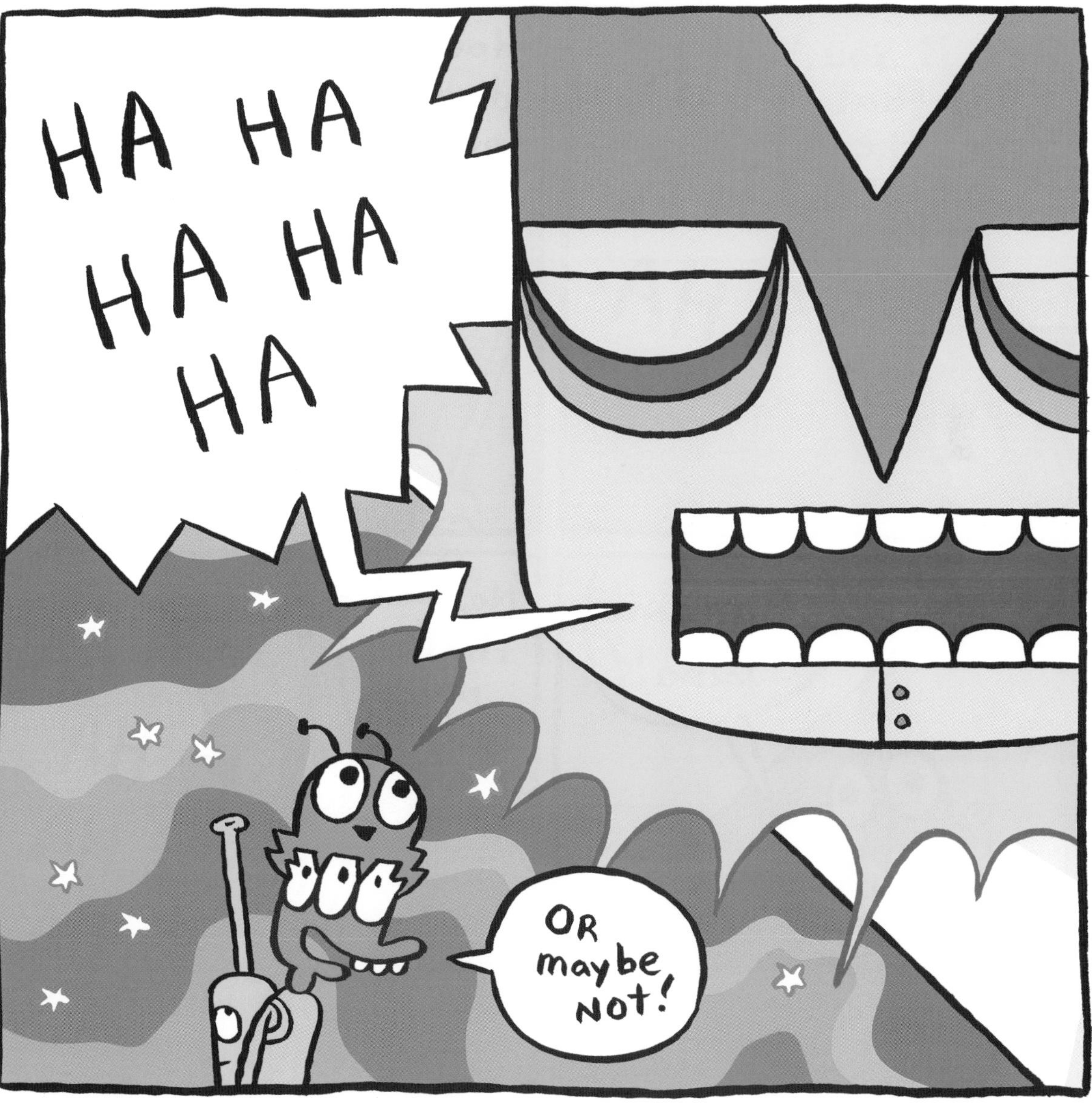
HA HA HA HA HA
OR maybe, NOT!

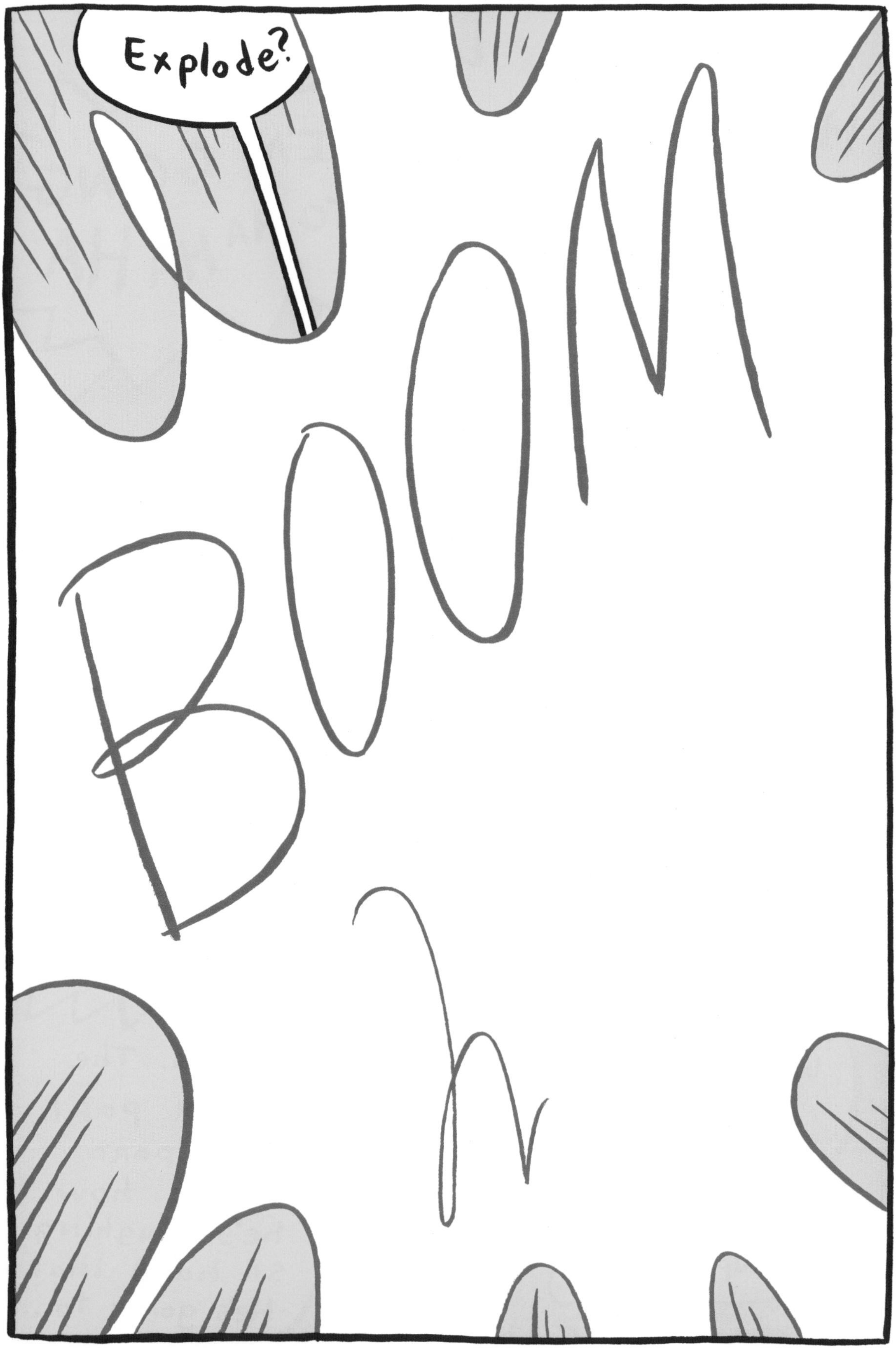
Explode?
BOOM

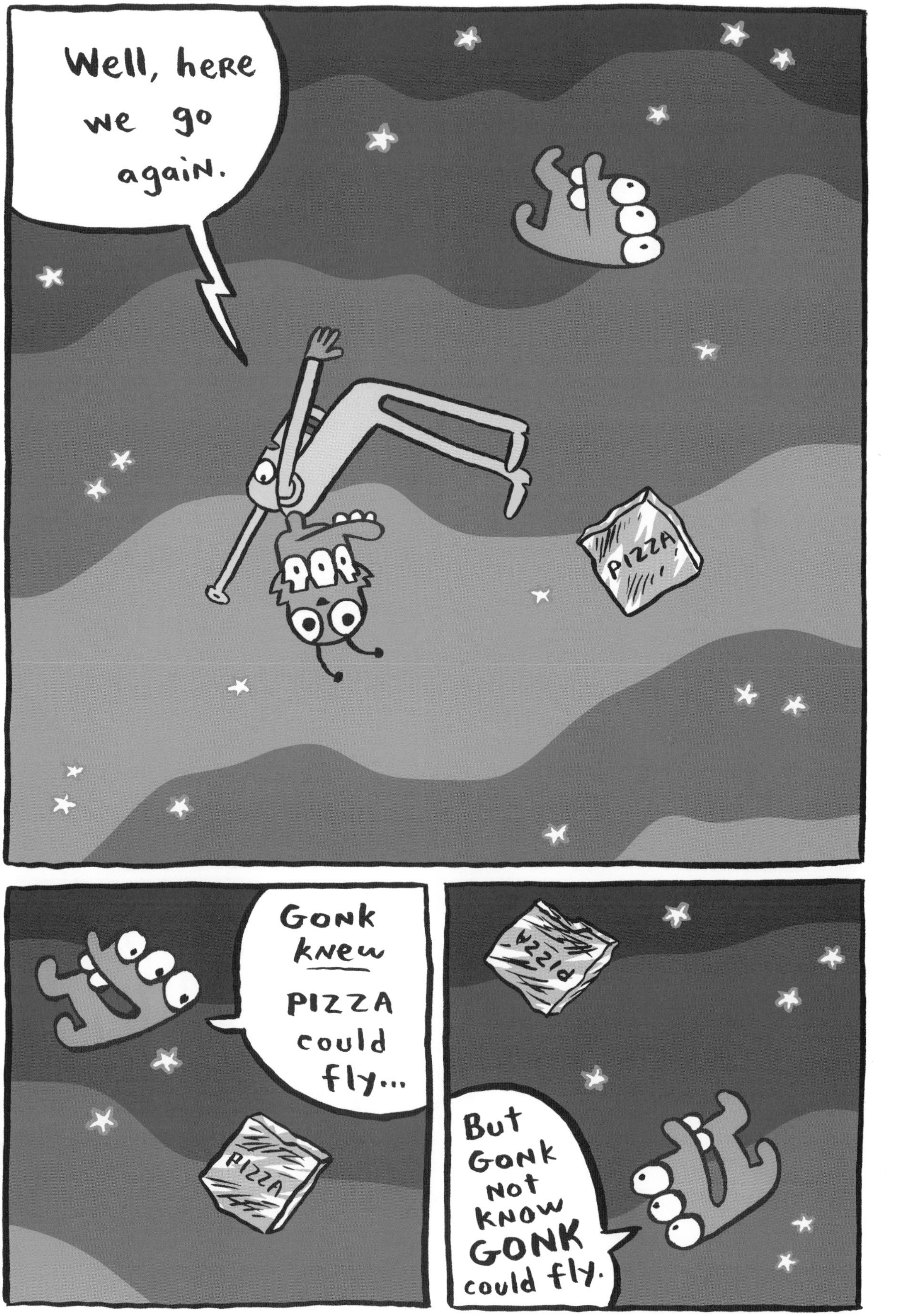
Well, here we go again.
PIZZA
Gonk knew PIZZA could fly...
PIZZA
PIZZA
But Gonk not know GONK could fly.

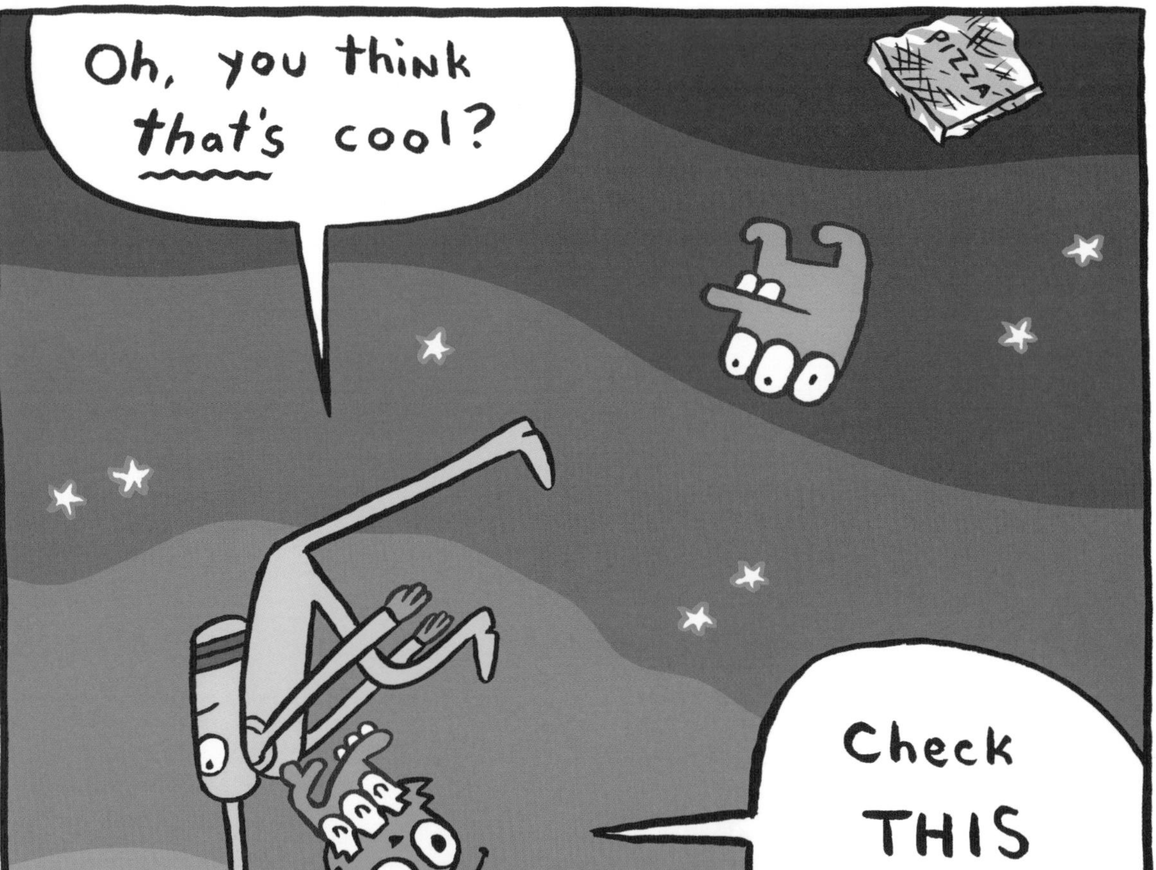
PIZZA
Oh, you think that's cool?
Check THIS out!

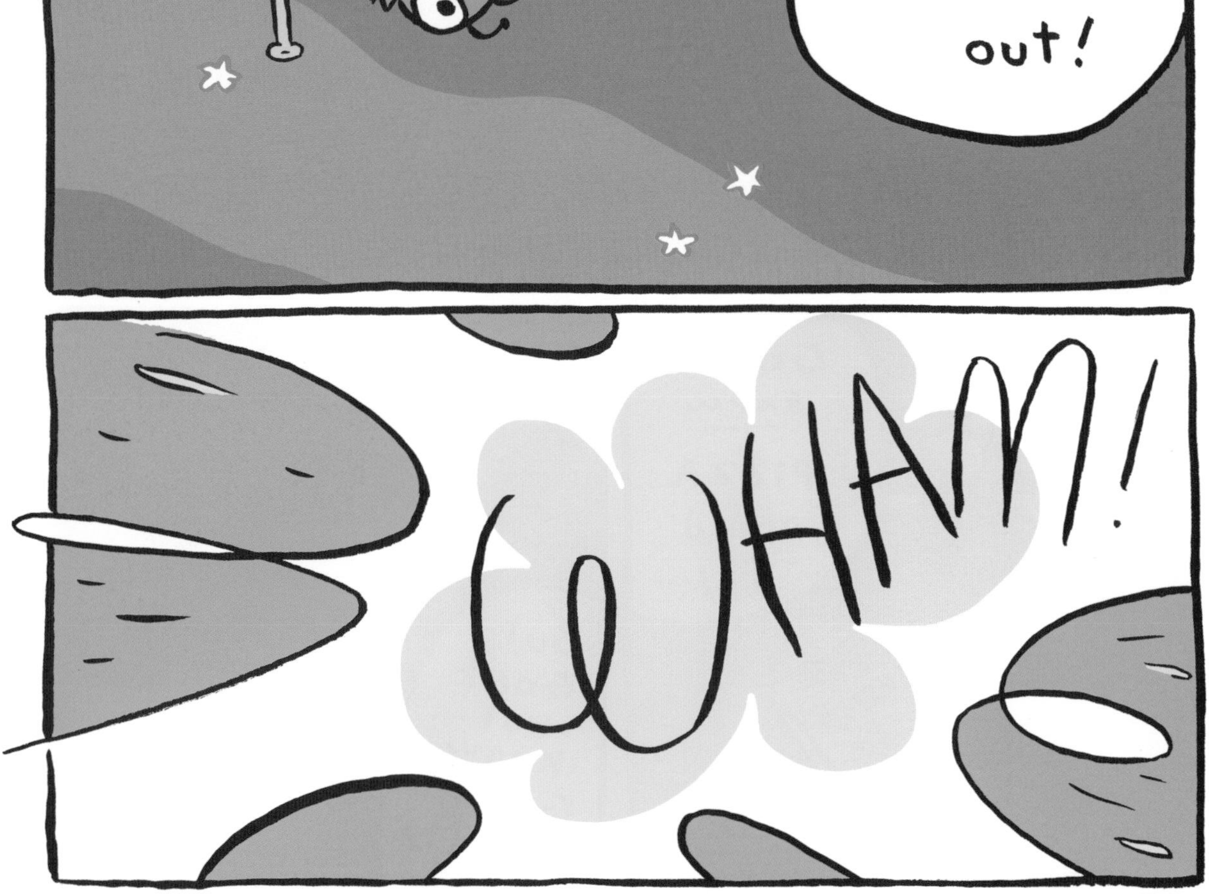
WHAM!

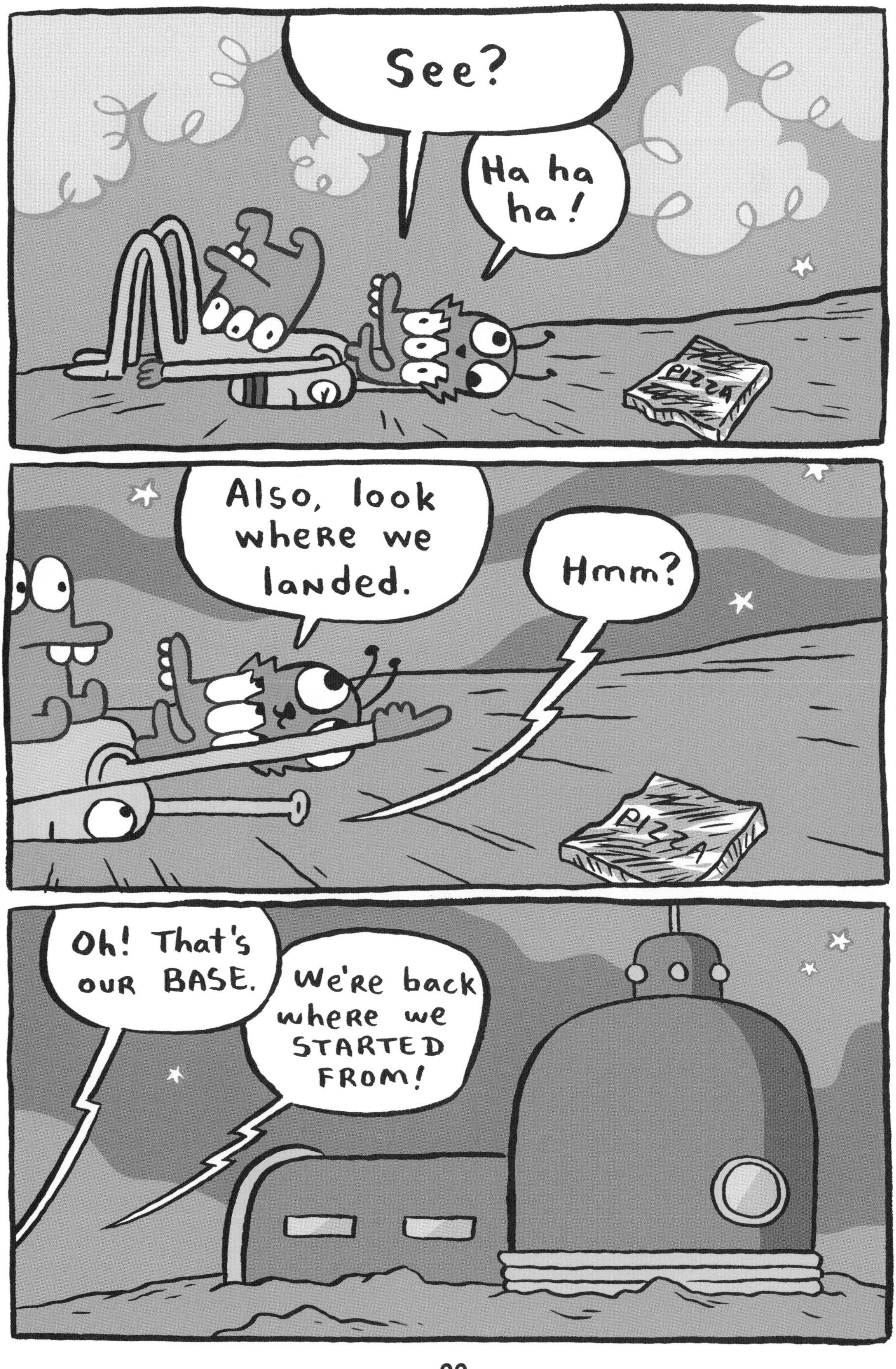
See?
Ha ha ha!
PIZZA
Also, look where we landed.
Hmm?
PIZZA
Oh! That's our BASE.
We're back where we STARTED FROM!

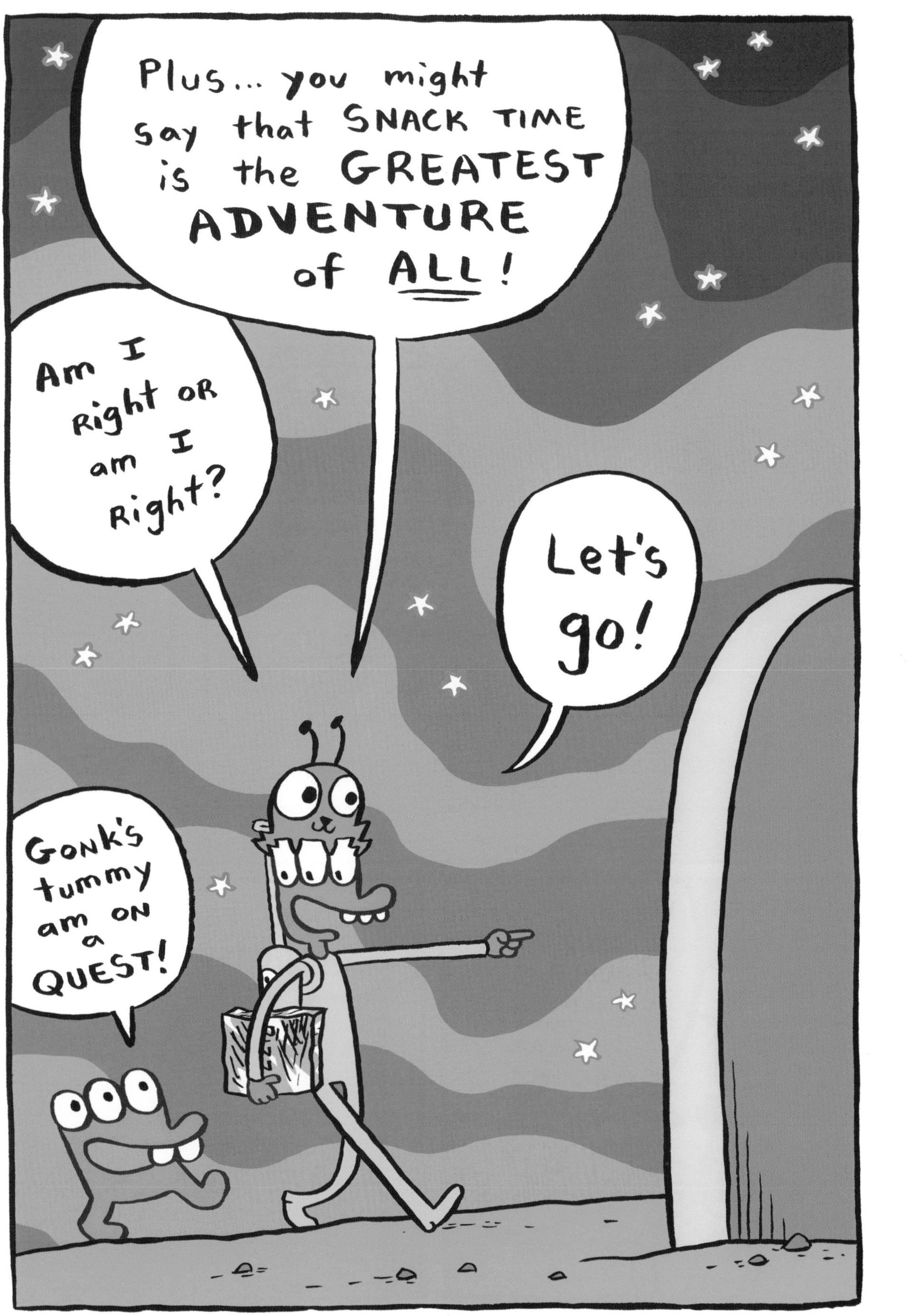
Plus... you might say that SNACK TIME is the GREATEST ADVENTURE of ALL!
Am I right OR am I right?
Let's go!
Gonk's tummy am ON a QUEST!

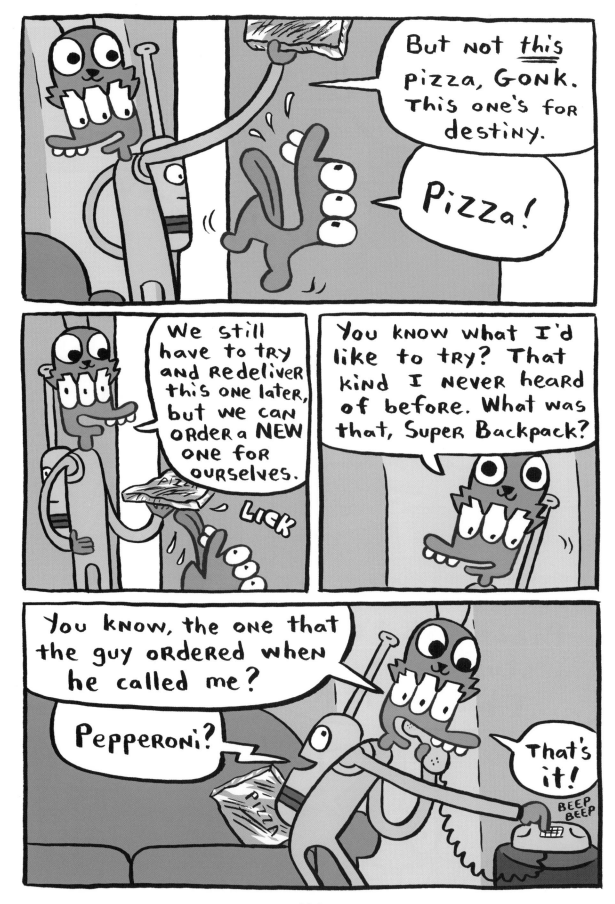

106